PENINSULA

PENINSULA

Sharron Came

TE HERENGA WAKA
UNIVERSITY PRESS

Te Herenga Waka University Press
PO Box 600, Wellington
New Zealand
teherengawakapress.co.nz

A catalogue record is available from the
National Library of New Zealand.

ISBN 9781776920242

Printed in Singapore by Markono Print Media Pte Ltd

Contents

Peacock   9

Hospital   27

Preschool   49

Anniversary   74

Horizon   98

Peninsula   128

Trailblazer   148

Tramp   174

Road   198

Survivor   227

Acknowledgements   255

Peacock

Jim Carlton didn't mean to close his eyes.

The barn's toasty warm and quiet thanks to its lack of ventilation and dried grass stuffing. A good resting place. When he hobbles in, wisps of hay and particles of dust yawn and float through the air to greet him. Speckles of light, glittering like jewels in the sunlight lasering through the gaps in the door, go unnoticed. It's the flash of colour that gets him. A surge of long iridescent necks and proud trains brush the grass. There's chatter. Shadows rise off the turf into the mouth of the mirror sky. Birds settle into field positions. They're taking their time.

Jim recognises the cricket pitch. He mixed and laid the concrete himself. Fixed netting at the batting end. Fence was supposed to stop the dining room windows getting smashed. On that point, it hasn't been a complete success. The pitch is overrun with weeds; not even the grandchildren use it. Jim likes to know it's there, a reminder. What he doesn't like is those bloody rabbits sneaking around feeding on the vege patch. A few weeks ago he brought his gun in, leaned out the lounge window to shoot a couple of them. Made a bit of a mess but he got the buggers. They won't be eating any more of Di's beans.

Now, at the crease, the opener uses his left wing to dig his bat into Jim's pitch. He stares into middle distance, checking the light and the fielder locations. A lefty, like Jim. Behind him the wicketkeeper's green cap bobs up and down. Any second, the cap could go. It's already got a drunken sailor tilt. Keeper's supreme confidence is all that keeps his hat locked to his quill. He sashays back and forth, gives his train a shake. Feathers unfurl like a colourful umbrella then close again. He deliberately scratches his talons across the concrete, clearing weeds. With studied casualness he extends his train, properly this time, inky eye spots absorbing the sunlight.

All eyes, including the wicketkeeper's, turn to the bowler. He's making last-minute tweaks to his field. Abrupt head flicks command a bird to move left or right. A nod or a shake compel a shift deeper or closer. He's mincing down the paddock, rubbing the blood red ball against his emerald plumage. Delivery already paced, he knows precisely where to halt. Before he starts his run, he pauses for a final look down the pitch. Batsman squirms. Keeper straightens. Bowler doesn't blink. Head cocked to one side he stares straight at Jim.

The corrugated-iron barn door slides open, flooding the interior with blatant sunlight. The screech is worse than any starling.

Jim jerks awake, squints into the light.

'Thought I'd find you here,' Jack says.

Jim stays sitting on his scratchy hay bale. Dog usually unleashes a trumpet bark. Where is his dog, why hasn't he barked?

'Dog tried to bite the dairy inspector again,' says Jack. 'I put him back in his kennel. If we get a grade, it's on the dog!'

In the early days every dog had a name but Jim's had so

many now he prefers to stick with Dog. The animal's energetic but useless at taking direction. Does its own thing most of the time. Jim likes that it's grateful. Grateful to be fed, grateful to be let out of its kennel to run around, grateful for Jim's company.

'Oh. I didn't know the inspector was coming today.'

'Yeah.' Jack takes one hand out of the pocket of his cobalt blue overalls and rubs his face. 'Neither did I.' He removes his hand to reveal a broad grin. 'Just pulling ya leg, but could've easily been an inspector. Buggers have started doing spot checks. At least the shed's clean. Good effort on that front.'

Jim nods. Jack, his eldest son, is all right. Worries too much about all the regulations. Too many strangers coming round and sticking their noses in where they don't belong.

'When you were a boy, we all drank milk straight from the vat. I'd grab a bucket full for breakfast. Take it to the house on the back of the quad. Di would take off the cream with a spoon and sit jugs of it in the fridge. Bloody good cream too.' Jim likes this story. Tells it frequently.

'Dad, the irrigation pump is playing up. I haven't got time to call the bloke. Would you ring and tell him we need a new filter?'

He's slow to haul himself upright. 'Filter, are you sure? I'll go take a look. I can probably fix it. It isn't going to rain. We need to irrigate.'

Jack doesn't know machinery. Jim can fix anything. Admittedly he doesn't always get it right the first few tries, but the irrigator is new, not like the baler. Jim's sure he could have kept the hay baler going. They'd only had it fifty years. It was a bit temperamental, prone to jamming mid-way through a paddock. Hard to find parts too, the newer models were different.

Last season the baler played up just when rain was

threatening and the haymaking crew was booked. Jim got his mate, a retired mechanic familiar with the particular vintage of baler, to scrounge through the parts he kept at home. Even then, the two of them couldn't get the machine to do more than a couple of bales without stopping. Jack called in the contractors.

This summer when Jim offered to check the baler, Jack had already lined up contractors. Jim was relegated to cutting and raking the hay. Still in charge of driving the tractor to collect the bales. The most difficult part, the part that took skill and years of practice, was backing the trailer. Nothing, not even a successful putt from the edge of the green, was more satisfying than inching a full trailer into the open mouth of the barn.

Jack's talking about the irrigator.

'Yeah, we need to irrigate. Not a case of fixing, the filter's old, needs replacing. If we talk to them today, they'll probably have a spare. You could collect it. That way, we can get the irrigator going, after milking.'

'All right.' Jim doesn't like it when Jack gets bossy, but he isn't keen on driving up to the irrigator in the heat of the day.

'I want to get the spuds planted, when can we do that?' Jim has old potatoes ready and the tractor set up. It's the bending down to push the spuds into the soil, plays havoc with his hips.

'Spuds? Where are you going to plant those? Not where the maize is going.'

'No, beside the maize. I've already ploughed some rows.'

Mention of maize reminds Jim of the peacocks up by the bush. He wonders if Jack has seen them. Peacocks are bloody lawnmowers. Peck through ryegrass and clover. Won't be able to resist the maize.

Jack is talking about the hay paddock.

'Yeah, I meant to ask you. That's a hay paddock. It was a hay paddock, before you ploughed it.'

'There's plenty of hay already. We need spuds.' Jim is up now, about to shuffle towards the barn door.

Jack sighs. He looks like Di when he sighs. Does he think Jim doesn't know it's a hay paddock, that he's an idiot? It's nice and flat and easy to plough and since he's bought the extra hectares up by the old airstrip, they have more hay paddocks than they need.

'Rach is up at the moment, why don't you get her in on a bit of planting. I reckon she'd be up for it.'

'Rachel? It's hard work.' Jim doesn't say it's men's work, he knows better than that.

'Yeah, Rach is bloody fit, fitter than me, maybe even fitter than you.' Jack shoots his father a sly glance.

Jim grins wearily. He knows Jack is taking the piss. Rachel, Jack's twin. He hardly sees her. She sneaks up without telling him or Di. Like one of those blue herons Di's so fond of. Perch in full view, but flighty, watchful. She never stays still for long, always off running.

'Well, tell her to come and plant spuds.'

'Tell her yourself. Give her a ring after you've rung the filter guy.'

Jim isn't sure why he didn't mention the peacocks to Jack. He doesn't like to think about the birds. Like gypsies that appeared from nowhere and set up camp in the bush-filled gully at the bottom of the airstrip.

At first, they'd stayed in the trees out of sight, but gradually they gained confidence, started coming out. It was hard to get a sense of their numbers. They flitted about, cutting behind and in front of each other, constantly on the move. Their spiky crests reminded him of fancy hats. Miniature emerald and aquamarine feathers infused with dark eyespots atop leathery, reptilian heads. Necks like swans, bodies like ducks. Eyes like searchlights.

As a boy Jim was fascinated by pūkeko, with their plumage the same colour as his school uniform. Their resemblance to the hens confused him. How come the blue birds were free to roam while the hens were kept under netting, he'd asked his father. The old man scowled, called them parasites. Within days pūkeko corpses started appearing, tied to fences like scarecrows. After that Jim took care not to comment on any birds.

He's kept pigs, highly intelligent waste-disposal units, good for bacon and pork, they like mud baths. He built them a pen. Sheep lived in a paddock, mainly for sausages and a bit of mutton, and Di spun the wool. Turkeys were a disaster. Making dust baths in the flower beds, nests under the hedges, piles of black and white shit wherever they roosted, as well as all over the lawn. Overnight the garden was overrun with tiny lemon chicks covered in brown freckles and emitting shrill chirps. The gobblers with their constant explosions – *gobble, gobble, gobble*, worse than roosters. Thought they owned the show. He had to get rid of the lot. He could see it would be the same with the peacocks.

He drove over a few times, studied their movements.

A fortnight ago, he steeled himself, took his gun to the paddock edge where the birds came out of the bush. The alpha peacock was in his usual spot at the front. The birds had gotten used to Jim's visits. The male came closer. His train spread out behind him as he paraded up and down the fence line. Staring at Jim with his beady eye, head on one side, watching.

Sitting in the driver's seat of his Mule, Jim had a memory of being back at school. His teacher was telling him his handwriting was beautiful but he needed to do more with it. Jim's father had snorted when he'd told him.

'Don't need neat handwriting to milk cows.'

Jim sat for a few more moments staring at the peacock staring back at him. Then he decided he'd given it enough of a chance to run away. He reached around and retrieved his gun, sighted the bird and released the trigger.

The peacock was warm, its eyes blank, body lighter than Jim expected, the plumage longer. He ran his finger down one of the iridescent emerald and turquoise feathers, the eyespots like silky paintings. He stared at the dead bird for a long time. He could chuck it in one of the holes where they buried animals but he didn't feel like disposing of it yet. He placed his hand around the bird's slim blue neck and lifted it into the tray of his vehicle.

It was past noon when he drove home. Inside, Di was picking at her lunch.

'Where've you been, you okay?'

'Sore hip.' Jim made for the couch.

'Lunch?'

'Not hungry.' Jim picked up the water bottle on the coffee table and took a swig, hoping it would satisfy Di so she'd leave him alone.

'Tui's coming round at three. Thought you'd be heading out to get the cows?'

Jim scowled. When Di and her friend Tui got together, they were like the high-pressure hose he used to clean the cowshed. Loved to pore over every bit of scuttlebutt in the district. He'd have to mute the television. Di was always trying to get him out of the house.

*

15

From his spot on the couch, a movement caught his eye. One of the house cows. Jim's father had taught him to identify the different types. Every herd had a few animals who liked to hide by the creek or pretend not to see open gates. Those ones were happy to kick or charge a cheeky dog, do anything but obediently file off to the shed. Jim glanced up at the family photo on the wall, wondered what his youngest son Willy was up to. The troublemakers had to be brought into line. The front-runners were the easiest. They'd always be quick smart at the gate to lead the way to the shed. Liked to get milked first and out again for first dibs on the fresh grass. Then there were the ones languishing down the back of the herd. They'd lost their ability to move quickly, usually due to age or lameness. They had little choice but to endure the humiliation of impatient dogs snapping at their heels.

'Watch for the lame ones. Put them in the house paddock with three or four calves and they'll feed and look after them, take the pressure off. Those ones deserve respect, they've earned it.'

The peacocks, they were looking for a place where they would be left in peace.

A scream interrupted Jim's musing. Di appeared in the doorway, hands on hips.

'Jim Carlton. What the hell is that peacock doing on the lawn?'

'Oh. Better move it.'

'Better had.'

Jim followed Di. He paused at the wash house to pull on his gumboots while Di carried on. Jim could see Tui through the window, her red head scarf, hard to miss. She was facing the rose bushes, her back to the peacock, fanning her face with her hand.

'I don't mind dead fish,' Tui said. 'Dead peacock in the

garden is a first, nearly gave me heart failure.'

Di poked the peacock with her foot. 'Oh my sainted aunt.' She walked over to Tui, rested an arm on her ample back. 'Sorry Tui. Did I tell you his nibs shot some rabbits out the lounge window a few weeks ago?'

The two of them turned round just as Jim finished negotiating the front steps.

Tui said, 'Hello Jim. I hear you've been on a killing spree. Am I safe to approach the house? You're not hiding a loaded gun behind your back, are you?'

'You're probably safe.' Jim flicked a glance towards the gate. 'Wasn't expecting visitors.'

'Why did you shoot it, mind me asking?'

Jim looked at the lifeless peacock as if he hadn't seen it before.

'Gang of them come over from the chicken place, up past the airstrip.'

Tui risked a glance at the bird and quickly looked away.

'Realise they're a nuisance but they're gorgeous. Alive. You know, people house them in enclosures as pets, feed them?'

Jim shrugged. He remembered Di's brother kept them at his place down south, along with various parrots and guinea pigs.

'You want a few? Might be a bit hard to round up now, they'll be wary.'

Tui said, 'I bet.'

'Don't encourage him Tui,' Di said. 'Where are you going to put it, Jim?'

Jim didn't answer.

Di said, 'Tui come on inside, we'll leave him to it.'

Tui said, 'How's things on the farm? You got enough going on, Jim?'

'Busy. Should be getting the cows now.'

'How's ya hips?'

'Good enough.' He waited for Di to contradict him, but to his relief she said nothing, at least not while he was within hearing.

Jim has everything ready. He's been waiting to plant his spuds for weeks now. Good to have some help, finally. Here's Rachel. She's wearing trainers.

'I'll pinch some gumboots?'

Di appears in the hallway, wearing an orange vest, ready for her daily walk. 'Use my spares.'

Rachel pulls a face. 'They'll be too small Mum. These ones look okay.' She settles on an old pair of Willy's.

As she pulls the boots on, she notices a tiny explosion of colour in the wash house window. She leans close to the windowsill, reaches for the delicate sculpture fashioned out of vivid blue and green feathers. She rotates it and the long quills curl over like a frozen waterfall. The feathers are set in a vessel carved out of wood and painted emerald.

'What's this? Peacock feathers. It's cool!'

'Your father made it. He shot one of the peacocks up the back, left it on the front lawn. Tui came round. Got a terrible scare. Dead bird on the lawn.'

Rachel calls out to Jim. 'How many peacocks are there?'

'I can take you later if you like. They come right up to the fence and stand there showing off their feathers.' Jim gestures with his arms to indicate how wide the peacock's petticoat extends. 'Pests. Too many, hiding in the bush and eating all the feed.'

Rachel's never seen her father make anything that doesn't serve some practical purpose. The ornament is as frivolous as it's striking. She returns it to the windowsill.

'I've made a few. Take one back with you.'

'Thanks. I'd like to.'

'Don't forget about the shortbread,' Di says.

Rachel glances from her mother to her father. 'I won't, Mum.'

'Your father should not be eating shortbread.'

'Someone shouldn't be walking on the road. Get flattened by those trucks!'

Jim clears space so Rachel can sit in the passenger seat of his Mule. She grips the handle above the window as he speeds along the races. Sunlight catches the grey gravel, gifting it a fresh complexion as if it's been there for months. Jim is careful to stick to the compacted tracks where the ride is smoothest. At the first gate he puts the Mule into neutral and makes to get out.

'I'll go.'

Rachel leaps out of the vehicle and opens the gate. Jim drives through and she jogs to the Mule, jumps in. They repeat this at every gate till Jim pulls over by a paddock of maize.

There is a strip of rotary-hoed pasture. The soil exposed to the sunlight is crusty and faded.

'Long way from the house.'

'Good soil.' Jim pokes his gumboot into the crust to show Rachel the dark, moist inner layer.

He gives Rachel instructions, hands her the reel so she can walk the nylon line the length of the ploughed section. He watches as she moves smoothly with a bucket of sliced potatoes, planting them in the loose soil two boot-lengths apart, burying them half a finger down. She's back and he's only just finished slicing up the next bucket of spuds.

'You're quick.'

'Usually sit at a desk all day so it's good to actually do something.'

Jim realises he has no real clue what his daughter does, only that she travels a lot. When she rings, he usually passes her straight over to Di. 'How is your job?'

Rachel screws up her nose. 'It's okay, pays the bills. It's not my passion. What's next? How many rows are we going to do?'

'Till we run out of spuds.'

Rachel glances at Jim's buckets and laughs.

'Good spuds. Better flavour than those supermarket ones.'

'Won't they go off before you eat them all?'

'No chance. Di gives them to the rural deliverywomen, the neighbours, Val Luxton, runs the sports shop. She takes them to the food bank. Take some to golf, for the raffles.' Jim is pleased to tell Rachel something she doesn't know, or perhaps she's forgotten. When she was little, she helped with the harvesting, all the kids did. 'You should take some when they're ready. You need feeding up. All that running.'

Rachel studies her dirt-covered hands. 'I know you love your mashed spuds Dad. It's better to eat complex carbs. Spuds and white bread are starchy, elevate your blood sugar. Lot of work planting them this way. You need a machine.'

'Got you.'

'Will you show me the peacocks?'

Jim drives past Jack's house to the base of the bush-filled gully. He slows down but there is no sign of the birds. He can feel his good mood retreating.

'I'll take you up to the airstrip, show you the chicken farm.'

*

When Tui turned up and he had to shift the peacock, he stashed it in the shed behind the garage. The ancient building was hidden behind a bamboo hedge. It was where he kept, preserved under layers of dust, rusty saws, slug pellets, the second freezer, redundant cricket bats, spare timber, partly used tins of paint.

A few days later he decided he would use the feathers to make ornaments. It was something his mother had done. She hadn't had colourful feathers to work with, resorting instead to staining chicken feathers. She was always making things, especially after the old man passed. Feather sculptures, they lasted longer than flowers. Flowers began dying the moment you picked them.

The former airstrip is the highest point for miles. Jim and Rachel have a bird's-eye view clear down the valley with its patchwork of fences stapled on rolling sine-curved hills. The undulations flow either side of the arterial road and the tree-lined creek, all the way to the state highway and Hereford. Two quarries, one next door to Jim and Di's house, the other down a side road. They look like toy sandpits. Diggers, cranes and trucks move around metal moats among bunkers. Out east, all that separates the Pacific Ocean from the orderly green pasture is a curly line of milky sand swished with waves, casual as a finger painting.

'Bit like the peninsula?' Jim glances at Rachel. She seems impressed. Whenever she visits, she borrows Di's car, drives to the peninsula, spends hours running and whatever else she does.

'This is higher, you can see further, but the peninsula's right on the coast, has trails. You'd roll an ankle running here. Is that Hen and Chickens?' She points to the lumpy sequence of landforms on the fuzzy horizon.

'Yep, and Whangārei Heads. Can see all the way to Marsden Point.' Jim shades the sun from his eyes with his hand.

'You used to point Hen and Chickens out, when we went Kontiki fishing.'

Jim gave up the Kontiki years ago. Had forgotten he used to take the twins along to help bait the line, get them out of Di's hair for a bit. The trouble with the Kontiki, it caught whatever was there, mostly catfish, which didn't taste good. The three of them had better luck collecting pipi and cockles. Rachel refused to eat them. She still ate meat then, but she didn't like the shellfish smell. Now Tui brought them fish caught by her son. He knew where to find the snapper. And Willy brought them whitebait.

Jim gestures towards several long, low buildings on the neighbouring farm.

'Used to be a sheep station down there, remember the Cliffords? Old man Clifford offloaded the flat land by the house to a chicken farmer. Those sheds are crammed full of chickens. Clifford sold us this hilly piece plus the former airstrip. Right on our boundary anyway. Soon this will be Jack's.'

Jim thinks about Clifford. His kids weren't interested in farming, nor was his wife. Two offspring, girls, used to share the school bus with Rachel and Jack until they were sent away to boarding school. The eldest lived in Sydney; Jim spoke with her at her father's funeral. The younger girl, chubby kid, ended up starving herself, bad business. He's been lucky, he realises; his kids have turned out all right, even Willy.

'Grandpa would be proud of you Dad, for expanding the farm. He'd have loved this view. You need a house up here.'

Jim grunts, allows himself a smile. He knew Rachel would like being higher, out of the valley. Maybe now she's seen it she'll come visit more often. 'Got a house. Too windy up here.

Old man wasn't interested in views. Your grandmother liked it.'

His father had a bad heart, ignored medical advice to slow down; rewarded with a stroke followed by a heart attack. Jim can still recall the frail shadow of a person, the rasping sound of his breath as he struggled to inhale oxygen from a machine. He was unrecognisable, gone within days.

Jim follows Rachel's gaze to the remnant bush on the farm boundary. There's a recently bulldozed road with half circles flattened on the sides.

'My guess is the chicken farmer's preparing to slice up his land and sell it off piece by piece, like the Wilsons.'

On the other side of Jim's place, a clutch of new houses perch on the ridgeline. Despite their prominent position they are only visible if you know where to look. Sealed off behind a locked gate, up a long driveway guarded by pine trees and regenerating bush. Dwellings with septic tanks, powerlines, privacy and coastal views. He doesn't know any of the new residents. For years the Wilsons leased their land to the local timber company, who kept it in pines. Jim used to get his Christmas tree by hopping the fence.

'I didn't realise the council had zoned round here for subdivision. You wouldn't do that?'

'No, nor will Jack.' Jim catches Rachel's sceptical look. For a moment he wonders, then bats the thought away.

Rachel is staring at the subdivision as if it's a problem she can solve. 'I'm thinking about getting a job with an environmental group, quitting the law firm. Sick of helping people do stuff like that.' She waves towards the bulldozing.

'Oh.' Jim isn't sure why she's concerned about the subdivision but not the chicken farming. He doesn't understand lawyers, what they do in their tidy offices, day to day. Always on the move, in Rachel's case.

It occurs to him that the peacocks might be refugees on his land, fleeing the subdivision. His dream started same time as the sculptures.

The wind is picking up, smearing the clouds like butter across toast, sweeping long strands of his daughter's feathery hair across her face. It's time to head down.

Jim drives slowly back past the bush, craning his neck, searching. No birds. They stop by Jack's place. His quad is parked outside so Jim follows Rachel in.

Jack is checking the weather forecast on his laptop. 'Spuds all planted?'

'Yep,' says Rachel. 'There must be ways to do it that don't involve literally bending over the soil? Spuds would cost a fortune if it was all done like that.'

'Course, but if you're only planting a few it's not worth the capital outlay. Dad's only planting a few, eh?' Jack turns to Jim.

'Yeah, yeah. Just need some elbow grease. Rachel was a big help, planted them quick as lightning. Seen the peacocks?'

Jack shakes his head. 'Why, did you see them?'

Rachel replies before Jim can answer. 'No. Dad was going to show me. We didn't see any. Sweet sculpture.'

Jack says, 'Think we should round them up?'

Jim helps himself to a glass of water from the kitchen. He puts the glass down. Doesn't look at his son. 'They eat the grass.'

Jack says, 'Hard to catch. They run pretty fast.' He gives Rachel a nudge. 'Faster than you sis!'

'Wouldn't be the only thing faster than me.' Rachel turns to Jack. 'I'm going to visit Willy this afternoon. You want to tag along? I can wait till milking is done.'

24

Out Jack's window, Jim can see the cowshed. The kids were eight when it was built, Willy must have been two, now the kids have wrinkles and streaks of grey in their hair. A movement catches his eye.

'You let the cat inside. You'll have cat hair everywhere.'

Jack says, 'I know. I tried to keep it out but Gemma and the kids overruled me. When the other one died, I didn't think the kids would be bothered, but they were. Had to bury it in the garden. We had a ceremony.'

'Oh.' Jim shuts his eyes for a moment. He and Di have attended a few funerals lately, people they've known for years. Some had a good innings, some like Di's sister Jean, out early.

He pictures his dog, the way it jumps, dashes away and circles back, using its pent-up energy. Black tail wagging like a yo-yo. The dog's oblivious; it ventures close for a second as if Jim might pat him, must know he never pats his dogs. He might grab one by the collar to shove it into the kennel, he might direct a gumboot in a dog's general direction in a moment of frustration, but no patting. Jim explains to the grandkids his dogs are working animals, not pets.

'Well, I'd better be off.' He can feel the twins watching him, like Tui and Di when he carted the peacock off.

'Shall I tell Willy to come round?' Rachel asks.

'May as well. Di's got some pruning she wants done.' Out by his Mule, he turns to give the twins a wave.

'Up to you.'

'What?'

'Up to you.'

Rachel and Jack exchange a puzzled look.

Jim raises his voice. 'The peacocks.'

*

Jim drives to the cowshed. His dog barks, beside himself with excitement at the sound of the vehicle. Released, the dog sprints in frantic zig-zags, as if determined not to waste a second of his unexpected, precious freedom.

Jim enters the little utility room, feels for the light switch, and closes the door. The space is airless, filthy and cluttered. He finds what he's looking for on the top shelf. The pile of notebooks, pages curling and stained. He pulls the bottom one out, tips it upside down over the bench. A piece of card drops out. A snap of the cowshed taken when the foundations were laid. He holds it close to his face. There is a properly composed version taken when the building was complete, sitting framed on the wall outside his and Di's bedroom. In this print nobody is where they should be. His father is pointing to something out of shot. Jim, with his shiny black hair worn like Johnny Cash, has his sleeves rolled up, baggy shorts, gumboots sinking into the earth. He's looking in the direction his father is pointing. The twins are wrestling each other, all elbows and pipe cleaner legs. A young, fierce-looking Di, with curly hair, is clutching a squirming Willy. The toddler is only wearing one gumboot, the other lies on the ground. Jim can't remember why. A stone, or perhaps he was wiggling and it slipped off. There is a shadow in the foreground, two arms curved like a heart. His builder mate leaning in taking the picture, the morning sun behind.

Jim doesn't know why he kept the snap, only that he's glad he did. He studies it for a long time before he returns it to the notebook, replaces the book on the messy shelf and opens the door.

Hospital

Di is riding on a magic carpet, floating in and out of consciousness. The carpet is beige, familiar, threadbare. She bought it with money she earned picking field mushrooms that appeared several autumns in a row. Creamy flat tops, fleshy taupe undersides, fragile, easy to bruise, stained her hands grey. Frantic Sunday afternoons in the garage filling paper-lined wooden boxes. As suddenly as they arrived the mushrooms vanished. No, wait, is she on a bed? Airport maybe, and the thought of travel warms her. Jim hates airports, used to tolerate the long-haul flights for her, now he scarcely leaves the farm.

Is it night? The hum of air conditioning is unsettling, sounds like her heat pump but she doesn't have it on in the evenings. Fluorescent light leaks in from the corridor. As her eyes adjust, machines move into focus, followed by their cables, dials, keypads. Faces for monitoring and gathering information. Full of computers Di supposes, hopefully easier to operate than hers. Often she needs Jack's help. Di smiles to herself. Hospital, not airport. The floaty feeling returns.

In her dream she was inspecting the carpet, could do with a vacuum. She thought she would get onto it later, needed fresh air. Hard to breathe, wheezy, must have slept in. Jim told the kids she got up at six to watch the news. She doubted they believed him. In her dream she thought they had no idea what it was like to see your sister bedridden, the wretched daily assessment of how much of Jean had leeched away.

She'd pounded the unflinching farm races. Asked the deep-fried hills, 'Why Jean?' They stared back, faded grass lifeless except for patches of vivid green kikuyu. Horrible stuff, consistency of a scratchy bird's nest. Colonised everything in its path. Like knitting with acrylic. Di saw every fence that needed fixing. Holes big enough for a cow to get its head stuck if it poked through. She cried till she and the land were both burnt out, dry as a wooden god.

Hospital wards, endless rooms without doors and cavernous corridors painted spinach green. When she'd worked for Dr Jury at the medical centre, before she got married, he told her the colour is supposed to have a calming, restorative effect on patients. Similar reasoning behind the practice of leaving an animal in the cowshed when you intend to shoot then butcher it. Relax them with a familiar place, then bang.

Di drifts off. When she wakes again, she feels like a scrubbed potato, all raw. Flimsy curtains divide beds, mobile walls crafted for convenience, not privacy. Adjustable berths like luggage trollies. Designed to optimise the movement of people who can't move themselves. She feels calm, relieved. If she has breathing trouble, the nurses will know what to do. When the kids were small, she knew what to do. There's something about having people depend on you, the responsibility a burden, but it gets you up. Di understands this is partly why Jim still goes to the cowshed every day. It's something he's kept, but she fears she's let go.

Curious to see what's going on, she climbs out of bed. She

has a new neighbour, missed the change. In the television area she uses the phone to call her friend Tui.

'I'm surviving. North Shore. Yes, I know, only just got out, talk about boomerang. For a minute there I thought I was at the airport. Got the cardiologist's attention this time, says they can put in a stent and I'll be good. Waiting till I get my strength up. There's more urgent ones to do.' Di listens. 'Oh, you don't need to. I'm sure you've seen enough of hospitals . . . Onwards and upwards.'

Di shuffles carefully to the nursing station. She looks in and salutes. The nurses smile and wave back.

'You ladies doing okay in there, bit hectic last night?'

The nurses roll their eyes. 'Yeah Mrs C. We'll be giving you a frequent flyer discount at this rate. Didn't we just send you home?'

'Got so many air points I don't know what to do with them. I'm hard to get rid of, came back cos I missed you all.' Di pauses, walks closer. 'Angus, she passed?'

The nurses look at Di, one of them nods. 'It was peaceful.'

Jim finishes his baked beans on toast, stacks plate and cutlery on the bench. He pulls the plastic container with his pills closer and flicks off its lid with his thumb. Selects one of the white pills and two of the little pale green ones, stuffs them in his mouth and reaches for the water. He thinks about doing a blood test. Lady quack said the morning one was the most important, if he wasn't going to do the three per day, do that one at least. Jim respects her, more clue than his usual useless doctor. She realises he's busy, no time to muck around trying to get a needle to pierce his finger. Lifetime working with his hands, his skin is leather, be lucky to get anything through it, those thin little needles don't cut it.

Long drive ahead, hot too. Better do a prick and make some sandwiches. He picks up the needle. After a couple of attempts he still hasn't managed to draw blood. He slaps the needle back on the bench. Gives the fridge door a frustrated pull, removes honey and the latest yellow spread Di bought.

Di. She hadn't looked good. Not good at all. He'd called Jack, hated using the phone. Jack called 111. They waited with Di, who was grey and sweating. The ambulance took ages. The doctor guy, what was he? Paratrooper, no, paramedic, rang the local medics, they didn't have any idea. Paratrooper didn't listen to Jim saying Di has had this before, the trouble breathing, gasping for breath, all weak. Paratrooper and his mate took her on a stretcher. It was a devil of a job to get her out, bit short of space, tricky down the front steps. She was gone.

People kept ringing once they got wind. He's stopped answering the phone. Endless questions he can't answer. Half of them only ring to complain that he hasn't told them, like he's a bloody magician hiding his tricks. Di is at the hospital, she doesn't look good. He doesn't know what to do with this information. Why would anyone else?

He finds four slices of Tip Top white thin-sliced, lays them on the bench and smears on a thick coat of the yellow muck. He adds honey then folds them into pairs like he does for his golf lunch. Slices them diagonally and chucks them in a plastic container. Last, he retrieves a small bag of jet planes from the coffee table.

The roads are quiet, though cars keep overtaking him at stupid spots. Jim refuses to increase his speed. Radio Sport turned up loud. Idiot host banging on about the Blues versus Chiefs match. He's plain wrong. Has he even watched the game? Selectors are nuts. Don't rate the Northland players, always overlooking them, stick with blokes their side of the bridge. If they'd picked Larkin, the Blues would have won easy. They need Larkin. Same flare and intuition for ball distribution as Sid Going. Coach probably never heard of Sid. Jim squints as the sun hits the front of the windscreen. Does he have sunglasses? If he concentrates, he can see. He's been down here often enough recently. Told Jack he'd have to wash the cowshed himself. Jack tried to talk him out of driving, said he'd go with him later. Later's no good. Beat the traffic. Sooner he gets to see what's going on, sooner they'll let Di come home. No point sitting on the farm doing nothing, unable to concentrate on any farm work. No point waiting for the hospital to ring, they're too busy to ring. They're like him, allergic to phones.

Jim drives past lines of houses. He hates the way they're springing up everywhere, invading perfectly good farmland. Used to be dairy all around here, good flat fertile land, should be in grass. The car park isn't full. Parks his ute near the entrance to minimise the walk. He glances at his lunch. He'll leave it, probably means he won't eat it, but the hospital café has pies. Not as good as Di's mince pie, and she'd give him hell if she caught him eating pies, but considering her current state he's pretty safe. She isn't in a position to give anyone hell.

Jim levers himself out of the ute. People keep passing him. A couple ask if he's okay, one volunteers to help him inside. He waves off all offers. 'I'm good thanks, just taking it easy.' He leans on the handrail of the ramp for a rest. At reception he asks for directions to Di's room. He's learnt the hard way not to wander the rabbit warren hoping to find her.

In the heart ward, Di's immediate neighbours are sleeping but a woman three beds along is struggling to reach her water. Di goes over to assist. The woman's name is Mavis. She's in for tests, has a son but he's in London. Di tells her, when she went to England, she couldn't believe how green the fields were or how grey the sky was. Mavis wants to sleep. Di decides she'll rest, then call Jack to update him, and he can tell Jim. Poor Jim, he should stay home. There are meals in the freezer, left over from when friends brought them last time. Jim prefers her cooking. He's probably already on the way down.

Jean had preferred her cooking too. Di was baking scones in her kitchen when Jean arrived with her youngest, born a week after Di's twins. Her sister smelt of stale smoke and disinfectant. Rachel, Jean's favourite, came running for a hug.

'Hello angel! You've grown, look at those lovely curls! Where's Jack?'

Di watched Rachel light up. She blushed, giggled and twirled. How old were the kids then, four maybe? Jean's boy joined in, wide brown eyes, curly dark hair, the spitting image of his mother. Jack poked his head around the corner, offered a shy grin, brushed his long fringe out of his eyes, his nose was covered in freckles.

Jean surveyed the kitchen. Di waited. Jean's house was as clean as a whistle, everything labelled and organised, fitting together like a jigsaw. Cigarettes were Jean's only dirty habit. Di hated smoking. She should have put her foot down and insisted it only happen outside. Instead, she looked around for a plate that could double as an ashtray. Pair of chimneys Jean and her husband, they lit up more than their parents. Di didn't understand it. Jean was a nurse for God's sake!

Jean set her black leather handbag down on the bench, but not before wrinkling her nose.

'When did you last clean the bench?'

Di sighed. 'Cup of tea?' She turned and excavated the stainless-steel teapot from the cupboard. It was at the back behind the plates and Tupperware. Some of the containers spilt onto the floor and Di stooped to retrieve them. Jean helped.

'Sorry I'm being a pain in the arse. Your garden's looking great. Those irises, mine look like they're going to die. You've got the green fingers of the family.'

'Take some when you go.'

'I brought you some shortbread.'

'Why? Mine's better than yours!'

The sisters shared a laugh.

'You know I didn't bring any shortbread. I wouldn't dare. You make the best shortbread.'

Jean wanted to see the latest stuffed toys Di had sewn for the Red Cross. She'd heard a lot about the teddy bears made of blue towelling with a pink flower print. Hippy bears.

When Di opens her eyes, Jim is hovering over her. He looks terrible.

'Asleep?'

'No, resting. I was going to ring. They're keeping me in for an operation.'

'Operation, what kind of operation?'

'Heart. Will be a few days, maybe a week.'

Jim is relieved. Not so bad, a pump, like fixing a blocked pipe. Not messy like chest infections and the stomach bugs Di keeps getting, or cancer. No four weeks to live then dead. He slumps onto the chair beside the bed.

'May as well go home, no need to stay,' Di says. She's glad to see him but Jim is not a good visitor, he doesn't like waiting around. If he lingers, she'll point him to the television room.

'I'm here now.' Jim folds his arms, prepares for a long wait. He needs a rest. 'Are they sure it's heart this time?'

Across in the nurses' station, the shift supervisor glances over at Di and Jim, wondering who the awkward, grizzly bear of a man is. Di's husband she guesses. Di's tiny, looks frail but she's a fighter, gritty. Like a solar panel, the way she teeters about drawing energy from patients and nurses, reflecting it back. Di's the kind of patient you remember. The man, despite his size, looks fragile, lost.

Di's in a room with a view. Lake Pupuke, heart-shaped, glistens in the sunlight. A few sailboats glide across its silky surface. She wishes the window opened, she'd love to feel the air, even though it's humid and laced with exhaust fumes.

'Di!'

Di turns to see a stout woman approaching, her hair encased in a cherry red headscarf, crinkles around her eyes, a bright grin. Tui bends and gives her a kiss on both cheeks, stands back, surveys the scene. 'Never mind that lake, you've got your back to all these gorgeous flowers.' She takes Di's shoulders and gently turns her around, giving her a wink. 'Anyone would think you were dead already!'

Di laughs. There is an abundance of flowers. Almost every visitor has brought some. On his last few visits Jim's brought roses from the garden, though they don't seem to like it in here, the petals keep falling off. She'd rather he brought his sweet peas. Di has carried several bunches of roses down to the other end of the ward for other patients to admire.

'Heard about the junior doctors' strike. Never rains it pours, eh?' Tui settles herself in the chair.

Di nods and lies back. 'Delays things by a week plus whatever new urgent cases come in.'

'Well, you and me, we're survivors. Hell, look at me, not only survived cancer, won the other Lotto, the money one!'

Di giggles. 'Better not say that too loud Tui, someone in here'll mug you.' Not many people know that Tui gave all her winnings to the Women's Refuge. She said it was to stop her family hassling her.

Tui touches Di on the arm. 'Doing okay here? At least there's folk to talk to.'

'Yeah, always something going on.' Her fellow patients and their visitors are interesting, some are infuriating. On the farm, she's alone and used to it, but people are a good distraction, as useful as the medicines, she feels. 'The food around here, Tui.' Di looks around to make sure there are no nurses within hearing. 'It's disgusting, worse than aeroplane food.'

'Temporary, eh. Long as they fix you up so you can get back to cooking your own stuff, you'll be sweet.'

'Yep, it's not a hotel. Want them putting their energy into the fixing. Long hours some of these doctors and nurses work, no weekends, same as us farmers. Jean, my sister, used to moan about the shifts. Got Jack to bring down some of my yoghurt. Stuff here tastes like sugary toothpaste.'

'How old were you when Jean died?'

Di blinks, wonders if she heard correctly. It's as if Tui can read her mind.

'I was thirty-four. Jean was thirty-nine.'

'You think about her?'

Di shuts her eyes for a moment. 'Only when I'm awake.'

Tui nods.

'Lately in my dreams as well.'

Tui stokes Di's pale arm. 'What's she telling you?'

Di stares into the distance, doesn't reply for a long time.

'I've had an extra lifetime.' She turns to Tui. 'I haven't told you. I wanted to be a nurse too, but I played up at school. Got sent up north to board. Hated it, quit soon as I could. First job I ever had was working for Dr Jury. Had a pharmacy job too. Medical centre was better. Here I am, need nurses to look after me, not the other way round. Kids would put me in a rest home given half a chance. Jim says they're to throw us in a hole up the back of the farm.' Di is smiling now, though her eyes are leaking.

Tui reaches out and pulls a tissue from the box and hands it over. 'Not the wildest idea Jim's had. Think of the mushrooms you guys would fertilise, they'd be mighty tasty. I'd come harvest them, sit down for my tea, get stuck into them. Raise a toast to you both. It's a long way off though, the time for that.' Tui looks down at Di. 'Can I tell you something else?'

'Do I have a choice?'

Tui reminds her of Jean. It's in the olive skin, dark hair, but mostly her directness.

'I don't reckon you'd have made a great nurse, Di. You like people in small doses, don't suffer fools gladly. Some folks would find it hard to take. What you've done raising your family, all the committees, sports organising, toy making, baking. I could go on, my point being, your path, sure, maybe you stumbled on it, but it seems like it's allowed you to use your natural talents.'

'You're trying to make me feel better, Tui.'

'Is it working? Maybe I should've been a nurse.'

*

Jim drives to the hospital every second day. Today the road is busy and he's tired. He wonders if he should pull over, never done that in his entire life. Where are his jet planes? Bugger, he realises they're on the coffee table in the lounge. Maybe a sandwich but he'd have to stop. Next petrol station, he'll turn in and get some wine gums, easier to chew. Good to have a stash to leave in the ute, one less thing to remember. Jim considers petrol stations, the old route through Orewa, mostly local traffic. He used to play cricket in Orewa. There's a station at the top of the hill, south of the town.

Golf the day before had fatigued him he supposes, plus a bit of worry stealing his sleep. He's been feeling out of sorts lately, especially first thing, normally his best time. He's like the old man, attached to the routine of rise and retire early, years after the need has fallen away. He doesn't like being in the house without Di, though not for the reasons everyone assumes. He's perfectly capable of cooking for himself. Doesn't bother with the frozen meals, except for the occasional pie he's smuggled into the freezer for emergencies. He's found his air fryer. Di tried to hide it, like she hides her baking, but Jim's not silly.

Jack calls by most evenings after milking.

'Dad do you want some quiche? We've got plenty.'

Jim points to his fryer. 'One of my golf mates told me about these. Gadget's a winner, cooks chips and sausages in a few minutes, tasty, no mess. You should get one.' He's told Rachel about it too.

Jack studies the fryer. It doesn't look particularly clean but at least Jim's eating. He glances at the needles and lollies on the dining room table. Jim notices.

'Damn hard to get the little needles in.'

Jack understands, faints at the sight of blood himself. 'You're drinking water and washing, eh?'

Jim doesn't reply. Main thing is for the animals to have their food and water. He showers when he's going to the hospital.

The aspect that bothers him with Di in hospital is being alone at night. The empty space in the bed. The only times in their long marriage she hasn't been beside him are when she's been in hospital. First to give birth to the kids, more recently due to illness. Di has always been fit and healthy.

At night he lies awake, his thoughts churning like a vat of milk. He isn't alone in this. The phone is always calling with demands from people who really want to talk to Di. Ring the hospital, he wants to say. Di needs a mobile phone. He's asked Jack about it. Jack reckons it's pointless, the valley has no cellular coverage. And Di loves to talk. If she had one, she'd be nattering all day. Talking holds no appeal for Jim, he's a doer like Rachel.

Rachel rings daily to tell him not to answer the phone. She rings at 7pm so Jim will know it's her. They've agreed that if he doesn't feel like it he doesn't have to pick up. They talk about golf. A quick check-in, no meandering waffle about some ailment the caller had five years ago, or some vague need to justify not visiting Di, as if he has the energy to figure out what the person really means in order to give the appropriate response. It isn't that he doesn't care. He isn't a bloody mind reader. If he was face to face he'd stand a better chance of figuring it out. Phone talk exhausts him, makes his head spin.

Yesterday, he and Peter played a round of golf with Lance and Steve.

'Your cart or mine? How's Di doing? Bit boring waiting.' Peter survived heart surgery a few years previously.

'She's all right, gossiping with everyone, bossing the nurses.'

'Oh yes, can imagine Di getting right into the swing of things. She'll be good as new after the surgery. Take my cart eh? You're going down the hospital tomorrow, be sick of driving?'

Jim hesitated. Peter's cart wasn't as good as his. He'd bought an almost new one from Gerard's widow. Waited a few weeks after Gerard passed, then rang her. He'd felt a bit awkward making the call but Gerard had said to him several times, it would make him happy if Jim had it when he went. Widow was glad to get rid of it. Asked if he could take the trailer too, it was blocking the driveway, she couldn't get her car into the garage easily. Top bloke, Gerard.

'Okay, you drive Peter, but shall we take Gerard's cart? Thing is practically new.'

'I know, good score there Jim. Okay, give us the keys.'

'How long did it take you to recover?'

'From surgery? Made it to the spring play-offs, only a couple of weeks of resting. Bit longer for my golf to get back to decent but I felt one hundred percent better after the knife. She'll be good as new Jim. Like we are now we have our carts.' Peter grinned. 'My bloody nephew keeps trying to borrow mine. I say to him, you're thirty-six, nothing wrong with your legs. Kids, like to save time, get a round in quick. Think carts are like those mobility scooters, only cooler.'

Jim mulled this over. Funny how the young ones were in such a rush. Best thing about golf was it took up half a day, time hanging out with your mates. He recalled the wheelchairs in the hospital. 'They'd be no good for golf those wheelchair things, they're for people can't walk at all.'

'No mate, not wheelchairs, the scooter things are like

skateboards with a long thin thing up front and handles.'

'Oh.' Jim had a way of saying oh that made it seem like an entire sentence.

Back in the clubhouse at lunchtime they checked their cards, though they all knew Lance had the lowest score.

'My round then?'

'Too right,' Peter said. 'Think we all need some chips, am I right gentlemen?'

Jim said, 'Too right. Tell Sandra tomato sauce, don't forget the sauce.'

When Peter and Lance got back, they fell into a discussion about club maintenance.

'Jimmy, you'll be off to North Shore tomorrow to see Di, so you're out?'

Jim nodded.

Lance raised his pint. 'Here's to Di, speedy recovery.'

The others raised their pints. 'To Di.'

'Need her home eh, Jim,' Peter said. 'I'm almost out of shortbread.'

'Lucky bugger,' Steve said. 'I haven't had any for months. She's forgotten me. Can you put an order in for me Jim?'

Jim said, 'She won't let me have it anymore, might have to pinch some of yours.'

'Why not?'

'Diabetes.'

'Jeez, most people our vintage got diabetes. You have those jet planes.'

'Yeah, yeah, gotta eat stuff most of the time, keep the blood sugar constant, lollies are for in between, emergencies.'

'Not all bad then.' Peter clapped Jim on the back. 'Though Di's shortbread. Worth dying for. Did you guys see Jim's inherited Gerard's flash cart? Remember we said when he got it, he could hardly play then, we said, jeez that's a big spend-up for limited time to use it.'

'Old bugger was loaded though, can't take it with you, may as well spend it doing what you love.'

'Another toast. To Gerard.' Peter raised his pint.

'To absent friends with great taste in golf carts!' Lance winked.

Okay, Orewa now, good. He's feeling giddy, vision isn't right either. There used to be a dairy at the northern end, they'd stop for ice creams on the way home from cricket, it was long gone, replaced by town houses and roundabouts. He doesn't like roundabouts. There on the right-hand side he catches a glimpse of the statue of the mountaineer, what was his name? Jim turned to get a better look, Hillary. Ed Hillary.

There's flashing lights behind him, where'd they come from, an ambulance? Better pull over.

Di thinks it must be lunchtime, the nurses are delivering trays of sandwiches. Jim usually comes on Wednesdays. He must have decided to take a day off. His anxiety about time, his compulsive need to be early, is a family joke. Tuesday's golf might have tired him out.

A nurse Di doesn't know comes over.

'Have you heard from your family, Mrs Carlton?'

'You can call me Di. No, I haven't. I don't have one of those cellphones. My husband comes down most days.'

There is something about the nurse. She seems distracted.

41

Di can feel her heart beating.

'What is it?'

'Nothing to worry about. I understand we've been trying to get hold of somebody.'

'Somebody? Is Jim all right?' Di looks at the nurse, who looks flustered.

'Contact details.'

'Phone number? My son will be out on the farm.'

'Does he have a mobile?'

'No. Gemma does.'

'Gemma?'

'His wife. What about Jim? He's my husband, just tell me!'

'Hi Mum.' Jack appeared behind the nurse.

'You're a relative?'

'Son. Will fill my mother in.'

The nurse looks from Jack to Di, lingers. Jack is waiting for the nurse to leave. When she doesn't, he turns to Di. 'Power pole has a few bruises and so has Dad, he's okay though.'

'It's no laughing matter,' the nurse says.

Mother and son look at her. There is a beeping sound coming from further down the ward.

'I'll leave you to it.' The nurse stalks off. Di and Jack watch her go.

Di shakes her head. 'That's one business-like nurse.' She was nuts to think she wanted to be one. 'Your father, what happened?'

Jack sits in the chair beside the bed. 'He looks better than he has in weeks, more sheepish than anything. Dehydrated. They've got him on a drip. Doctor reckons blood sugar, tested, and it's through the roof. Has to overnight.'

'He's here?'

'Um, he knocked into a power pole in Orewa on the way

42

down, nothing serious, probably shouldn't have been driving though.'

Di sighs, her colour returns. 'You try telling your father not to drive.'

'Yeah well, the ute's a bit banged up according to Willy. He's going to sort it. The ute, I mean.'

'Willy?'

'Yeah, when the hospital couldn't reach me, they got hold of Willy. He came down. He'll be in later.'

Jack doesn't tell Di what Willy had said when he'd called his brother from the crash site. 'Lucky the old man drives like a snail or we'd be stashing him in a coffin. Thought he wanted to cark it on the farm.'

Di considers this. She hopes Jack is not going to raise the rest home idea. She and Jim can look after themselves, they just need to get home.

Jack says, 'Mum, it might be a good time to have another think about living options.'

Di has her eyes shut, pretending to be asleep.

'Mum.'

'I'll be fine after my operation, cardiologist said so. We'll be fine.'

Di remembers standing with Jean and her brothers, apple trees behind. They're all squinting into the glare, bodies dappled by sunlight. Di looks like Goldilocks, long-legged and skinny in her pale green frock. Her mother insisted on dressing her in green. She's never worn it since.

'Perhaps you don't remember my father in the rest home. He was miserable. Aged overnight. Place killed him.'

'They've improved.'

'I don't want you kids to go through what I did. It was bad enough Aunty Jean and then your nana dying at home but at least they were in their lives. It's not right to be in some spinach green room with flowers and one family photo like he was. Waiting and imagining in the company of strangers. I should know. I visited him every day, my brothers lived too far away. We both died a little bit every day.'

Jim is glad they're heading home on the motorway rather than through Orewa. He has no wish to revisit Hillary Square. The expressway is flanked by rolling green hills he's taken for granted all his life. On the flat sections the first signs of infection are visible. Circular cul-de-sacs laid out like Lego pieces someone's forgotten to put away. A few bulldozers, orange cones, packets of concrete blocks, their plastic covers spilling out around them. Patches of bare earth like enormous divots. In a few years the houses will take over the grass. He might not be around to see it.

He wiggles his hips, trying to manufacture comfort from the peculiarity of his situation. The seat is pushed back as far as it will go but his knees graze the glove box. He glances at Jack, whose hands grip the steering wheel. Jim can't remember the last time he sat in the passenger seat. He doesn't like it. The left-hand seat is for Di.

'The ute will be back in a few days. Might be best to stick to short local trips, eh Dad, when it's back?' Jack glances across.

Jim grunts. He feels like a suitcase plonked in a plane or a bus. The weird music spilling out of the car radio hurts his ears.

'You could still go to the shops and golf.'

Jim wants to get back on the golf course before rust sets in. He looks over at his son who he taught to drive, first on the tractor, then in the car. The boy has never been confident, prefers automatics. Gemma does most of the driving.

'Ellen drives the car around on the races to feed the hens, she's pretty good.'

'Ellen? She's only fourteen. Why doesn't she walk?'

'She's nearly fifteen. It's a place to practise. We can see her from the house.'

'Oh.' Jim can remember when Ellen was born, tiny white doll, big eyes, first grandchild. Those little fingers that curled around his index finger. Her fingernails the size of the point of a tee. Mouth opening and closing silently like a fish. He'd forgotten how warm and soft babies were. It was like starting all over again except he got to sleep at night.

When Jack finally leaves him alone on his couch, Jim flicks through the television channels. Too early for the rugby. He doesn't feel like watching the grand prix thing. He should get his drink bottle out of his Mule, bring it inside. Opening the front door, he pauses to smell the freshly mown lawn. Jack must have cut it. He makes his way down the path, avoids shortcutting through the garage with its black hole where the ute should be. Past the bamboo hedge, his dirty white Mule sits waiting where he left it. The familiar dents on the corners of the tray where it's run too close to a fence post or a gate, or more likely the side of the barn. He hobbles up to it and looks through the driver's window. There's his grimy water bottles, an old rag he uses for wiping the window when it fogs up, and a half-consumed packet of jet planes. He touches the door handle, the metal cool on his fingertips. He feels like giving his Mule a pat. After a moment he lets his hand fall away. Tonight he can drink from a cup, tomorrow go for a drive.

Di returns to the farm as bleached and light as driftwood, but she isn't about to be swept away. She tells Jim to go to golf. He doesn't need telling twice. He's plonked one of his peacock feather things on the bedroom dressing table. Di can see it from the bed. Worse, it's reflected in the mirror behind it. Glossy. Kind of thing that gathers dust but won't turn to dust. She doesn't mind the vivid blue, pity about the green. Living flowers in the garden are better, not that she's about to tell Jim.

Di has her medical instructions and her own plans. Movement, she walks as soon as she feels able. A little bit further each day. Between the flowerbeds alive with weeds. It doesn't matter. The last of the runner beans she picks and a few grapes. Jim's vegetable garden is doing okay. He's watering it first thing, till he gets back to washing down the cowshed. The slugs, slaters and snails are holding munch-ins. Gorging on the lettuce and silver beet before the sun scorches them the colour of hay and they disintegrate. Nourishment for the soil at least. A clutch of white butterflies rises up from their midst.

'Are you going to eat those lettuces?'

Jim pretends not to hear. Di understands it's the planting and growing. He offers them to Jack but he has his own vege garden. Jim used to grow passionfruit at the cowshed, replaced by sweet peas. Di loves their fragrance, the delicate colours, the crunch of their thin, pale green stalks when she cuts them with her scissors. You can't snap them, the stalks just bend and squash, bleeding sap while the sweet pea remains stubbornly connected to the branch. Strong attachment, those sweet peas. The way the flowers climb together up their lattice, turning back towards each other, spreading and weaving. A network of intimacy and growth. Don't last, they have their spectacular season then crumble to dust like the lettuce.

Jim thinks she should get back into driving. The doctors said she could after two months, it's three months now and Di hasn't been beyond the passenger seat. She's walking out on the farm most days now, sticking to the races, enjoying the timeless order of grass and animal. The way the days start out crisp then soften, the smell of autumn – remnant hay, dry mud mixed with fresh cow shit, the cicada soundtrack.

Every paddock has a purpose. The night paddocks, where the milking herd rest close to the cowshed for early morning starts. The flat, fertile hay paddocks. The rush-fringed paddocks prone to flooding. The paddock with the oxidation pond and mud runnels. The ones housing beehives. Calf paddocks, a pig paddock complete with sties, more mud than grass, a bull paddock with muddy trails round the edge where the animals pace sniffing for cows in heat. Paddocks for sowing potatoes and maize, full of old stalks that haven't finished dying. Steep paddocks for the steers. Bush-filled places where ragwort, foxglove and scotch thistles stand proud and belligerent while peacocks, possums and wild pigs skulk.

Di's paddock map is different. Mushroom paddocks, paddocks sideswiping the creek where ducks float and where many years ago the risk young children might wander in kept Di on high alert. The paddock where Jack's house is. It used to be covered in blackberries. Those berries turned her hands purple and the kids' lips and tongues blue. Jack earnestly claiming he wasn't eating more than he'd picked. Blackberry and apple pie.

One day Di notices a white patch in one of the paddocks. Is it what she thinks it is? She lets herself in through the gate, bends down for a closer look. Her knees ache with the effort, she rests them on the ground. A pair of mushrooms, so well established the grass has grown across their flat tops, forming bindings that cut into their flesh. Skin originally soft, now leathery thanks to the sun. They're too old to be worth picking, but there will be others nearby.

Di changes her route to take in the mushroom paddocks as she circles back towards the house. If she spots some more she'll come back with a bucket. She thinks about driving, how it isn't necessary. She can walk, escape through television, the internet, books, phone calls. Her family and friends can come to her. In hospital she missed the farm. Gratitude swells inside her like a sweet pea. When she finds mushrooms, she'll take some to Tui.

Preschool

Felix is tugging at Kiri's shorts.

'Kiri, can we go look for eels now?'

Kiri looks over at Julie, who makes a swigging motion with her mug. In six months, Kiri can't recall ever getting a chance to finish a coffee. She drinks hers in the car on the morning commute. Dropping to her knees, Kiri ruffles Felix's black curls. 'Yeah man, let's go outside.'

Kiri still can't believe she's landed a job at the new preschool with its smell of freshly sawn pine mixed with hand sanitiser. Tiny concrete pavers pale and exquisite as baby teeth mark the entrance. Come winter they'll be coated with a lick of green slime and someone will have to hose them down. For now, every time Kiri walks over them, they're a fresh start.

Julie picks up the cane basket full of sunhats. Kiri grabs the blue sunscreen bottle.

'Steal a hat guys. Come to me for your . . .' Kiri pauses, gazes at the bottle, waves it about. The kids turn to watch. 'Oh, magic bottle, what shall we call your creamy insides today?'

Voices gush into the room. Kiri puts a hand behind one of her ears and leans forward, eyes wide, eyebrows skywards.

'What?'

'You're supposed to say pardon,' Cayla says.

'Toothpaste!'

'Sticky white!'

'Snow cream!'

'Ice cream!'

Kiri winks at the brunette behind Cayla. Her pigtails are coming undone, her face is a splatter painting of freckles. She reminds Kiri of herself.

'Good thinking Bree, let's call it toothpaste today. Someone else can name it next time.'

'Toothpaste belongs to the teeth fairy!' Felix tries poking a finger into Alex's mouth. Alex bites.

'Hey stop that,' Julie warns. 'No eating each other. Come get a hat, then toothpaste.'

'I'm a teeth fairy!' Kiri spins in a tight circle, clutching the blue bottle until, feeling pleasantly dizzy, she settles on the floor. Pointing the bottle at outstretched palms, she whispers 'Toothpaste' each time she pushes the dispenser. The kids wipe the sunscreen on their faces and arms as they've been taught. Julie moves around helping the strugglers, using the opportunity to make sure sunhats are properly fastened.

'Pairs, tamariki, remember we need to pick a person and hold their hand, make sure we stay safe so the eels don't get us. What's the name for eels?'

'Tuna!'

'Ka pai. What do we say about the tuna?'

'Slippery?' Bree looks up at Kiri.

'Yummy,' Felix says. Cheeky little bugger.

'Mahinga kai.'

Cayla wears her 'I'm always right' pout. There's a line of sunscreen on her forehead. Kiri is tempted to ignore it but she leans across and gently rubs it in.

'Wow, that's a good one Cayla. Slippery is good too Bree. Yes Felix, people eat tuna sometimes, as kai.' An image of feeding pieces of eel to her cat pops into her head.

'Let's go check on our mahinga kai.'

Kiri hadn't always wanted to be a teacher. Way she saw it, teaching was a major contributor to her parents living apart. When Kiri was a teenager her mother's birth family got in touch, pleaded for her to return to the north. It was as if a boulder had dropped into a still pond.

'What about it? We'd be helping my whānau with marae-based projects,' her mother said.

'I can't run away at the drop of a hat, I have a paid job here. Someone has to provide.'

'Don't get all hōhā. Hell of a difference between tūrangawaewae and running away. You have skills we could use, if you were better at feeling people, not talking down.'

The arguments spun around Kiri, creating a whirlpool of conflicting pressures and desires.

Kiri's mother ran out of breath first, waved her hand vaguely. 'You know, never mind. I'm sick of this kōrero. It's time.'

The only thing the two of them agreed was Kiri should remain at school in Hereford. Her father taught at her secondary school. His attempts to persuade his pupils to catch the wisdom he was so eager to pass on failed to land. Kids could smell his neediness a mile off. Respect was reserved for the sports and woodwork teachers, the funny ones.

'Soul destroying,' he complained to Kiri.

'Why do you do it then?'

'I shouldn't burden you with my issues.'

51

'Probably not.'

'Too many kids who know their future lies outdoors, working the land. No interest in broadening their minds.'

'You mean they want to do practical stuff?' Kiri thought of her friend Shayne, good at fixing cars, solved people problems with his fists.

'Some of those brats are going to end up in prison.'

Listening to his complaints was like giving blood without the reward of a chocolate biscuit. 'That's a bit harsh, Dad. Doesn't Mum help kids who need to be taught in less structured ways, learning that relates to their, you know, circumstances, relevant stuff?'

'Kiri, you're smart, you need to use your brains, focus on a career, rise above the trash.'

He meant her boyfriend. Willy was funny, laid back, smart-arse and sporty. His devotion was the best thing. That Kiri Rd sign he'd pinched from the side of the road. He'd wrapped it in pink tissue paper, tied it together with one of his hockey socks and presented it to her for her sixteenth birthday. The fried bacon sandwiches he whipped up for breakfast. He followed her to Auckland when she enrolled at training college. She wasn't sure who she was, let alone what she wanted to do, but she loved kids and figured the way to avoid her father's disillusionment was to teach preschool. Willy started a horticulture course, quit to follow her back home.

Kiri could see she'd been in love with the power she had over Willy. He wasn't like her self-absorbed father, who wanted to debate each point and plan. And Willy enjoyed her mum. They were like kindred spirits, a connection Kiri struggled to emulate.

*

Julie leads the kids towards the river, Kiri holding Felix's hand, bringing up the rear. The main road is quiet without the weekend day-trippers and bach owners. It seems like only a few years ago, but probably longer, the village consisted of a few rickety houses, a butchery, a timber mill and a dairy. Now entire suburbs exist. Cul-de-sacs dotted with mansions. Driveways stuffed with boats, trailers, utes and Nissan Leafs. The main street has cafés selling chai lattes and wheatgrass smoothies. A flash pub, a cinema complex, boutiques peddling designer brands, an organic bakery. Kiri marvels at the new residents. The way they swim upstream wielding their influence, like pinking shears, sawing effortlessly through bureaucratic inertia to secure broadband, seal the hill road, set up the preschool and medical centre, plant native trees, build trails. Jobs for those born locally like Kiri, Julie and Jadin.

She glances at her phone. Jadin will be tackling his latest agriculture assignment. It's his last year juggling study with work. Then it's her turn. Sports management degree. Small surges, but she feels she's swimming in the right direction, like the migrating eels she and Julie have been teaching the kids about. She just needs to model the focus and confidence of the new residents. The cycleway is testament to their capability. Fine gravel surface, the colour of her Rhode Island Reds, the texture of the poultry pellets she feeds them. Her trainers produce a satisfying crunch as they press into the surface, like biting into a carrot. She soaks up the light touch of the warm breeze against her face. Higher up the same wind rearranges a few clouds, tidying the sky.

The kids start out in orderly pairs till Alex spots a white butterfly. It's a signal for the line to dissolve and hunt for eel food. Worms, snails and any insects they can find. Julie glances over her shoulder. Kiri shrugs. It doesn't matter, they can see all their charges. Bit of fresh air, burn off some energy then they'll head inside.

Below the path, past fruit trees decorated with candyfloss blossoms, the stream bank is fringed with clumps of harakeke. Rushes colonise the indeterminate space between land and water, their stalks poking up like antennae. Pond weed cruises the stream's surface. A khaki plant catches Kiri's eye. She stops. Felix gives her hand a tug.

'Hey Felix. Let's check out the green stuff, I think it's puha.' Felix looks puzzled. 'Watercress?' Kiri leads him to the water's edge and bends down, reaches out to feel the dark green leaves. Plucks a tiny sample, brings it to her nose. The peppery smell. She bites and swallows, feels its mustardy tang, slightly bitter. 'Mum,' she hears herself say. She picks another piece, offers it to Felix. He puts it in his mouth. Spits it out. 'Your mum yucky!'

Kiri shakes her head. There's no way she can explain to Felix.

It was spring, her final year at school, when her mother was diagnosed with cancer. Willy did his best to distract her, took her for drives, persuaded his mother to make her strawberry cheesecake, located alcohol, weed, whatever she wanted. He took her up north to see her mum, made them both laugh so they could cry.

'Dear Willy. Thanks for bringing my Kiri to see me, thank you!' Her mum would kiss her and Willy on both cheeks.

'Only reason I brought Kiri is cos she was already in the car, needed her to act as look-out while I was lifting some beef from the old man's freezer.' Willy winked at her mum. 'Grabbed some puha while I was at it.' He held up a newspaper package of greens. 'Larceny's bloody hard work, long-term plan is to find something easier. We'll have a boil-up.

Get ya people over if you feel like it. How's the old lady doing?'

'Old lady is dog-tired,' her mum said. 'Don't make me laugh, hurts me stomach. You're a devil. Where'd you find puha? Scarce as hen's teeth round here. All the waterways polluted.'

'We got it on the farm, in the creek. Don't look while I wash the cow shit off it. Really hot this lot, burn ya tongue good, better than a smoke.'

'How'd you know puha's me favourite?'

'Your daughter filled me in. Did Kiri tell you about her netball last Saturday?'

'Kiri?'

'Can we get you anything, have you been sleeping?' It occurred to Kiri that her mother preferred talking to Willy over her. She pushed the thought aside.

'Don't wanna sleep, gotta have this puha. You making fried bread too Willy? Tell me Kiri. I wanna hear about this game, come sit beside me while that rascal makes us a feed. Make it good.'

Kiri hesitated, ran her fingernails through her hair, digging at her scalp, searching for purchase, some new scab to pick at. She didn't know if she could get through a story. What she really wanted was to sit back and listen to her mother's stories. There was so much she didn't know, didn't feel she could ask, might never know.

She sat beside her mother. The old couch sank low even though her mother hardly weighed anything. As she studied the blood under her fingernails Kiri focused on the kitchen smells, the dankness of wet newspaper, the sweet aroma of butter caramelising in the pan. She sucked a fingernail clean, summoned her story voice for a blow-by-blow account of her netball game. Casting her net, she fished out the choicest embellishments just at the right moment. She wove the story together to prolong her mother's anticipation and pleasure, while luxuriating in her attention, conscious it could slip away in an instant. Kiri wasn't sure how much her mother was taking in, but she held Kiri's hand, preventing her from scratching her head, and lightly squeezed it from time to time. When Kiri glanced across to Willy bent over the frying pan, he would meet her eye from the side and nod.

'You always were a good storyteller Kiri, ever since you were little. Ka pai.'

Kiri felt a surge of relief, maybe it was happiness. She wished she could ask her mother for a story but she looked exhausted and Kiri's throat felt like it was full of mud.

Kiri gives Felix a pat. 'Sorry little fella, bit spicy for you. Shall we race? Ready, set . . .' Kiri lets go of Felix's hand and he's off without waiting. 'Go!' She jogs after him, wiping tears from her eyes with her arm. On the landward side of the path, short white posts appear at regular intervals. Each stamped with a koru. She catches Felix after two posts.

She leans over to catch her breath. A couple of the kids are knelt by the stream where they spotted sprats a few days ago.

'Don't go in the water guys!' Julie is getting nervous. The golden rule of child minding is never voice what you don't want the kids to do. The entire group peers into the water. Kiri picks up a pebble off the path and chucks it into the stream ahead of them. It lands with a small splash and heads turn.

'Is that an eel?'

Kiri again hastens to catch up but Bree is sitting on the path, one shoe off. Half an eye on the activity ahead, Kiri kneels to help. Bree pulls at Kiri's top.

'Tight.'

Kiri studies the shoe to figure out the strapping system. It's unnecessarily complicated despite being pink and cute when paired with the girl's yellow socks. The village kids have nice shoes, multiple pairs, though some of them aren't suited for walking. Chloe has silvery sandals. When her feet get sweaty, they slide out the side, making her walk as if she's wearing flippers. Last time Kiri gave her a piggy back, but then they all wanted one. She reties Bree's pigtails. At her old preschool the kids mostly wore jandals, hand-me-downs or bare feet.

Her previous job was only on the other side of the district but it felt like a different country. The long commute added a couple of hours to her day. Half of her lousy pay went on petrol and car maintenance. Her boss was okay but they were only ever an education inspector visit away from being shut down. The ancient farmhouse was more crumbly than stale bread. She never knew which kids were going to turn up. Some arrived with rumbling stomachs and bruises that didn't look like they'd been acquired from horsing around. She'd often shared her packed lunch. Started bringing leftovers from the fridge, stuff the Carltons gave Willy and her they didn't really need. It was better than wasting food.

The other carers kept a wall between the job and their lives but Kiri found herself thinking about the kids all the time. She longed for her mother then, wished she could ask her what to do. Didn't want to admit to her father, or Willy, she might not be cut out for preschool. Wine camouflaged her distress, made her a shapeshifter. She could turn into something else and swim away from her fears.

Kiri smiles at Bree. The kids' energy, their optimism, it's contagious. The pressure of paying the bills, wondering whether she and Jadin will ever be able to afford a house, her guilt about Willy, melts away. Kids, especially these ones, born to parents with money, plenty of kai, all the latest gear, chirpy as tūī. Kiri licks the inside of her mouth to clear the puha taste, looks at her phone.

'Intrepid explorers, it's time for us to head back. The eels must be on holiday today.'

The group clustered at the edge of the stream ignores her. Bree toddles towards them. Julie turns around, mouths, 'Eel.'

Kiri is amazed. For weeks she's regaled the kids with eel stories, describing how they float to Aotearoa on ocean currents. 'Like specks of seaweed glitter, sparkling in the sun! Whole schools of them. The babies are called elvers.'

'What do the babies look like?' Cayla had asked.

'Like glass, or plastic, see-through.' The kids look at her blankly. 'Like a fairy window.'

'When will we see an eel?' Bree asked.

'We'll have to search with wide eyes and open hearts. The eels can sense how we're feeling, our mauri. They hide down in the mud on the bottom bunk of the stream where it's dark. We'll have to look really hard, and be super quiet to spot them. Ninja mode. They're the opposite to us, sleep all day, work at night.'

Kiri and Willy were nineteen when they got married. They were the first of their cohort to commit, had no clue how to do it. It was supposed to be a party but it was more like a wake. Willy looked like a peg in his grey skinny suit and good shoes. Kiri decked out in an extravagant white frock. They were a pair of kids playing dress-ups, after childhoods spent in shorts, singlets and jandals.

Her mum arrived in a wheelchair. It was just before she went into the hospice. Although she had assured Kiri she looked lovely, her attention was directed at Willy. She called him over, gestured for him to get down on his knees, then laid a palm on each of his cheeks.

'Willy, you love my daughter heart and soul. She has found the right man, bless you.'

Her mother kissed Willy and the two of them embraced. They hugged for ages. The room cried, especially Kiri. She wept for the mother she was losing, who had been drifting away for years. The comforts, advice, unasked questions she was taking with her. She cried for Willy who was replacing her. Her dad, flustered at being sidelined, tried to shift the limelight by making a joke about how paying for all the alcohol was going to bankrupt him. Willy's parents seemed content to remain in the background, unsure how to arrange their faces. They didn't do hugs in that family.

The kids whisper and lean towards the shallow water. They remind Kiri of newborn calves, precarious on wobbly legs, jostling each other, waiting impatiently by their trough for milk. Felix can't resist, he slaps the surface with his hand. Energy pops like a balloon. Several kids slap the water. Cries of disappointment float towards where Kiri stands.

'Hey, hey. Come on. Mr Eel has gone now. He didn't like your splashing, Felix,' Julie says.

A flotilla of splashes fluff the water till it ripples, flopping water onto the grass. Thank you, Julie, Kiri thinks. Working together they collect up the deflated kids and point them towards the centre.

'I'm wet!' Cayla announces. She glares at Felix and turns her expectant blue eyes on Julie, who ignores her.

'I wanna see the eel.' Bree remains by the churned-up water.

Julie grasps her hand. 'Next time darling. You can help me lead the way.'

Kiri says, 'All good Cayla? We can dry you off when we get back. Felix didn't mean to splash you, did you Felix?'

Felix pokes his tongue out at Cayla. Kiri suppresses a chuckle. 'Hey Felix don't be mean. Grab hold of Alex's hand.' Cayla pouts, looks for someone to walk with.

Kiri says, 'Chloe, how about you with Cayla.' Chloe tilts her head to one side, considering. 'Worth a try eh. If you slip in your sandals, I'll give you a piggy back.'

Chloe smiles. 'All right.' She offers Cayla her hand. Cayla looks at it, as if she's checking whether it's clean, then takes it.

'Was it an eel?' Kiri asks Julie.

'Yeah, a big one.' Julie spreads her hands. 'A local must be feeding it.'

'No way.' Kiri studies the stream. It looks like someone has puked up duck weed into the swirling grey water. There aren't any trees or dead wood to provide shade but she knows the bottom is carpeted in mud and silt, perfect cover for eels. When she turns away from the stream, Cayla and Chloe are the only kids holding hands. Julie has her palm resting on Bree's back, steering her forward. Bree's pigtails keep swivelling back towards Kiri.

Kiri remembers the period after she and Willy married as a slow rusting. It took four years of exposure to the elements before the bond between them snapped. Her father supplemented his teacher salary with rental properties, and he sold Kiri and Willy a one-bedroom unit in a remote coastal settlement. Reckoned the location was up and coming. He was right, although it wouldn't happen for another ten years, too late for Kiri and Willy. Back then, it was a place folded in on itself, inhabited by nautical castaways. Boats, faded buoys, vintage nets, plastic packing cases, rabbits, retirees, alcoholics and fishermen. Many of the ramshackle baches saw only intermittent occupation, though the local pub did a good trade.

Meeting the mortgage was tricky. Willy's orchard job was minimum wage. He worked hard, got on well with his boss, but the offshore owner used Willy's lack of formal qualifications as an excuse to deny pay increases. She and Willy fell into a rut of collapsing on their exhausted couch, barely enough energy for TV. When Kiri complained about cricket taking all day, Willy gave it up. They were trying for a baby. Kiri's craving to be a mum wasn't satisfied by her job, or their two dogs and cat. Nothing grew in the garden Willy made, the soil was mostly sand.

One evening Willy's best mate Ritchie called with the news he'd landed a job in Brisbane.

'I'll miss you guys.'

Kiri had a sensation of being on a netball court, arms lifted, poised to land the ball in the ring. An unseen defender elbowing her in the ribs.

'Kiri?'

'I'm happy for you Ritchie,' she said.

'You don't sound thrilled. How's Willy?'

Through the window she could just make out the shape of the cringing, brown tomato vines crumbling off their bamboo stakes. The last play in a game they were doomed to lose.

'Yeah. Willy's down the pub. Ritchie, do you think we should have stayed in Auckland? He could have finished his diploma.'

'I dunno Kiri, you guys didn't warm to Auckland. "Shitty concrete jungle prowled by motorways breathing petrol fumes, vacuous malls, try-hard skyscrapers, undersized volcanoes and pretentious people with big hair." That Kiri-ism. Willy couldn't have said it any better. I'm escaping the place too.'

Kiri remembered Ritchie's flat, the suffocating humidity laced with traffic fumes drifting in from the window she'd managed to wrench open to let in some air. She'd knocked over a bottle of red wine, catching some on her denim shorts. The stain had faded but it was still visible, like a scar.

'Ha, true.'

Her gaze drifted to their wedding photo, the only decorative item she and Willy possessed. She wondered if this was it. Pushed the thought away.

Ritchie said, 'It's not too late, you can do courses extramurally. I'll come visit. We'll stay in touch I promise.'

His words reminded Kiri of her mother before she headed north, when she'd thought the shift was temporary. 'Come see us before you go.'

'Let's draw pictures of eels.'

'Better get them toileted, find a towel and dry the wet ones first,' Julie says.

Kiri notices Julie glance at the tin of instant. 'After the toilets, you grab a coffee, Julie. I can dry them.'

Julie shoots her friend a grateful look. 'Didn't get much sleep last night.'

'We got this.'

'Hey! Anyone with eel juice on them come over here, I'll dry you off.'

Kiri lays a couple of towels on the ground and invites the kids to roll on them. Amid the squeals of delight Cayla stands off to one side, arms folded.

'Cayla?' Julie puts down her mug and moves towards the girl.

'I don't want to roll on the floor like a dog!' She stamps a foot.

Kiri and Julie exchange a look. For a second Kiri is reminded of her father. She points to the roll of paper towels. Julie nods. Grabs it, and gathers up a big sheet of paper and crayons.

'Cayla, how about we dry you off with these paper towels? Could you help me with the art materials? We're going to do drawing. You're a terrific artist.'

Kiri wonders if Cayla will demand a real towel, but she follows Julie. Cayla's parents donated a piece from their sculpture collection to the preschool. 'Nymphs cuddling a dolphin,' Kiri told the kids. The plaque accompanying the piece describes how it references the symbolic associations between life forces and the sea. The inscription is obscured by the copper plate announcing Cayla's dad's name, where to find the gallery, and its opening hours.

All the kids, except Felix and a couple of his rowdy mates, tire of doing forward rolls and drift over to Julie. Revived by caffeine, she's getting their snacks out. As Kiri picks up the towels she glances across at the clutch of blonde, red, black and brown heads. Pigtails? Kiri feels a rush of confusion, drops the towels on the chair and gives the child she is drying a nudge.

'Go get a snack and help with the eel drawing.'

She checks the toilet, pushes open the front door, scans left to right, returns inside, panic rising in her like a flame.

'Julie!'

Julie comes over.

'Bree?' Kiri is trying to keep her voice low.

'Shit. When? She came back with me.'

Kiri checks nobody else is missing. 'Stay here with them.'

Willy spent more time at the orchard, working weekends and taking on responsibilities for which he wasn't paid. Kiri started coaching netball and flirting with the guys in the touch team. She caught herself snapping at Willy.

Willy's twin siblings came to visit. They'd all crowd in the lounge, which doubled as the dining room and spare bedroom, drinking cups of tea nobody wanted.

'What you been up to?' Jack would ask.

'Same old, same old.'

'Playing touch?'

'Yep.'

'How's the garden?'

'Useless. The salt gets in everything.'

'Old man's planted enough spuds for an army, wasting the best night paddock.'

'No change there then, don't worry, half of them will get blight. Wait till he cuts loose with the maize.'

Jack liked to give wry updates featuring Jim's latest bouts of stubbornness. Kiri sensed Jim stressed him out, but he didn't clash with him the way Willy did. Jim didn't appreciate Willy's ideas for doing things differently. The old bugger seemed to have Jack where he wanted him.

Willy laughed when she asked him about it.

'You forget, Kiri, Jack was captain of the first eleven and opening bat. He knows a thing or two about playing the long game. Openers the good ones, stay at the crease whatever the bowlers chuck at them, whether it's sledging or the ball, whatever, they suck it up. He'll be there till the end, the dutiful son.'

Kiri thought about her parents pulling in different directions, the distance opening up, solidifying, her inability to bridge it. Willy had connected with her mum better than she had, better than with his own dad. She put her arm around him.

'Mum thought you were a pretty good son.'

The crunch of her trainers on the path sounds like a series of small explosions. As she sprints along the cycleway she has a sense of racing to the rescue, wind in her hair, as if she's rushing through a tunnel propelled by forces she can't see. It only takes a few minutes to pass all the white posts with the koru pattern and reach the point where they turned back less than half an hour ago.

'Bree!' Nothing. The path is blank. The stream's surface unreadable. Kiri can feel her stomach rotating, like it wants to take off. A coldness spreads over her. For a second, she has an image of a car being winched out of the creek. Water gushing off it, mud and sticks everywhere. She scratches at her head, digs her fingernails in. When she pulls her hand away there is blood under her nails. She breathes. *Think.* She pictures their return from the stream. Cayla and Chloe. Julie with Bree. Did they close the building door? She can't remember. They always closed the door, it's the kind of thing you do automatically. Like kissing your boyfriend goodbye in the morning, assuming he'll be there when you get home. But it doesn't always shut properly, you have to slam it. Bree isn't inside, which only leaves outside.

She crunches back, scanning the stream and the fruit trees on the other side of the path. Nothing looks different except for a couple of tīwaiwaka in the harakeke. They watch her progress, their eyes demanding to know why she didn't keep the kids inside. Kiri drags her nails through her hair again as she walks around the centre, more for something to do than with any hope of finding Bree.

The preschool rests in the middle of a piece of undulating land reserved for public enjoyment. The developer had pondered this. The council likely had green space or a playground in mind, but they were expensive to build and didn't generate an ongoing revenue stream. Landscaping was scheduled, but the construction sector was going nuts so the local bulldozer guy got the call up. Kiri remembers Blackie from school. The big fight during a bullrush game, after he was mean to Ritchie. More accustomed to doing drainage jobs than landscaping, Blackie had attempted to flatten the hill. Realising his mistake, he'd tried to cover up the sticky clay mess by sprinkling grass seed. It had been a particularly wet winter even for Northland. Some of the grass grew tall and green no problem but, like a half-hearted Mexican wave at a boring game, the majority held off or didn't bother. The result resembled a grassy beard, scraggly and uneven.

The Residents Association came to the rescue with a working bee. Designer gumboots were located. Shallow trenches were dug, filled with compost and sprinkled with bark. Lines of hebe, harakeke and miro were planted.

Kiri searches the bushes, shaking the biggest ones. She finds a green plastic bag containing dog shit, but no lost girl. She looks around. Part of her wants to throw the bag back where she found it. She hangs it on the dolphin sculpture. Below the landscaping lies the main river, car parking, a boat ramp, and the new public toilet. Kiri bet Julie the loo was designed with some architectural competition in mind. Aqua and orange tiles over a structure shaped like a surfboard standing vertical. A loo that epitomises, celebrates even, the glossy ambitions of the village.

Descending from the preschool requires climbing down the grass or a hike around to the pavement. Where else? In the other direction the main road and the village shops sit silent. The kids are used to arriving and leaving that way. Bree may have gone looking for her mother.

Kiri thinks of Bree's pigtails swivelling. She'd wanted to see the eel. Kiri stares at the steep grassy slope and recalls Bree's shoes. She might have been able to climb down thanks to Kiri's efforts with the straps. Kiri again looks across to the shops. Both routes involve crossing a road, but the street by the loo only gets traffic on the weekends. She skids down the grass, not bothering with the footpath.

The car park is deserted. The loo stands empty and unappreciated. Kiri walks to the river. Early settlers used it to transport goods between villages. She struggles to imagine how they managed; the channel is narrow and willow trees overhang each side. The water is bark coloured, unlike the creek all those years ago. There is nothing to see. Kiri turns and heads back up to the preschool.

Jadin was a hot guy in Willy's touch rugby team. His main attraction being he didn't love her like Willy did, they hadn't grown up in each other's pockets. He saw her as a mature woman. He obviously lusted after her. Willy didn't notice. It was true, they were careful. Kiri was sure a few people had cottoned on, although nobody said anything to Willy. Initially Kiri kind of enjoyed the illicit nature of what they were doing.

But she couldn't sustain the duplicity. When she and Willy had one of their arguments, she told him.

When she opens the preschool door, the kids are still drawing. Kiri shakes her head.

'Shit. What do we do?' Julie makes no effort to keep her voice down. A couple of the kids look up.

'Where is Bree?' Cayla turns her blue eyes from Julie to Kiri. She uses her little hand to brush her blonde hair away from her forehead.

'Good question Cayla. Has anyone seen Bree since we got back from the eels?'

There is a general shaking of heads. The pile of damp towels catch Kiri's eye. The sunhats are back in their basket mostly, a few lie on the chairs in the corner. Julie's coffee mug is still sitting on the bench, half full.

'What happened to the sunscreen?' Kiri asks.

Julie says, 'I didn't shift it. It'll turn up.'

Kiri scans the room again. 'Hey team, the teeth fairy is missing her toothpaste, has anyone seen it?' She flaps her arms as she says it. The kids turn to look.

'Bree has it.' Alex is busy with his drawing.

Kiri stiffens, walks over and crouches beside him. 'Can I see, Alex?'

Alex leans back. The boy has drawn several eels and some stick figures.

'Great eels, Alex. Where did Bree take the toothpaste?'

'My painting is better.' Cayla is peering over Kiri's shoulder at Alex's effort.

Alex frowns, puts down his crayon and rubs one of the eels with his finger. 'That one is a worm not an eel, it's a mistake.'

'It's beautiful Alex, don't rub it out. How about you come with the tooth fairy and show her where you saw Bree and the toothpaste?'

Cayla is holding up her eel picture. 'Great work Cayla, show it to Julie.' Kiri helps Alex up. Her hands are shaking.

'Can I come too?' Felix wants to know.

'Do you know where the toothpaste is?'

Felix is already at the door. Alex tugs Kiri's hand and points to the door. Kiri tells Julie, 'You guys stay put.' To Felix she says, 'Are we going outside?' He nods.

'I'm showing!' Alex insists.

'The tooth fairy needs two helpers.' Kiri yanks the door open, then the three of them are outside. Kiri snatches Felix's hand. The last thing she wants is to lose another kid.

Willy gave her a look like he'd never seen her before. The blood drained from his face. He shouted at her to get out in a voice that could cut steel. He wouldn't stop shouting till she left. She stayed with Jadin.

'Bit of a mess,' her father said when she called him.

Kiri waited for the *I told you so.*

'I'm sorry.'

'Me too.' Kiri could not believe how numb she felt. She knew she was someone else now.

Kiri stands blinking into the sunshine.

'Where's Bree?'

Alex and Felix let go of her hands.

'It's important you help the teeth fairy find her.'

'She's hiding,' Felix says.

'I know. Teeth fairy can't find her. Will you help me?'

'You haven't looked,' Alex says.

'Worms,' Felix says, pointing to the grass.

Kiri feels like strangling them both. 'Bree!' She starts to yell, realising as she does that she probably should have tried yelling earlier. Alex and Felix join in. 'Bree!'

'She's hiding,' Felix repeats. Kiri turns to him. He is looking past the sculpture back at the preschool. She glances at Alex; he too is looking at the preschool.

'Eel,' Alex says. Felix giggles. 'Worm.' Kiri has no idea what they are on about. She lies down on the grass, stares at the sky. 'I'm an eel,' she announces in a flat voice. The kids join her.

'Hi Bree,' Alex says.

'What?'

Then she hears it. A faint voice. Scrambling upright she rushes to the preschool, drops to her knees. There is a gap, it isn't large, but it's enough for a toddler to crawl under.

'Bree!'

'You found me.'

'Come out here now Bree.'

'I'm cold.'

'Come out lovely and we'll warm you up. It's sunny out here.' Kiri reaches her arm under the building, hoping it will encourage Bree to wriggle towards her, hoping the child isn't stuck.

'Can you wriggle this way like an eel?'

'Eels stay in the dark. You told us.' But the girl moves towards Kiri slowly.

'Well done. You're doing good Bree. Eels come to the light, the surface to breathe when it's nice and quiet, remember?'

Above her Kiri can hear the door of the preschool opening, then footsteps as Julie comes down.

'Oh my god. What are you doing?'

Kiri turns her head to the side. 'She's under the building. Get a broom.'

'Is she stuck?'

Kiri hears Julie's steps as she goes back inside. Beside her Alex and Felix are also looking into the underground space. Felix makes to wiggle under.

'No, Felix. Bree can do it. Bree, can you wriggle some more?' Bree wriggles a bit closer but she is still too far away for Kiri to reach.

Julie returns with the broom.

'Bree, I'm just going to get a stick for you to hold on to, and we'll pull you out. Stay right where you are, can you do that?'

'Okay.'

Kiri uses both hands to push the broom under the building, handle first. 'Can you see the stick, Bree?'

There is a long pause then Kiri feels Bree touch the broom. 'Can you hold on really tight, keep your head low near the ground, and I'll pull you out.'

'I'm scared.' Bree's voice wavers.

Kiri glances around. 'Hey Felix and Alex, why don't you sing for Bree?'

'Bree, Bree!' The boys are yelling not singing but their tone is encouraging.

Kiri gets up on her knees and pulls on the broom but it comes out without Bree.

'Shit.'

There is a thump. The sunscreen bottle appears, followed by Bree's face.

'Hello.'

'Wowser. Hello Bree.'

'Eel.'

71

'Well, hello eel!' Kiri reaches for Bree, pulls her into her arms and away from the building. The girl is covered in soil and sunscreen. She wipes her grimy hand across her face to get hair out of her eyes.

'I saw worms underneath. Why are you crying?' Bree asks.

Kiri bites her lip, but the tears are flowing freely. She looks into the girl's freckled face, one hand strokes Bree's dirty hair, a finger combs a cobweb and draws it out with a flick. The pale thread clings to her nail, even as she rubs her fingers against each other to get rid of it.

'Shit.'

Kiri turns in the direction of the voice. Alex has commandeered the sunscreen and is smearing it on the sculpture. Felix is shaking a green plastic bag, intent on releasing its contents. A dark lump remains stubbornly attached to it. He moves to put his hand inside the bag.

'Felix! It's stinky dog poo. Alex, the dolphin doesn't need toothpaste. Come here, you eel hunters.' She opens her arms to include Felix and Alex.

The four of them huddle together long enough for Kiri to inhale the salty taste of her tears, the pungent odour coming off Felix, the gritty, sticky sensation of soil mingling with sunscreen. For a moment she's reminded of her wedding in all its glorious craziness. Tears where there should have been laughter, the awkwardness that somehow fitted them both.

'Thank goodness.' Julie is coming down the stairs with a towel in each hand. 'Felix, Alex, Bree, let's get you cleaned up.' She pauses. 'What's that smell?'

Kiri points to the green bag below the sculpture.

'Hunting eels and worms is messy work, but it's worth it eh,' she says, letting her hand rest on Bree's head.

She considers the white smears on the sculpture. Willy

would probably say the baked-on sunscreen lends the stylised dolphin an originality it didn't have before. Julie's right, they need to clean up the kids before the parents arrive. It won't take long.

Anniversary

Ritchie's heart is full of questions but the sky has nothing to say. The moon's a rugby ball kicking the dark as he scrutinises the splatter of luminous pinpricks that form the Milky Way. He clears customs well after midnight, isn't tired. The borrowed car feels strange, foot brake, he's used to hand, old model. It only takes a couple of blocks before flashing lights infuse the darkness with purple and blue light. The giant hypodermic needle of the Sky Tower pierces the stars. He susses how to lower his window, inhales the cool air. If he tried this in Brissie he'd cop a sticky cocktail of eucalyptus and exhaust. On the bridge he sticks his head right out. 'Welcome home, mate,' he yells. Five years since his last trip, twenty since he lived here, twenty-five since the creek. He catches sight of his stomach reflected in the windscreen. Same shape as the moon.

By the time he hits the Helm Valley he's divorced the radio. Thick smudges of bush grease the roadsides. Wait, there's a clutch of handmade signs. Ritchie slows the car, dips his headlights for a better read. Placards denouncing plans to build a landfill. Spelling's a bit off. But too right, cities eh, like to chuck their rubbish out of sight in the sticks. Company will own a network of tips. Probably bought the land a few years back and quietly waited for the right time, after a council election's a goodie. Secure consents, next play, dial in an outfit like his for the clean-up. Good coin in rubbish, not like recycling.

The range of the car's headlights fails to illuminate the complex tangle of trees and shrubs Ritchie knows lurk beyond, familiar as a good mate. He sighs, exhaling a puff of nostalgia and regret. His school buddies Shayne and Willy hadn't shared his interest in trees. His interest eventually grew into passion, driving him to study ecology, ditch Northland for Brisbane, and grow his dream company specialising in ecological restoration.

They must have been fourteen. The walk wasn't long, but the trail was muddier than a rugby field post-match. He can picture the ponga fronds like big green umbrellas, collecting the rain, broken twigs and decaying leaves, and funnelling them onto the path where the runnels of saturated debris sought refuge in the dips worn by foot traffic.

'I bloody hate this bush. I'm dying.'

Shayne's voice was like a chisel rasping on wood. He dropped off the track, letting other kids past. Everyone else had day packs. Shayne clutched a supermarket bag, but his jandals were the problem. They were no match for the track, a tree-root-infested bog, and steep. Sturdy shoes featured on the list of things to bring. Ritchie was sure his friend didn't own sturdy shoes. His rugby boots were borrowed. Shayne dropped his bag. Sweat drained off his ample forehead.

'How much further you reckon?'

'Come on Shayne, you're not munted yet, even with those flippers,' Willy said. 'You look like a mountain dolphin!'

Ritchie raised his eyebrows at Willy.

'Yeah, man, I'm tail-end Charlie,' Willy said.

Willy was so deadpan Ritchie wasn't sure if he was joking. He reminded Ritchie of a young rimu, lean, dark, a bit prickly. Willy gathered up Shayne's bag and stuffed it into his own. 'Make that mountain whale.' He pretended to give Shayne a punch on the arm. Shayne glared at Willy for a second then his shoulders slumped and he bent to yank off a jandal. He inspected the thick undercoat of mud and dead leaves.

'Jeez, ya supposed to look at the bush, not nick it. Whale turned leaf lifter,' Willy said.

'We're nearly there.' Ritchie was worried about Shayne's short fuse, knew he sounded like his mum, sensed the *yeah right* coming from his mates. 'Big pūriri. Not many left.' He pointed to the old tree a few metres off the track. Its rosy flowers sprinkled on the edge of their path like lolly wrappers.

Shayne looked up. 'Good timber? Good as tōtara?' Shayne's old man worked at the timber mill.

'Nah mate, stick with those pine trees,' Ritchie said.

'You liar, Ritchie, pūriri's a good hardwood, same as tōtara,' Willy said. 'Bloody greenie.'

Ritchie's face turned the colour of the flowers. Shayne was about to sit down when they heard the teacher's whistle.

'Shit, they're at the top.' Willy glanced at Ritchie. 'Shayne, you go in the bush there, outta sight, we'll pick you up on the way back. Me and Rich'll leg it up.'

Shayne peered into the bush. 'Okay.'

Willy and Ritchie sprinted up the hill, leaving Shayne leaning against the pūriri scraping mud off his jandals with a branch.

When he got home Ritchie learned his dad had done a runner.

*

When his old man shot through, Ritchie assumed they'd all leave. He hadn't wanted to go, but his father had abandoned his bank job in Hereford for a similar gig in Brisbane. Whether it was naivete or denial, it took a few days for him to catch on to what everyone else knew. His dad's departure had been prearranged. A sheila, also with the bank, waiting for him. They'd met at a training thing in Auckland a year prior. His aunt stormed the bank, interrogated her second cousin, a teller. He fessed up. There was hell to pay. Lots of yelling and crying, and that was just Ritchie's aunt.

'I want to go and live with him!' Nicole wailed. For a moment Ritchie's mother looked like she wanted slap his sister, but she recovered and tried to comfort her instead. Maybe it was worse at sixteen. Nicole was their father's favourite, good with numbers. He reckoned she should follow him into banking.

'Come on Nicole. He spent most of his time at work anyway.' This was something Ritchie had only twigged to when the old man's absence became official. For years his dad had hardly been there. His mother's grey eyes met his. He'd nearly started crying too.

'Oh Ritchie. Don't be like that. Come here, let's all have a cuddle.'

His mum had family in Hereford and further north, otherwise they would have moved to Auckland for sure. She started helping her sister with her catering. The work was irregular, dependent on sports events, weddings, funerals, church-related jobs, a few school and business gigs. There were weeks when there wasn't much going on, so money was tight. But it gave her something to do.

In the excruciating days, weeks and months after his family blew apart, Ritchie had no appetite for school, let alone home.

Without the old man it was like a channel had been altered from clear reception to static. There were things he didn't let himself see. He was afraid he'd be laughed at. He underestimated Shayne.

During lunchtime bullrush, Ritchie lunged for one of the Blackford twins, who easily sidestepped him. As he landed on the ground the twin yelled out, 'Can ya run as fast as your old man?' Shayne turned and punched the boy in the face, floored him. There was a bit of a pile-on after that. Shayne, Blackie and Ritchie were summoned to the principal's office.

'No sweat bro. Wasn't your fault.' Shayne's chest puffed out like a rooster. He looked over Ritchie's shoulder to make sure Blackie wasn't listening. 'Bugger's a can short of a six pack. Maybe two cans short now.' He slapped Ritchie on the arm. Ritchie's arm was stinging from the missed tackle and he tried not to wince.

'Thanks, mate.'

Shayne didn't care about school rules. He enjoyed a fight. Ritchie had seen his homemade tackle bags fashioned from offcuts from the mill stuffed into old mash sacks. He liked to watch boxing on television and follow along with the moves. 'It's not the same as a live match,' Shayne said, but he practised most nights if he wasn't at the mill. Ritchie had seen him punch a few walls in moments of frustration. Biceps the size of watermelons. Shayne was in with the principal longer than Ritchie.

'What did he say,' Ritchie wanted to know.

Shayne rolled his eyes. 'Blah blah blah.'

'He wanted a lesson in how to deliver a decent right hook, eh Shayne?' Willy said. 'Hope you didn't give away any of your trade secrets, mate.' He clapped Shayne on the back.

The whole class had to do detention. Word got around. Kiri,

the looker in Nicole's class Willy had a crush on, spotted Ritchie and broke away from her netball mates to give him a big hug.

'You hang in there!'

Kiri had some idea. Her old lady disappeared up north the year before. Got the call-up from her birth family. Ritchie felt sorry for Kiri and glad she hadn't gone away too. Everyone could see why her mother might want to bugger off. Kiri's old man, he wasn't like Kiri, probably the most uptight, strict and humourless teacher at their school. Kiri copped a fair bit of flak because of it. Ritchie recalled watching with Willy from the fringes of a group of senior students. Brainbox, real name Sophey, was venting away in her bitchy voice about Kiri's dad. For a few minutes, her arms folded, Kiri listened patiently. Then she unfolded those arms and fixed the girl with a hard stare.

'Can you not handle the jandal?'

Brainbox had fat pink lips like a snapper. She opened them, shut them again.

'My dad's responsible for me,' Kiri said. 'I'm not responsible for him, okay.' She turned her back and walked off.

Willy started clapping. It was genius. Ritchie joined in. In the wake of the Brainbox takedown Kiri and her posse started hanging out with Willy, Ritchie and Shayne. They saw more of Willy outside school. He managed to swing a deal where he'd go to his uncle's place after work. Persuaded him he needed help on his orchard. The orchard was near the mill, but the real reason was so he could see Kiri.

Ritchie fell into the habit of hanging out with Shayne. He and his dad lived to the north of Hereford, in a mouldy, run-down villa permanently shaded by a line of spiky macrocarpa. Every time Ritchie visited he nearly tripped over the ugly brown seed cones scattered across the front lawn like golf balls on a putting range.

Shayne hitchhiked out to the timber mill on nights he didn't have footy practice. Ritchie started tagging along. They were supposed to move strainers and fence posts, but Shayne liked to hang out in the equipment shed where the forklifts were parked, along with the stocks of spare parts. Apart from boxing, his other interest was tinkering with machinery abandoned by the day shift. If nothing needed fixing, Shayne was happy to take something apart just to recreate it. Ritchie watched, impressed by this mill version of his friend, the way his chubby fingers moved nimbly over metal, fitting pieces together like a jigsaw puzzle. Ritchie wished he had that for himself, something he could lose himself in that was actually useful.

Shayne noticed him watching and grinned.

'That heavy lifting shit might be good training for rugby, mate, not like there are gyms round here, but I like engines, they save you from shitty sweat jobs. Wish we could drive those forklifts eh, would be cool.'

Ritchie wasn't keen on lifting either, but machinery was an enigma to him. In the absence of other options, he appreciated the way the physical activity left him too tired to dwell on his dad's absence or his mother's silence.

What Shayne's old man did was a mystery. Something to do with security. When he wasn't out the back in the restricted area, he presided over the smoko room. Every time Ritchie entered the room, he was sat in his special chair he'd furnished with an old sheepskin, sunglasses protecting his eyes from the fluorescent light, chain-smoking and reading a paperback.

'Shayney works magic on the metal. Reckon he can hold his own in a fight, but more than that eh, he's a born grease monkey. Like his old man.'

Ritchie nodded, though he'd never seen Shayne's dad touch any of the hardware.

'Shayne's mum,' he pointed his finger to the ceiling, 'up there she'll be watching him and proud eh.'

'Yeah, totally.' Ritchie hadn't known what else to say.

'You look like a numbers guy Ritchie. Reckon you'll end up in a fancy office eh.'

Ritchie hadn't wanted to contradict Shayne's dad. Sometimes he was given handwritten orders to check against computerised records. He didn't object, though the task was boring and he was surprised to be given the responsibility. Ritchie wondered if the mill was short-staffed and using kids to avoid paying the minimum wage, or if Shayne's dad had hired them on the down-low. They were paid in cash. A couple of times he told them to make themselves scarce.

The cemetery behind Hereford's main drag is dismal but at least the grass is freshly mown. Ritchie places the flowers he bought at the local market beside his mother's headstone. Although he thinks of her often, the place where she is buried holds no significance for him and he wishes he hadn't bothered.

He's meeting Kiri at eleven. It's not the primary reason for his trip home but like the anniversary thing it's important. He's looking forward to it and he's terrified. *Calm down.* He wipes his palms against his jeans, runs nervous fingers through what's left of his hair.

'Ritchie!'

A woman jumps up from the corner table accompanied by a shriek as her chair scrapes the concrete floor. She waves both her brown arms. Ritchie smiles at Kiri's exuberance, conscious of curious eyes following him as he makes his way towards her. Here they are, in their early forties. They've both got a few streaks of grey in their hair and loads of crinkles round their eyes, sun spots, a bit more weight. Her capacity to spark up a room, buzz his heart, remains. He feels like he's smashed a short black and he hasn't even sat down.

She hugs him, releases him, pulls him close again.

'So good to see you in person Ritchie. It's been too long.'

'Yeah. You want something?' He looks at the counter. Kiri waves a menu at him and he studies the laminated sheet. Kiri points to the scrambled eggs. When he returns with their coffees most of the patrons are back to minding their own business.

Kiri has her phone out.

'Do you mind?' Before Ritchie responds Kiri has asked the women at the neighbouring table to take a photo of the two of them. She leans in beside him, beaming.

'Thank you!'

'No worries. He your brother?'

Kiri blinks. 'Ah no, well kinda I guess.' She glances at Ritchie sideways, ducking her head so her hair falls over her face. 'The brother I wish I'd had. No, better than a brother.'

He can feel his face heating up even as his heart sinks. Kiri is thanking the women again, which gives him a few seconds. He looks at the photo, doesn't recognise the startled man with Kiri.

'So much of the past is fucked up, want a photo, store some happy stuff you know?' She rests her hand on his arm for a moment.

'Okay.' He realises he still struggles for words around Kiri.

She is swiping through her phone, squinting to read the screen. Ritchie notices that like him she's long-sighted. She shows him a series of photos.

'Karena, she's nine. This is her team last year, winning the Northland netball under-ten competition.'

Ritchie looks at the pictures. 'She takes after you Kiri.'

'I love being a mum. Took long enough. Don't you wish you had kids Ritchie?'

He's glad the food arrives then. He feels like he's still catching up, had been prepared for small talk, he should have known Kiri would knife right in.

She's staring at him. There is an intensity to her look, as if she is trying to locate the eye of a needle.

'Mate.' Ritchie picks up his fork, puts it down again. 'Maybe there was a time, but you know, the old man didn't set a great example and the consultancy takes up all my energy. I guess the trees are my kids.' Ritchie realises as he says this that it's actually true.

Kiri laughs, though he can see she isn't totally convinced.

'How's Jadin?' He figures if Kiri can be direct, he can go all in as well.

She tilts her head sideways, studies him. For a second, she looks irritated.

'Not important Rich. We're doing okay, I've got a great job at the village preschool. I coach netball. Karena goes to the poncey school round the corner from my work, she's happy, loves it. Dad's mellowed, spoils Karena rotten. That's it, ten years in three sentences. Your turn.'

'Don't be like that. I didn't mean anything by it.' Kiri is still prickly about the Jadin business. Fine. He stares at the table. Jadin is about as interesting as a pepper shaker. He's moved on too, though perhaps not to the extent she has.

'All good at my end. Development is mega in Brissie. I'm run off my feet doing ecological restoration projects for the new housing schemes, got twenty-two staff now, second office out in the suburbs.'

'Your dad?'

'He's okay, silent partner, just pumps in money from time

to time, stays hands off. Figures eh. Why break the habit of a lifetime?' Ritchie can't resist throwing that in.

She chuckles, takes a big gulp of her coffee. 'Do you see him much?'

'Nah, sometimes we talk on the phone. I might see him in person once every couple of months.'

'Single?' Kiri doesn't look at him when she asks.

His heart leaps. *You still fancy her you dumb bugger.* 'Me dad? You're kidding me Kiri, he's never single! Yeah, I've had a few relationships but they haven't worked out. Pretty focused on the business.'

Kiri looks like she's about to say something but changes her mind. Then she shoots him a sceptical look. 'If you don't want kids then there's no great need to settle down is there?'

He meets her gaze. 'No.' But it depends on the person. His thoughts turn to Willy, all the bad relationships he had post-Kiri. Willy doesn't like to be on his own, nor does his father. Kiri, it seems to him, is the same.

'Will you catch up with Willy?'

He studies the toast crusts on his plate. 'Tonight, assuming he shows.' He's horrified by this slip. 'He will show,' he says firmly. 'He's in a good headspace now. It's the anniversary.'

Kiri nods slowly, a pensive look on her face. 'Don't –'

'I won't.' He knows she doesn't want Willy to know she and Ritchie stay in touch. He doesn't want Willy to know either. His friend would not like it one bit.

Kiri reaches across the table, touches his arm. 'I think about Shayne every time I pass the creek on the way into Hereford. We used to hoon along that road at night. We hit a possum once.' She shudders.

Ritchie nods, remembers the Kirimobile, the faded orange Holden. Shayne's mechanical genius and Kiri's optimism were all that kept it on the road. He tries to lighten the mood. 'Possums are pests. You did good.'

She pulls a face. 'I know. They look cute though. And the bump.' She shudders again.

'Speaking of night rides, what's going on in the Helm? I saw the signs when I drove up yesterday.'

She explains about the Helm landfill. They argue about the bush. Kiri thinks it's poor quality, Ritchie thinks it provides a vital transition zone.

'Well, you have the degree in ecology.' She says this lightly, accompanied by her face-igniting smile.

'Too right. You stick to sports management and early childcare.' He's proud of her for doing the extra study to get the sports management degree. She's a survivor.

She laughs and touches his arm again. He can taste the chemistry, bittersweet, almost soapy like a ripe feijoa. He knows she can as well. He needs to leave before the moment decays into regret.

'Hey I've gotta go and pick up Karena. Shame, woulda been nice to talk for longer.'

They stare at each other for a moment. Kiri breaks eye contact first, digs her fingernails into her hair.

'Remember that old dunger, when we first got our licences? Was always breaking down. Only Shayney could get it going.'

'The Kirimobile,' Ritchie says.

She laughs even as she uses her serviette to wipe her eyes. 'Drive a Toyota now, always gets its warrant first time.' She stands up.

Ritchie rises as well, comes around so they can hug, though this time in the noisy café the gesture feels awkward.

'Holdens, never trust an Aussie, eh. Bloody unreliable.'

Kiri snorts. 'Ha. Still the comedian. Good luck with the

anniversary. If he liked you he had your back eh. Real fighter, Shayney.'

'Reckon that's why he left school.'

'Mill was his happy place.'

'When he wasn't partying.'

'We all liked a good party. Young and stupid. No parties for Karena!'

Outside, they pause for a moment. The late afternoon light is behind Kiri so Ritchie can't read her expression.

'Next time you come over, don't leave it ten bloody years, eh.'

Ritchie has a couple of hours to kill. There's a little kauri reserve behind the town where his mother used to take him and Nicole for walks on Sundays, when she wasn't helping his aunt with catering. They were often the only visitors. Now the car park is almost full. Kauri dieback has sparked fresh interest in the trees. Typical, people don't value things till they're nearly gone.

Ritchie hadn't appreciated his mother. The effort she put in to keeping their family going when the old man left. The subtle way she nurtured his interest in ecology. She liked to point to trees and ask their names, the reason for their leaf shape, colour or some other feature. Careful to keep Nicole entertained with math problems she could calculate in her head – the distance covered, density of leaves per square metre. He knew she wasn't a big fan of either Shayne or Willy. It was there in the tightening of her face whenever he said he was off to meet one of them. She never tried to stop him going, even suggested he have them round to their place.

When she begged him to prioritise school work over the mill, Ritchie listened. He was tired of the heavy lifting and spreadsheets by then. Although he didn't like to admit it, his study also took his mind off the displacement he felt when Willy hooked up with Kiri. Plants, they were his equivalent of Shayne's machines. When his mother catered rugby functions, she seldom embarrassed Ritchie in front of his friends the way Di Carlton did. His mum would pass by when it was obvious he'd had a few drinks, deliver a whispered inquiry about a lift home. If it wasn't for her, he would have been in the car with Shayne that night.

Ritchie approaches one of the volunteers supervising the visitors.

'How are the trees faring?'

'So far the disinfectant washes seem be keeping the fungus out. I can explain what we're doing.'

And he does. Ritchie is reluctant to tell him he has studied the disease.

'What about a rāhui?'

'Ideally, but we also need people to engage, to understand, see what is going on, it's a compromise.'

Ritchie nods. The time for compromise is past, yet here he is. His feet soggy from their bath and brush. The minor discomfort falls away as he dawdles through the remnant forest, grateful to the locals who had the foresight to band together and purchase this tiny piece of land. The kauri themselves are heart-melting. He strokes a trickle of liquid sap that hasn't yet congealed to form tiny gum tears. He lifts his finger to his nose, shuts his eyes and inhales the tangy scent. Was a time he thought the sap meant the trees were crying. He returns his hand to the trunk, traces the mottled, smooth bark with his index finger. It occurs to him this is what he misses the most about Northland. He stoops to pick up a few golden branches with the familiar pointy leaves. He should visit the big one while he's in the country.

Are things changing? Kiri says the new residents, the affluent lifestylers, are big on protecting the trees, planting natives, restoring ecosystems. Problem is there's too many of them, and development hasn't kept pace with the conservation ideals. Everyone wants their big house, boat storage, cafés, pubs, shops, schools. They all take up space. Car parks too. Ritchie sees it in Brisbane, where there's more land to work with. Vast swathes of pasture and eucalyptus forest decimated to make room for highways and new subdivisions, so if anyone wants to experience wilderness they have to drive for days or take a flight. Even getting to wild places amounts to killing the goose that lays the golden egg. Carrying on as if the planet's capacity to absorb the carnage is infinite.

On the way out he pauses by a stream, listens to the water trickling over the rocks. The sunlight grates the canopy, giving the water a ruffled texture. At least it looks clean.

Willy will have finished work. It dawns on Ritchie as he returns to his car that avoiding the creek will require a massive detour.

Where the road meets the valley Ritchie turns inland, past the Carlton farm. Willy's parents took a close interest in what he got up to, everything from grades to sport. Helicopter parents before the term was invented, or as Willy called it, with characteristic exaggeration, 'Full on micro-management.'

'You gonna play rugby mate?' Shayne was good at rugby, big for his age, had the physique for the front row. Ritchie was okay at the game, more interested in the camaraderie than winning, was tolerated because he was Shayne's mate.

'Can't bro,' Willy said. 'Old man won't let me. Have to play bloody hockey.'

'Can't you just skive off?'

'Mate, we live like half an hour outta town. I'm under house arrest till I'm old enough to get my licence.'

'You're not really the right shape for rugby anyway,' Ritchie pointed out.

'Not like there's a local basketball team,' Willy said.

Ritchie could imagine Di Carlton acting mother hen with her orange quarters and barley sugars for half time. Her loud, partisan sideline commentary. Jim would take coaching seriously. Willy complained about them nonstop.

'It's a real buzzkill. Old man is never satisfied, even when we win by miles, on the way home he's going over every wrong play, all the might-have-beens. Then we get home and watch games on the telly and he's doing his own bloody commentary, ruining it.'

'Yeah, sucks but least he shows up. Only sign of my old man is a monthly line in a bank statement,' Ritchie said.

Shayne rolled his eyes. 'My dad's all I've got.'

There was a pause. Ritchie and Willy exchanged a look of shame. Shayne's mother died giving birth to him. It was the only time before the disintegration of his marriage to Kiri that Ritchie could remember Willy being lost for words.

Ritchie follows the school bus route back towards Hereford. He can't resist glancing out his side window. The creek isn't obvious. When not in flood it's nothing more than a ditch. If it wasn't for Shayne, Ritchie doubts it would register.

They all got their driver's licences when they turned fifteen. Kiri's lot, including Nicole, being two years older, already had theirs.

It was golden having your licence, ticket to go anywhere you wanted, provided you could score some wheels. They'd started going out to the lake and the surf club, all kinds of places for beers and a bonfire. They kept tabs on where the older guys were partying so they could freeload. The local pub sponsored the after-match functions, plenty of other illicit gear about as well. Shayne seemed to be able to get hold of as much as he wanted.

Mid-winter in the winterless north, and it had been pissing down. Rained for days, most rivers and creeks were up. Even Hereford had surface flooding. The sports fields were submerged, all games cancelled. Ritchie took the opportunity to get a bit of revision in, had assumed Shayne would be at the mill. By the time he headed to the clubrooms it was late afternoon. Pulling open the door the volume of the noise told him the boys had been there for some time. Ritchie felt uneasy, conspicuously sober. There wasn't much on Sky Sport, too early. Some of the guys were playing pool.

'Ritchie!' Shayne charged towards him and enfolded him in a warm hug.

'Oh wow. G'day mate.' Ritchie could tell from Shayne's eyes he was high. On what, he wasn't sure, didn't want to know.

'Have you seen Willy?' Ritchie asked.

'Nah, haven't seen that dude. Where is he?' Shayne couldn't stop grinning. Ritchie used the club phone to call Willy but got an engaged signal. He scanned the room for anyone who might have an idea. He spotted one of the quarry guys who worked next door to Willy's house, went over and asked him.

'Phone line's probably down mate, if it ain't the phone lines it's the electricity, plus the creek will be up, easy to get cut off, even with the new bridge.'

Someone was yelling.

'Ritchie. Phone for you.'

His mother was on the line. Could he call in at his aunt's place and collect some trays on the way home? She needed them for a job the following day. Ritchie wanted to refuse but he had her car so he'd have to do it. He glanced at his watch. It was getting ridiculous. Where was Willy? He picked up the phone and tried him again. This time there wasn't even an engaged signal. Ritchie returned to Shayne. He had his arm around one of his teammates and a huge, vacant smile on his face.

'I'll just go. Pick up Willy on the way.'

'Nah, wait for me, I'll be back in half an hour max.' Ritchie put a hand on Shayne's shoulder, leaned in so close he could feel Shayne's beery breath tickle his cheeks. 'Wait here man. Have another game of pool, then we can all go together.'

Ritchie pulls into a driveway, unsure if he has the right place. Someone is standing on the front porch. Ritchie can't make out any of his features in the twilight, it could be a burglar for all he knows, though the silhouette looks right. The figure strides down the steps, comes round to Ritchie's side of the car and stoops to open his door.

'Valet service. Rich my man. Jeez, you've put on the beef.'

Ritchie gets out. 'None of that cheek.' He pokes Willy's stomach. 'You've got a bit of a spare tyre going on as well mate.'

'Yeah, you should have seen it last year. I've stopped with the booze, it's going down. Come in bro.' Willy gestures towards the house. 'Did I mention I gave up the booze?'

'No. You didn't.' They've been emailing regularly. Haven't upgraded to video calls, standard in Aussie, a struggle here till broadband gets rolled out properly. Willy must have saved up the news to give him in person. Ritchie feels stoked, it makes it more precious. 'Never thought I'd see the day.' He hopes he doesn't sound condescending. 'Well done bro, since when?'

'Beginning of the year, so only five months. Come in. The missus is out with her girlfriends, just us.'

This overt hosting thing, the politeness, is new too, and it's messing with Ritchie's head almost as much as the teetotalism. Willy leads the way to the lounge. At last, something familiar. Ritchie recognises the old couch he offloaded to Willy when he left, the big flat screen that takes up half the wall, Sky Sport on mute.

'I got a pizza, gonna heat it up in the oven. Get onto it now, eh? Can I get you a cuppa or something?'

Ritchie isn't sure if this new version of Willy is taking the piss. 'Sure, why not? We're geriatrics now, eh.'

'I was pulling your leg, Rich. I got a slab of Lion Red in there if you fancy some beer.'

'Nah mate, I'll keep you company.'

'Sure? Unlike you to turn down a beer.'

'Mate, it's Lion Red. I live across the ditch now, I'm a Foster's man.'

Willy stops. 'Get out of here this minute and fuck off back to Aussie. Wash ya mouth out with soap first, bathroom's down the hall. You uncouth bastard!'

They both laugh. Willy continues on into the kitchen, Ritchie follows. Willy puts the pizza in the oven. 'Got a vegan one specially, Hereford's big on vegan.' He pulls a couple of ginger beers out of the fridge. 'Some non-alkie bevvies I prepared earlier. Wanna glass?'

'Nah, I'm fine.'

They clink bottles and return to the lounge. Ritchie is enjoying the banter but perhaps because of the anniversary, or how he's spent his first day back, it isn't enough.

'How ya been, Willy?'

Willy shoots him a look of recognition. Must have been thinking the same, the banter is automatic. Start-up mode, the way other people do small talk.

'Good eh, things are good these days Rich.'

'Went to Mum's grave this morning.'

'Did ya? Whole of Hereford's a grave, must've had trouble finding her among the debris.'

Ritchie shakes his head. Willy's incorrigible. 'Ah yeah, the place hasn't changed much.'

'Yeah, but everywhere else has. Good old Hereford. Skipped the recession vaccination, caught the decline early on and it's never managed to shake it. I'm working up north, long commute, partly why I gave up the booze. Gotta get a house out that way. Good work, loads of orchards going in out the West Coast. How's Stralia?'

'Good, busy as, was gonna say you should come over. But you seem settled here?'

'Yeah, nah. I tried Adelaide remember? Got real homesick. God knows why. Missus likes it here, she's real close to her family, her kids are here, she'll never leave. Her folks are cool. We spend a lotta time with them. They have a beach place up north good for camping.'

Ritchie nods. He met Willy's partner at his mum's funeral, liked her. Willy has told him he enjoys being a stepdad.

'How are the Carltons?'

Willy grimaces. 'Mellowed a bit, frail these days. The old man's still pretending like he runs the farm. The old lady's taken to walking up and down the road. She's looking to get skittled by a quarry truck. He's leaning towards dropping dead in the barn. That's how they want it eh, they don't wanna leave. How's Nicole?'

'Still number-crunching in Sydney. Comes out to Brissie

every month or so, mostly to visit the old man not me.'

Willy gets the pizza and a couple of plates. They sit down again. Ritchie's glad they're drinking ginger beer. He was about to say he'd driven past the creek. If he had, Willy might have realised he's been to see Kiri. Willy is studying the muted telly. 'So it's the anniversary eh.'

'Yeah. Is what happened to Shayne part of it, why you've stopped drinking?'

They sit in silence for a moment.

'No. All a bit hazy but probably I drank even more after that. Now that you mention it, s'pose I could add it to the list of reasons.'

'I should've taken his car keys.'

'Mate.' He says it quietly. 'We both know you wouldn't have pulled that off, not without a massive beating. He was taking quite a bit of shit besides beer, off his head he would've been.'

'How long had he been taking stuff?' Ritchie has wanted to ask for years but never found the right moment. 'I mean, I sort've clocked on to it, but not the scale.' He isn't sure how much he genuinely didn't know versus what he chose not to see, and whether he really wants to go there, to dig up the past.

'Dunno. His old man was a dealer, you know I got stuff from him. I should've driven round the long way and met yous. Old man was pretty insistent I stay put. Knew the creek would be in flood. That road was a nightmare even when you're sober. Lot of tight corners, the one he didn't take was the worst one. I mean, it's better now, they straightened it, you know.'

Ritchie is about to agree, catches himself just in time. 'Have they?'

Willy gives him a hard look, frowns. There's a pause, finally he says slowly, 'Yep, didn't you know that? Maybe you shot through before they did it. Fuck, I think of Shayne every time I

94

drive past and there ain't any other way to get to the olds' place.'

Exactly what Kiri said. He licks his lips, knows he's a bad fibber. 'He was a good mate.'

Willy raises his bottle. 'To Shayne.' Ritchie reaches across and clinks his bottle against Willy's. Willy raises an eyebrow. 'Remember the Kirimobile?'

Ritchie almost drops his bottle. It dawns on him in a bolt of guilt and admiration that Willy knows about him and Kiri, possibly has always known. 'The Holden?'

Willy stares at his bottle. 'Only person loved that piece of shit more than Kiri was Shayne. Legend, way he kept it going.'

'He'd be embarrassed by us toasting him with ginger beer.'

'Good thing he isn't here then.' After a pause he adds, 'You've been a good mate to me, bro. I know it hasn't been easy and I've been shit at keeping in touch.'

Ritchie wishes they were driving around. It would be easier to talk without looking at each other. Wonders when their friendship reached the stage where they could lie to each other but still trust. When things stopped being black and white and took on this complexity. 'We're all human bro, all deal with shit in our own way.' Ritchie raises his bottle again. 'To mates.'

'Jesus.' Willy clinks his bottle, takes a final slug of his ginger beer and sets it down. 'More coherent when we're running on alcohol aren't we? Turn the sound up?' He points the remote. They both turn to watch the game.

At half time Willy mutes the TV. 'You still hugging trees and shit?'

'I'm gonna go see Tāne Mahuta tomorrow, wanna come?'

He braces for Willy to lash him with a witty put-down. Instead, he offers one of his James Dean looks. 'Maybe. Could show you me orchard, it's out that way, and the financial apartheid going on up there. Bloody glamour zones where the rich fellas hang out. Buggers take choppers, no traffic jams for them. The locals living in shacks and motels. Thought of you, bro, the big forest up there, possums been eating the rata.'

Ritchie thinks about the first time the four of them rode together in the Kirimobile. Kiri wanted to have a bonfire at the beach, watch the sunset. They were running late. Any idea of catching the last of the light seemed optimistic, unless Kiri drove like a rally driver. Willy had wanted to sit in the front but he couldn't get the passenger door open.

'Bro stand back, give me a go.' Shayne had broken off a piece of bracken and used the stem to press the lock mechanism.

'Mate, if we don't hit the road we'll miss the sunset. Don't worry, I'll slide in from the back.'

The lock mechanism clicked and the door opened. Kiri gave the roof of the car a thump.

'Shayney fixed it. He gets to sit in the front!' Ritchie wasn't sure if she was teasing. Willy scowled but gestured to Shayne to jump in.

'Now Kiri, babe, I can't be sitting in the front with you, Willy's ya main man.' Shayne winked at her as he said it.

She tossed her hair and rolled her eyes. 'Shayney, I think getting the passenger door working is just one of the issues with this car, so I need you close at hand. Willy's good for other things.'

'True story mate.' Willy had climbed into the back. Ritchie followed, leaving Shayne to get in the front.

Kiri looked over her shoulder into the back.

'Whatcha waiting for?' Willy asked. 'Sky's already colouring up babe.'

'Seat belts.'

'This thing's got seat belts?'

Kiri started the car. The sky was the colour of sunburn, it

hurt to look at it. When they realised they had no hope of making the beach in time, Kiri pulled over. They piled out, watched in silence as the sky glided from pink to tangerine. Fragments of light caught on the edges of Kiri's and Shayne's hair like a golden net.

'Same colour as the Kirimobile!' Willy had an arm around Kiri, the other was shading his eyes. Shayne sat on the bumper. He was using one of his jandals to swat mosquitos. Over the jandal slap a mournful sound rose from the roadside tōtara behind them, rising in intensity before fading, only to repeat. Ritchie turned away from the colour show for a moment to see if he could locate the bird even though he knew korimako were tiny. All he could see was tōtara and the dark space filled by the creek. When he turned back again the light show was over.

Horizon

Melissa lies in bed. Her eyes are venetian blinds. She opens them slit by slit, searching for the horizon. A wake up, gather her bearings, check for ghosts ritual she's had since childhood. Thick, impenetrable curtains. Is her brain playing tricks? She rolls, white ceiling. Seems the surface is blank and silent today, no dancers or leopards, more importantly no rippling. The rippling triggers waves of nausea. There is a stale vomit smell rising from the basin under the bed. She needs to pee. Her stomach keeps roaring. The sound is like farting. She may have a headache, it's hard to tell, everything aches. Daylight hassles the curtains. The digital alarm clock beside the bed smirks 1:35pm.

In the bathroom, her mirror's an accusing parent. Disappointment reflected in her chalky thirty-eight-year-old face, brown eyes bloodshot. Only her pupils look normal. Tea bags under her eyes. Her hair's lumpy like chutney. The thought has her leaning over the sink, retching. She splashes water on her cheeks. Cautiously runs fingers through unresponsive hair. Her hands aren't shaking. Good sign. No diarrhoea, something to be grateful for. She can always find something to be grateful for, it's her super power. Gives her the strength she needs to enter the kitchen.

Thank God she left the windows open. No stale fry-up odour, its presence would have necessitated a return to the bathroom for sure. The room's busy storing emptiness. Cutlery bisects dirty plates and cups like a game of pick-up sticks, hollow cans, flattened painkiller packets. She shakes the Milo tin, silent, weightless, hollow as her guts. She thinks of her dog Milo, she can't help herself. Although the physical reminders are gone, her memories are right here.

The fridge is bare except for a few cans of Red Bull squatting down the bottom. There's probably food in the freezer, would need defrosting. She goes back to the bedroom and pulls on her jeans and a jumper. Finds the car keys, phone and wallet. Jandals are by the back door. Figures she'll drive to the Four Square or the service station and get a pie.

Shit. The car's nearly out of petrol. Hunched over the steering wheel, like an old lady concentrating, squinting into the sun. Ignores her beeping phone, surprised it still has battery. The village is empty. Petrol first. Inside she selects two steak pies from the warmer. Hands over her mother's petrol card, digs around in her wallet for change. Relief she doesn't know the guy doing the serving. Back outside she drives along the road till she finds a park. Hoovers one of the pies while sitting in the car. Should call her mother, stop being a pussy. Rummages around looking for water, locates a crumpled plastic bottle. The liquid has a dusty warm tang to it, stale. Some runs down her chin, wetting her jumper. Okay, she needs coffee, is there any at the house? She isn't sure. Checks her wallet, fingers a twenty.

Inside the Four Square she clutches a basket, litre of milk, ancient bananas, instant lurking with the tea, the sole loaf of Tip Top, a dozen eggs and a packet of salt and vinegar chips.

At the checkout a couple of Moros jump aboard. Her collection is more than twenty.

'Can you put it on Mum's account?'

The cashier glances at her. 'Barclay?'

She nods, recognises his face from parties, eczema where his collar creases his neck. He looks doubtful, but checks his list. The account is there. Her mother obviously hasn't gotten as far as instructing them not to serve her. He scrutinises her small pile of goods and nods again. If he's checking for cigarettes or painkillers he's out of luck, she isn't that stupid. Figures to make hay while the sun shines.

'Actually, can I add a couple of things?'

The cashier shrugs. She goes to the fridge to get the juice and Coke and brings them back.

'Um, I need a bag too.'

'We don't sell bags.'

'Shit, okay. I'll take the basket and bring it straight back, car's just down the street.'

The cashier can't see any way around it so he nods. As she's lugging her loot to the car she wonders if she should have grabbed some ice cream now her appetite is back. No. She's probably stretched the counter guy's patience as far as she can. When she pops the basket back where it belongs, she gives him a wave and shouts, 'Thanks mate.'

Back at the car she checks her phone. She turned it off while she was detoxing, so while she expected the missed calls from her mother, the texts from people checking in are surprising. Maybe she does have friends. She sends off quick replies saying it's all good. What else can she say? She eats the other pie. Damn, should have gotten more. She takes her wallet and heads to the ATM. Checks her balance. It's not good. She'd better ring her mother.

Her head aches. Sleep, she could do with more. When she sees the black ute parked by the house, she considers doing a uey and heading to the beach. It's too late. She's been seen.

'Hi Mum.'

Jennifer Barclay's calm nod somehow conveys years of sorrow and stoicism. Melissa wonders, not for the first time, what her secret is. Her face has a smooth, plumped-up gloss to it, impenetrable. Her pale brown eyes remind Melissa of Andy. Melissa forces a smile, conscious she looks like death warmed up.

'Darling, I was between meetings, thought I'd pop over and see how you were doing. I took the liberty of putting the dishwasher on, cleaning up a bit. Looks like you could do with some groceries.'

'Thanks Mum, I was going to get onto that. Groceries in the car, just need a bag to put them in.' Melissa looks around, wondering where she'd find a recyclable bag. Thinks better of it, doesn't want her mother to see all the junk food. *Stop acting like a child Mel.*

'Do you want a coffee Mum?'

'No, dear. I've got a committee session to get to. I was thinking if you're feeling up to it, come round for dinner. Your father and I are free tomorrow night. We can discuss next steps. It's about time, don't you think?'

Melissa sees it isn't a suggestion.

'Sure, okay, what time?'

'As you know dear, we have dinner at 6pm. We'll see you then. Good you're up and about.'

Jennifer takes a few steps toward her, rests a manicured hand on her arm briefly. Then she climbs into her ute, and Melissa lets out a sigh of relief as she drives off. The judgement that her mother's so careful to edit out of her talk leaks out in other, silent ways. In her meaner moments she thinks of her as being like a sprinkler, the type her father runs from the cowshed to spray diluted cow shit onto the paddocks.

She needs a job. Start fresh. Daryl's goneburger. Long-suffering parents stubbornly refuse to chuck her under the bus. They're in it for the boys, for her too. They don't approve of her but can't bear the thought of losing their remaining offspring. That'd be another level of careless. Melissa might be the black sheep but she's still in the flock. Isn't sure she can handle it. She almost laughs and cries at the same time at her attempts to convince herself. She wipes her eyes with her arm and plugs her phone in to charge.

Daryl. Their first encounter was almost two decades ago, at the local squash club. She was twenty-one, back from beauty school and interning at the spa down the road. Despite their age difference – she discovered later he had ten years on her – she was down on the draw to play him. She thrashed him in straight games, then, still dripping with sweat, asked him what he did.

'I'm a firefighter, babe.'

'Really?' He was good-natured about losing, smooth tongue on him, matched his unlined face. No perspiration, as if he'd hardly made an effort.

'For real. They sent me up here to manage the northern business, stock agency mainly, bit of buying and selling farms. Been out to your coast, bloody gorgeous, reckon real estate side will grow like wild fire.'

'So that red sports car outside is yours then?'

She learned sex in a sports car is overrated. Lotta bruises. Totally impractical set of wheels, not least because he preferred tall chicks. He had a way of making her feel like she was his co-conspirator. He could hold his drink. Party central old Daryl. She failed to immediately spot the shrewdness behind his easy charm. Ironic really that the professional beautician in her didn't see the make-up straight away. She should've listened to Dana.

When she fell pregnant, she kept working at the spa. Daryl did a deal with her parents – they'd tie the knot in return for accommodation in the spare farmhouse. She'd been keener on the kid part than living on the farm.

'Wouldn't a place in town be better? Big commute, isolated out by the coast.'

'Babe, you wanna have kids, I'm on the same page. We're gonna be, like, grownups. Your folks, they're kinda cool. Your dad's in the thick of it, Fed Farmers, Lions, council, good contacts. I'll be working my arse off. Olds can help out with baby stuff. They're gasping to be grandparents. We can always get a nice place in town later.'

Daryl's own parents had been killed in a car crash when he was a teenager.

He got on well with her parents. Bugger got on well with everyone except Dana. Ever since Melissa started at the spa as a trainee, she and Dana had been close. Dana was a couple of years older than Melissa, flatted in the neighbouring town with a bunch of women with short spiky hair and tattoos. Dana. Her long pale pink mane sheathed in a ponytail, lovely olive skin. She had a way of lifting her sculpted eyebrows to flirt with Melissa, like a feathery tickle.

'He wants you to live on your parents' farm for their benefit? He doesn't strike me as a social worker type.'

'He's sexier than any social worker Dana. And my parents adore him.'

'Better he adores you, honey,' Dana said.

Melissa felt stupid, as she sometimes did around Dana. It was all right for her. She didn't seem interested in getting married and having kids. A sticking point between them. When she'd first mentioned that she and Daryl were dating, Dana had been unsurprised but unenthusiastic.

'He's a step up from your previous boyfriends, for sure.'

Melissa recalled the way the wine had caused Dana's cheeks to flush the colour of her hair. She looked like a pink goddess.

'Dana, he's hot, and smart.'

Dana shrugged. 'Yeah, kid, we know it's slim pickings in Hereford. Unemployed drug addicts and farmers' sons who think because they're going to inherit a farm local chicks should be happy to put up with their beer guts and chauvinism.'

'They aren't that bad! Anyway, even more reason to hang with Daryl.' Melissa felt the alcohol warming her skin too, like a mohair sweater, not that she'd ever had such a sweater, but she imagined it would be like that, all scratchy yet comforting.

Dana fiddled with her wine glass.

'Spit it out.'

'Babe.' Dana was looking at her like she was a puppy she was about to kick. 'You don't think your parents see him as a kind of Andy replacement?'

'Daryl as a son-in-law? I sure as hell don't see Daryl as a brother!'

Dana held up her hands in surrender. 'I'm being a bitch. Having a baby is a shitload of commitment, be the making of you guys. Where you live is not that big a deal.'

Melissa wasn't listening. Her brother had vanished fifteen years ago, when she was seven. She'd spilled her guts to Dana because she trusted her. It wasn't something she told most people.

'Of course, remote rural is better for his side hustle,' Dana added.

She can't avoid dinner with her parents so her goal is to get through it. His tight smile indicates that Hamish Barclay is on his best behaviour and likely feels the same way. He has a couple of tiny lesions on his face where melanomas have been removed. But the worst is on his forearm, a finger-length scar. He takes sunscreen as seriously as he takes farming and parenting now. Jennifer has made some kind of casserole. They all pick at it as they push small talk around the table. Melissa notices her parents prefer the wine over the food. She's careful to stick to one glass.

'The boys have school holidays in two weeks,' Jennifer murmurs.

Melissa nods. She knows what her mother is doing. Pretending it's up to her, Mel. Like she isn't embroiled in a tug of war between her sons, Marty and Lucas, and her parents. The boys want to remain in Auckland with family friends. The Grahams have two boys who are also fifteen and sixteen, a tight four. Mel considers the Grahams saints, the way they're willing to accommodate her two. She can't really blame her boys for not wanting to hang out in the sticks with their embarrassing mother. It stings, but she has a high pain tolerance.

'Yeah Mum, I'm planning to ring them. Judging by our past chats I think they'll stay with the Grahams. Maybe come up for a weekend.'

Hamish colours up, looks like he's about to say something. A glance from her mother keeps him silent.

'I know the Grahams are lovely people, inspirational. Are you sure the boys want to stay in Auckland? They wouldn't just say that because they think it's what you want? It would be a pity to push them away or give in to their every whim. It's so tricky, isn't it? Your father and I would love to see them of course. It would be such a shame if they lost their connection with the district.'

Anger is bubbling in Melissa's belly, but she's anticipated this.

'I'll call them, see what they think. They'll probably be keen for a weekend. Maybe we can all go out for dinner.' It's a compromise, a pragmatic solution that satisfies nobody, but she can see all parties agreeing to it. The Grahams will surely want a weekend to themselves.

Hamish glares at her, red in the face. 'It's what you as the parent thinks. Those boys will do what they're told!'

'Hamish.' Her mother's voice is pleasant but tight.

Melissa studies the fan of blue veins that form little mounds on the backs of her hands. Her white knuckles. For a moment she's a small girl in navy gumboots with stripy toothpaste tops, red and white. A dark shadow falls across her feet. Her father has found them. He's admonishing Andy for taking her down to the creek. Andy's squeezing her muddy hand. It hurts but not as much as the shouting back and forth. She cries to make them stop. She shakes the memory free, looks up at Hamish.

'Melissa.' Her mother uses the same voice she used for Melissa's father.

'Oh, come on, Mum. Let Dad have his say, you've had yours. You guys are such good parents. Heard from Andy?' Melissa can feel her heart scrabbling against her chest like it's trying to push open a door.

Hamish pushes back his chair and leaves the room. He seems more resigned than angry. Jennifer, Melissa notices, doesn't even glance in his direction, she keeps her puppy eyes on Melissa.

'That was unbelievably cruel.'

'Sorry Mum.' It's hard to breathe, like she's encased in Gladwrap, fighting to remove it so she can get some air. She pours herself another glass of wine. 'You guys are killing me. Please stop. I'm doing an excellent job without your help.'

'What do you mean?' Jennifer looks startled, though her eyes quickly return to their resting state of sorrowful empathy.

Melissa drains her glass.

'You think I can't look after my own kids, but you want them up here. I'll get a job, get back on my feet. I need to get my health back. I've got enough to deal with without you two telling me how to parent.' She pauses, searching for a conciliatory place to land. 'Gotta hand it to you guys, sending them to Dad's old school, it's been the making of them. They're well-adjusted and protected from all the stuff going down round here.'

What she means is they won't vanish into thin air on the way to uni like Andy did. It's hard to focus. *Look at your hands Mel.*

Jennifer reaches across the table, touches Melissa's arm.

'Melissa, I've been very careful not to tell you how to parent. Your father, he has the best of intentions, we will support your choices, as we've always done.'

She nods, resigned. *Enabled my choices.* Not that she'll admit that aloud.

'I am sorry about Milo, dear. So is your father.'

Melissa stares at her mother. 'You're sorry about Milo.' She shuts her eyes for a moment and bites her lip to stop herself crying.

*

When things spun out of control in the days after Daryl was arrested, she'd stayed in bed mostly, listening to Milo barking, whining and scratching at the door. His soft eyes imploring her to get up, asking to be walked. With each day he got more desperate, tugging on her sheets, pushing his spongey nose into her face. He wouldn't eat his food if she wasn't eating. His constant presence felt less comforting and more like a millstone. She called her parents and asked them to take him.

'Just for a few weeks, Mum. I can't look after him. I've got no energy for walks. He needs company.'

'Darling, I'll talk to Hamish, the issue will be the other dogs, you know what Milo is like, very territorial, a Blue Heeler thing I believe. We'll work something out.'

Milo hid under the bed. Mel had to drag him out.

'A handful.' Hamish's mottled hands gripped Milo's collar. The spider veins crawling on his cheeks seemed to be spreading. Mel put it down to the physical effort of wrestling Milo, but she suddenly felt a rush of sympathy for her father. If she was still at the spa she could have gotten him some retinol cream. Milo whined, lay spreadeagled on the lino like a drunk. 'Better not linger,' Hamish said gruffly. He looked at her for the first time since he'd arrived. 'You don't look too flash eh, sing out if you need anything.'

Mel cried for a long time. Part of her knew she should go outside, walk, let time pass. Not think about Milo or Hamish's red face. Rosacea, if she recalled correctly, got worse if left untreated. Everyone has a point at which they can no longer absorb pressure. Hamish, like her, had a breaking point. There was a packet of Tramadol in the bathroom. Her shaky hands ejected a few pills. She collapsed on her bed as the room spun.

A couple of weeks later, she asked her mother about Milo.

'Oh darling, we didn't want to upset you.'

'Is he okay?'

'Oh yes, he's thriving. He's lovely but he isn't used to other dogs. There was a bit of trouble, well quite a bit of conflict actually, your father got stressed, Milo too.'

'He can come back now. I think I'm ready. Sorry he's been a hassle.'

'Um yes, dear, the thing is, your father, we, decided the best course of action was to give Milo to one of Hamish's colleagues who was looking for a dog.'

'I can take him back now.'

'Well, actually it seems Milo and Frank, that is the chap who has Milo, they have really bonded. I think it would be very difficult to change the arrangement now. I'm sorry dear, we didn't anticipate things turning out quite like this, but Milo is very happy –'

Mel hurled her phone onto the couch with enough force for it to bounce to the floor. Anger surged through her chest as she clenched her fists. She pictured Milo being pulled towards Hamish's ute. She was right to have felt guilty entrusting him to her parents. They'd abandoned him like he was nothing.

She shut her eyes for a moment and imagined Andy walking through an airport departure gate, like a godwit about to wing his way to another hemisphere. He had taken his future into his own hands. Milo too had escaped to somewhere better. Frank, whoever he was. She unclenched her hands. She could do that. She could get out.

'Do you need money?' Jennifer is looking at Melissa, her eyes watery too.

Melissa knows she should prefer understanding to money. Her parents don't get her, even if she can acknowledge their effort. The sense of being cling-wrapped, she can't get rid of it. Part of her doesn't want them to understand. She's used to being misunderstood, and maybe it's easier to exist under the radar. All the searching and protecting since Andy disappeared. Their anguish was diluted when she had the boys, and deflected by all the trouble with Daryl, but now it's creeping back to full focus.

'Money would be good, just till I get a job. I'm going to get one now I've detoxed. It might take a few months, there isn't much around here. I'll get a gig in a café or a supermarket, till I find something in a spa.' She says it even though she isn't sure she's ready to return to the world of facials and dermal fillers, whether she even believes in it anymore.

Her mother nods. There's a hint of an expression Melissa can't read. She's unsure whether her mother believes her or is back to being empathetic. She wants her mother to believe her, is annoyed at herself for wanting this, angry with her mother for being so patient. Her fingernails bite into her clenched fists.

Jennifer leans forward again, her face a mask though her voice is animated. 'Actually dear, I've heard there is a new spa opening in the village in the spring. Now the gated community is fully subscribed, and the developer has released tenders on a second one, there are fresh business opportunities.'

'Right.' Melissa imagines her mother's heard about this at one of her community board meetings.

'It would be handy, wouldn't it? A situation where you can use your training and expertise, and minimal travel time.' Her mother's smile could have been a rainbow of compassion, hope and anxiety, impossible to tell.

She can't remember the point at which she could no longer turn a blind eye to Daryl's meth hustle. Knowledge seeped in the way the epidermis absorbs pollutants, toxins, sun damage. Skin will seemingly tolerate half-arsed application of sun protection and moisturiser, cursory removal of makeup and other crap for years. There's a tipping point when the signs of aging surface, spread, and hey, all that denial was for nothing. No amount of corrective action can make it right again. Even the latest and most expensive treatments only slow the damage, they can't reverse the march of time.

Marty, her first-born, absorbed her completely. It was tiring but she didn't miss her beauty work as much as she'd expected. When she took him into the spa to visit her workmates, she saw they occupied different worlds now. Daryl's stock agent role was delegated to others so he could pursue the firm's real estate interests, which had morphed into subdivision and financial advice. He was shoulder-tapped to set up the new regional office, started commuting to Whangārei and Kerikeri. They had a second son, Lucas. Marty took after Daryl in looks and temperament, but Lucas, with his blue eyes and serious manner, reminded her of Andy. Her parents too, he was their clear favourite. Melissa struggled to keep up with the boys. Daryl always seemed full of energy, although increasingly he was away overnight. His absence, coupled with her parents' suffocating presence, made her feel anxious.

'Your parents are kind of hands on. I like it. Better than the alternative, babe.'

He said it to remind her of his own parents, to remind her to be grateful.

'Reckon your brother skipped across the ditch, India or something. Doesn't get in touch cos he doesn't want to be found. It's cos you were only seven, you hardly knew him, he's a ghost. Reckon he's captain of his own ship, if he was dead or in trouble you'd have heard.'

Melissa wanted to believe him. The private detective her parents hired said the same thing – her brother had covered his tracks, consistent with the actions of someone who wanted to disappear. Her parents had been controlling. No doubt they'd had Andy's path all mapped out, commerce and law at Otago then back to run the farm businesses. More than anything she wanted Andy to get in touch, to give some sign. She thought again about trying to find him but she wouldn't know where to start. It was the not knowing that sat inside her skin. In that respect, Daryl's notion of haunting rang true. And Lucas's resembling Andy caused the hurt to flare up like a rash she couldn't soothe.

When Daryl was home, they had an active social life. It was good for his work, and her parents were willing babysitters. Their habit of reaching for coffee and alcohol to stay sociable and awake escalated seamlessly into pills and later, a bit of meth.

They agreed no more kids. Melissa returned to work. She thought adult company and the sense of making a difference at her job would help soothe her disquiet. It wasn't the same. The spa had expanded to cater for the influx of affluent arrivals drawn to the region's rolling green pasture, pristine beaches and coastal wetlands. Boutique retail experiences, artisan bakeries, wineries, chocolatiers, sculpture parks and tiny potteries doubling as art galleries reeled them in. Horse trekking, bird-watching, guided fishing and yoga retreats. Golf courses with helicopter pads and luxury accommodation.

Before, Melissa would provide face massages, try to minimise sun spots, pluck facial hairs from the bashful wives of retired farmers. The newcomers – retired, working from home, commuting to Auckland, or in the country over summer – were more sophisticated and demanding. Their company was more exhausting than invigorating. Where the farmer's wives had been respectful, trusting, above all appreciative, the new customers barely acknowledged her existence and when they did it was to compare her service, usually unfavourably, to that they received in their city salons.

During her time away, the treatments had changed too. She had to learn about new procedures. She got Dana to help her, experimented on herself at home. The latest methods seemed more invasive, more directly aimed at hiding the client's age rather than helping them de-stress and feel better about themselves.

'It's like it isn't okay to show your real age,' Melissa remarked to Dana as she inspected her bright red face in the mirror. She looked like she had a bad sunburn. Her forehead stung, her skin felt too tight for her head.

Dana laughed. 'A day or so, the redness fades. You need to keep out of the sun. Slap sunscreen on like shaving cream or you'll undo all the good work. It's worth it. You'll look ten years younger. No one will know you're a mum with two kids.'

Melissa frowned. 'I'm okay with being a mum with two kids.'

'Yeah mate, I feel you, but most of our clients are ancient. Adult kids, husbands take 'em for granted or want to trade them in for a later model. They wanna look young to hook a new bloke, or land or stay in their job. Pining for the good young days. Get your hair dyed, get your face pricked all over with needles or scrubbed with chemical sandpaper. You've gotta rip it up so it'll heal and look fresh. It's like any other reno, bloody expensive and probably not going to turn out like you hoped, loads of ongoing maintenance. Not for the faint of heart or light of wallet. Pretty mint business model for us, keeps us in pin money eh.'

Melissa snorted. She'd missed Dana's rants. 'P money.'

'Eh. Too right.'

Not that she and Daryl were short of money. The boys were away in Auckland at her father's alma mater, even though Melissa hadn't been sure about the idea.

'Dad's keen for the boys to go to his old boarding school in Auckland. Is that weird? We would hardly see them.'

'Babe, it's a great idea. Hereford's shit. How many of the kids you went to school with are doing stuff now? This'll broaden their horizons. Free us up a bit.'

'Wouldn't you miss them?'

'Course but I've got you to keep me company! They'll be back between terms and all of summer, plus they'll meet different people, families in business, lawyers, doctors, better sports teams. Hamish offered to pay for it too.'

'So, you and Dad have already talked about it?'

'Ha yeah, he's mentioned it a few times.' Daryl grinned at her and winked. 'Separately eh. Mentioned to us separately, the old divide and rule trick, sly bastard.'

They agreed they would ask the boys what they wanted to do, though she knew with Daryl doing the asking they would be sold on going.

They fell into a routine of work and parties on the weekend. People she knew from school, people Daryl knew. It was a way to fill the void left by her boys, to elbow out the unpleasant feeling she was wasting her life on ungrateful, unlikeable clients. When she was doped, she could almost forget the bafflement of Andy's absence, her inability to fix her parents' grief. Turning a blind eye to Daryl was easier. Don't ask don't tell was their most important marriage vow, and she hadn't realised it at the time. When she wasn't thinking about getting high, Melissa was thinking about getting a puppy. Daryl wasn't keen.

'What about a cat? They're more independent. Puppy you'll have to train it and stuff, like another kid.'

Melissa felt that was the point. She started researching dog breeds.

'Ever think of going overseas?' Dana and Melissa were enjoying a furtive toke outside the squash club.

'No. My family's here. Kinda missed my chance, I guess.' She looked across at Dana. She had in fact considered going to Aussie when she finished school, in part to look for Andy, but she didn't have any money. Dana's ponytail glowed where it caught the late sun. Her face was cast in shadow. 'Why do you ask? You're not thinking of leaving are you?' Melissa clenched her hands then released them.

'Inevitable I'll blow this popsicle stand mate.' Dana shifted so Melissa could see her eyebrows arch. 'I'm thinking maybe Queenstown or across the ditch. I'm getting restless, like I've been here too long. This place doesn't feel as chilled out as it used to. Too much dodgy stuff going down, changes people, changes the vibe.'

'Oh.' Melissa could feel currents swirling in her stomach.

'You could always come with me.' Dana laughed at the look on Melissa's face. 'Jokes, babe. You and the lovely Daryl, you're going the distance.'

'I'd visit you.' Melissa clenched her hands again, willed her stomach to calm. *Don't leave.*

Daryl was strict with meth use. Only long weekends, or when there was a lot going on.

'There's a difference between needing the stuff and using it

115

to tide you over, babe. Don't wanna go overboard. Like at the spa, you don't go round giving clients Botox injections every five minutes, do you? There's a limit.'

'Honey, we don't do Botox. You have to go somewhere bigger for that.'

'Right. Your place is probably missing out on custom then. S'pose it's risky eh, need special insurance and shit. Anyway, there's a line. Thing is to keep on the right side of the line.'

One night in the Hereford pub, waiting for the toilet queue to drop off, she spotted a guy in a pale blue shirt and navy slacks, a uniform almost. He didn't belong. Didn't seem to care, wasn't making any effort to fit in. It was like he was studying the scene for an assignment. She half expected him to pull out an iPad and start noting stuff down. Worse, he looked familiar. She stared at him, willing herself to place him. She prided herself on knowing faces, that was her job after all. Samuel? Simon. Simon Connor. He'd lost his hair, his glasses, a ton of weight. Chest muscles under the shirt for sure. Good skin, minimal sun damage, could be the shit lighting of course. He'd had acne at school. Wasn't he a cop now? He caught her eye and came over.

'Hey, Melissa.' He looked sober.

'Simon. Sup?' She focused on not twitching. It was something she did when she hadn't eaten.

He gave her an appraising stare and she squirmed, shifted from one foot to the other. Hopefully Simon would think she was just busting for the loo. She hadn't gotten on with the geeks at school, wasn't likely they'd have much in common now. What was he doing here, of all places? He'd recognised her immediately.

'What are you up to these days Melissa?'

'Um. Still working as a beautician in town, kids at school in Auckland. Mum and Dad keeping local government ticking over and stuff.' Aware she was prattling, she looked around for Daryl, half wondering why she was doing it.

Simon followed her gaze, raised an eyebrow. 'Looking for someone?'

'Yeah, nah. What did you say you were up to? Haven't seen you round these parts for ages.' She hadn't seen him since school as far as she could recall.

He seemed to be studying the room rather than concentrating on their chat. Melissa was about to edge away. It wasn't like she needed an excuse. The room was so noisy conversation was difficult, and the toilet queue wasn't moving.

'Visiting my mother –'

Her shoulders slumped with relief.

'Illicit substances.'

She wondered if she'd heard correctly. 'Drug squad?'

'I'm a detective, look into certain things.'

'Like P and hash and stuff?' Melissa meant it as a joke, realised the second she'd said it that she should've kept quiet.

He gave her a hard look. 'You should be careful who you mix with. It's easier than you think to get out of your depth. Things have changed round here since we were at school.'

Melissa could feel petulance hovering within her, like the red phosphorus head of a match striking the powdered glass on the box. It flickered into life every time someone talked down to her. 'No kidding. I'm pretty good at swimming!' She made goofy swimming motions with her arms, and he raised an eyebrow again.

Why was she scared of Simon Connor? He was just visiting his mum. A geek. A fit-looking geek these days, granted.

He was still on her mind the next day when she and Daryl

were medicating their hangovers with coffee and painkillers. She told Daryl about him. 'He's a cop now. Real nerd at school, wasn't sure if he was at the pub for work or to chill.'

'Built, bald guy in blue?'

She was surprised he knew who she meant. 'Yeah. Didn't fit in.'

He pulled a face. 'Seen him a few places. Whaddya reckon he's up to?'

'Who cares?' She said it lightly but she studied Daryl. It was unlike him to take an interest in built bald guys.

He shrugged. 'P is in the news a lot now eh, people cooking in houses and stuff.'

Neither of them slept well. Daryl often got up in the night to go for drives – he told her it helped him plan work stuff. Sometimes he'd only return at dawn. She was glad of Milo's company. In the end she'd worn Daryl down and bought a Blue Heeler puppy. He slept on the bed. She spent hours training him, took him for walks in the local scenic reserve, which helped both of them use up surplus energy. She reached out to give Milo a rub. Daryl smiled. She scrutinised him. His face had a slack, slightly greasy appearance that reminded her of a discarded meal. Tiny lines rippled his forehead, his blue eyes were hooded and bloodshot, his stubbled cheeks and chin like mouldy bread.

'Good we've got Milo. You were right about getting a dog, babe.'

As Melissa stroked Milo she noticed her blotchy hands, their prominent veins. Funny, she didn't feel old, she felt full of energy, hyped up. Daryl reached over and stroked her cheek. His hand felt moist, the humidity maybe. 'Even with Milo, leave no gear around the house.'

*

At the spa her boss introduced new security measures. Said the head office decreed it. A local locksmith installed bars over windows, tested the deadlocks. An IT guy reviewed access codes and a more granular stock ordering system was implemented.

Melissa found the new systems irritating, and complained to Dana.

'Well, you know, continuous improvement, gotta be agile, curious, solution-focused, your best self,' Dana said.

'How do more audits help the clients look younger, remind me?'

'Ha. Rumoured surge in break-ins. Pharmacies, medical centres and a couple of spas up by Kerikeri. People looking for cooking ingredients.'

Melissa shuddered. 'The stuff we put on people's faces, you can't inhale it!'

Dana raised her eyebrows. 'Don't tell the clients. What we slop on 'em, it's all wholesome wellness shit, gloves are for hygiene, eh. Ha, but yeah, bit of a mind fuck. Reckon the usual supply chains must be disrupted at the mo.'

Melissa smiled but she felt a rising tide of unease. 'You should be a business analyst.'

'Mate. I am a business analyst. Buy shares in spas baby, and move to Oz.'

Six months later, Mel was sleeping off a hangover when a persistent pinging of her phone dragged her into semi-awakeness. Her head hurt. She kept her eyes shut and put her pillow over her head. Beside her, Milo gave her hand a lick. More pings. She lifted her head and reached for her phone, rolled onto her back and scrolled down, half expecting to see pictures from the party last night. The first message was from Dana.

'Hereford!'

'?' She closed her eyes, reached for the water bottle she kept on the bedside table.

'Your BP!'

She could feel sweat trickling down her back and sticking to her T-shirt as she went to a news site and started reading. She checked several other sites. Daryl didn't pick up when she called him. She went to the kitchen to make an instant. Explosion in a P lab at an old farmhouse less than thirty kilometres away. Two guys. A woman took them to the village petrol station, then the local medical centre. Four Square's entire supply of Glad Wrap commandeered. Airlifted to Middlemore's burns unit. The regional police and health authorities launched a massive decontamination effort, hazardous substances specialists everywhere.

The jug boiled and switched itself off. She sat staring at her phone. Gradually she became aware of a soft rubbing against her legs. She reached down and pulled Milo up onto her lap. He licked her face and she hugged him so tightly he let out a yelp. She relaxed her grip, releasing him to the lino. He watched her, tail going left and right as he glanced from her to the door and back again.

'It's all right boy,' she whispered. Milo let out a couple of sharp barks. They sounded like a rebuke. Mel went into the bathroom in search of painkillers.

For the next twenty-four hours, the news spread the story in the manner of a low-flying top dressing plane dropping its cargo of dark grey superphosphate. The loud drone impossible to ignore, wiring her nerves, giving rise to itches that refused to abate. One of the blokes died from his burns, the other remained critical.

Months later at a party Mel remembered her comparison

with top dressing. She mentioned it to her mate Willy Carlton.

'At least with top dressing, the noise and dust results in a subsequent boost in grass growth.'

A month after the explosion, the boys came home for the school holidays. Melissa took some time off intending to hang out with them. At first Milo regarded them with suspicion, nipping their outstretched hands and growling. He needn't have bothered. Whether it was boarding school or teenage hormones she wasn't sure, but something had changed in her boys. They'd grown a coat of bland politeness she couldn't seem to penetrate. Both were unmoved by her spa stories, unresponsive to her questions about their lives in the city, showed zero curiosity about Daryl's farm deals. Their eyes glazed over when she suggested activities.

Once Milo got used to them they took him for walks, but otherwise they seemed content to mooch around the house. They clearly missed their Auckland friends, never letting their phones out of sight, checking for messages, or forever on their iPads, gaming, lost in their own worlds for hours. They had a way of communicating with each other and the wider world that only heightened her feeling of exclusion. She found herself taking more pills than usual, washing them down with white wine. The time when her boys had needed her were fading. Like she'd been made redundant and had slept through the notice period.

She mentioned her feelings to Dana.

'I'm a bed and breakfast provider. Except no breakfast, they sleep in till noon.'

'It's a phase,' Dana said, with a wave of her hand. 'Teenage thing, they'll be more attentive in a few years I reckon. You pay much attention to your olds at that age? Don't think I did.'

'Maybe. They aren't keen to visit Mum and Dad either. Always on their devices.'

Dana raised her rainbow eyebrows in Mel's direction. 'Little junkies eh.'

'Don't say that!'

Dana was right. The Barclay household was in a state of constant craving, a den of iniquity, a soap opera that should have been canned a few seasons back. The boys primed for the next electronic notification, her for the next sweet chemical high, Daryl always working. Even Milo got angsty if he hadn't been out for a walk for a few hours. Realising this didn't dampen Melissa's disappointment. Preoccupied, she forgot meals. Marty and Lucas deployed their recently acquired independence by making themselves nachos and toasted sandwiches.

'I can't compete with Minecraft. I expect you and Dad are in the same boat,' Melissa told her mother, when she asked when the kids were popping over to visit.

After they'd returned to Auckland, Melissa went to a party at the Rugby Club. She looked around for Simon, something she did automatically now, though she hadn't seen him since her first encounter. She knocked against Willy Carlton.

'Shit, sorry!'

'No worries, Mel.' Willy grinned at her. He looked the same as always, skinny and freckly, pretty good skin, Willy, considering he didn't take care of it.

'Hey, seen your other half?' He was checking out the room, same as she'd been.

'Not for a bit.' She was surprised, didn't think Willy had any time for Daryl. She'd had a few yarns with him at parties when they were both outside enjoying a vape. He tended to be a bit dark on those he called 'wankerpreneurs'. Once, they'd argued about whether Daryl counted. 'Daryl works for the man, so he doesn't count,' Melissa said.

Willy had shaken his head. 'Daryl,' he drawled. 'Taking into account his extracurricular activities, career adjacent business interests – definitely a classic wankerpreneur.'

Now she looked at Willy more closely, and felt tension lurking behind his smile. He touched her arm. 'Never mind. Stay safe chicky.' She watched him stride off, then finally went in search of a drink.

A few weeks later someone broke into one of Hamish's barns. Her father heard them, got out of bed and drove down. Whoever it was fled when they saw his headlights. Nothing was taken. The would-be burglars left some lime-green tags on the side of the shed.

'What did the cops say?' Melissa asked her father.

'Said there's been a few break-ins. Hoons looking for drugs. Chap told me not to go confronting them, too dangerous. I'm going to get alarms for the sheds, same as the house one, don't want machinery going missing.'

She was glad she had Milo, her small parcel of comfort she could open when needed. She was trying to ration her other comforts but it was proving difficult. She was driving miles out of her way to find new pharmacies that would sell her painkillers. Consulted several different medics to obtain the necessary scripts. Daryl was out at night more often than he was home, and when he did return he'd sit in his car talking on his phone before coming inside to shower and head back to work. He carried his phones with him everywhere, along with his various laptops. Seemed distracted, irritable and distant. It had been going on for weeks.

Dana was applying for jobs. She had a Zoom interview with

a recruitment agency in Sydney, then handed in her notice at the spa. Melissa cried when Dana told her, but she was angry too.

'Everyone's leaving me!'

'Don't be silly. Change is all. Once I've settled in, you can come over for a visit. Even if Daryl is busy. Come yourself, before the school holidays. Change of scene. And don't tell your parents, they'll try to stop you.'

Melissa thought about it, but she couldn't leave Milo. She didn't mention it to Daryl or her parents.

Then Daryl announced he was going up north for a week or so, however long it took. Urgent business, some wrinkles with a sale that needed to be sorted. He needed to be on hand 24/7. Place was remote, accessible only by boat, no cell or Wi-Fi. In disbelief, she watched him throw a few clothes into a suitcase.

'I'll call you when I can babe. Don't worry. Go hang with your olds if you get anxious.'

'I'm not a child. What's going on? Milo and I could come as well.'

'No. You're better off out of it, you'd be bored. And you've got work remember? It's nothing, babe. Nothing that can't be sorted.'

She cuddled Milo as she watched Daryl leave. When she set him down, he ran outside, chased Daryl's car down the drive. It was only later, in her darker moments when she was hating herself for being so weak, stupid and blind, that she imagined that Milo was trying to protect her from Daryl.

She has only the haziest recollection of the months after he left for good. Some of the time was lost to self-medication. She stopped turning up at the spa and stopped answering her phone. The local police searched the house and questioned her endlessly. She could tell them virtually nothing. Eventually they gave up, warning her they would keep her under surveillance but she wouldn't face charges. She talked to the school, along with her parents, to make sure the boys were okay. They wanted to stay in Auckland and everyone seemed to think this was for the best. Stability, routine, minimum of disruption.

Asking her parents to take Milo was a turning point of sorts. She had no energy for walking him, was too nervous to leave the house to buy his food. Jennifer insisted she see her doctor. And counselling twice a week. Melissa hated it, but her mother made it clear they would only take Milo if she complied. Her parents paid for the counsellor to come to her for the first few weeks. She agreed to do it for the boys. When Dana or anyone else tried to call or text her, she told them she was detoxing and getting her shit together, that they should stay away. She turned off her phone. If anyone came round, she didn't answer the door.

Gradually her pain and cravings subsided. She started leaving the house for counselling and to get groceries. She talked to the boys twice a week. She learned her parents had given Milo away. On top of losing Andy, Daryl and Dana, it was too much to bear. Her counsellor told her dwelling on loss was unhelpful, not that she put it as bluntly as that. She was paid big bucks to let her clients come to their own conclusions. Melissa came to the conclusion her counsellor also had an eye on who was paying the big bucks. Melissa was not the only one relying on her parents for financial support. She decided she'd had enough counselling.

It's the day after the dinner with her parents. She's spent the night staring at her bedroom ceiling. It's close to 5am when the dawn light reveals the first hint of its shape. She blinks, feels the faint brush of her eyelashes against her skin. With each blink the ceiling gains a little more focus. She breathes as she blinks, open and shut, in and out. Through her open window she hears a distant barking and for a moment she holds her breath till she remembers Milo is with Frank. Her rhythm is broken so she decides to go to the beach.

She doesn't know why she stops by the Four Square, it's too early for it to be open. She sees a handwritten note taped to the window. Helen is eighty-six and lives in the gated community. She's had a fall and gets about with crutches, so she needs someone to exercise her poodle and help brush his coat, bathe him, trim his nails. Helen is so relieved and pleased with Melissa's efforts she tells all her neighbours. Soon Melissa has several dogs to look after.

It's a part-time gig that only works because her parents subsidise her existence. It's not independence, but it does afford some freedom. It's a start. She likes that she got the job at her own initiative. Jennifer, when she finds out about the dogs, offers to ask around to see if other people need help. Melissa begs her not to. She wants to manage things herself, thinks she'll build up slowly, step by step.

The dog owners are grateful that there's someone local who can come and take their pets and deliver them back without them having to do anything. The dogs are less demanding and more pleasant to deal with than her former clients at the spa. So long as she establishes a clear hierarchy, with herself at the top, they fall into line. She finds their haphazard chasing after scents endearing, and while it's tiring, the sense of being worn out is not unpleasant. The exercise is helping her fitness. Dogs and children. She's a young mum again.

She could post about her services on the community Facebook

page. There are probably some stressed-out professionals living locally and commuting who need someone to look after their pets.

She thinks about Marty and Lucas. They stay in touch via text and Zoom. So far, they seem to have taken their father's incarceration in their stride. The school seems to have done so too. She finds this incredible. It surely cannot last. In two years, Marty will be the same age Andy was when he headed off to university. She lets thoughts of Andy and Daryl come and go, like they tell you to do on the meditations she follows on YouTube sometimes. In good moments she believes she might start doing yoga.

The dogs aren't allowed near the estuary, but when she tires of the scenic reserve there's a little bay further east. Ivory sand melts to caramel where it's stroked by the tide. The tepid water has a light head of froth that bubbles over her feet like warm beer. Once, she finds herself thinking Daryl was right about this place. Its beauty is a sight to behold, constantly changing with the light. She looks towards Maratere. The islands are slightly out of focus as they often are, but she knows where to find them. She can call Dana anytime, but she needs to find her own feet. There are clouds on the horizon. Late afternoon sun is casting a few lines through them, God rays.

All her life she's stayed here. People she's loved have gone away. She has her scars and her hopes. She'll hold on to them for as long as she can. The sun will continue to shine. The clouds will shed their water vapour, gather moisture again and again.

Peninsula

Driving east, the car headlights make little impression on the tentacles of mist conducting a quiet exploration of the valley floor, poking every crevice and groove. Heavy, saturated air languishes near the creek, waiting for the dark sky to lighten. Fog blurs night and dawn, bewitches earth and sky. The sun shakes itself awake with a shudder of warmth, gets its glow on, orange today, and sets about sweeping away the clutter. In a few hours the fog will be gone, though Rachel can't shake the fog in her own head.

Returning to the valley, one of the most reliable sensations is of the past seeping in and around, sticky, hard to shake off. Coming home, it seemed to Rachel, is instinctual, like opening a hot oven with your glasses on and being surprised when they steamed up. You feel silly when it happens but the insight doesn't stop you from doing it again.

Like running. Rachel enjoys the way running dependably shifts her mood, enables her to think inside things, while also getting outside herself. It's hard to put into words. She loves to run in beautiful places where there are forests and coast, but a blank strip of asphalt or the cobblestones of a bustling town are just as good, harder on the joints perhaps but meditative, the endorphins pumping around her brain like oxygen delivered by her blood. Sometimes all she does is ruminate, her thoughts churning over on a feedback loop going nowhere. But on a good run, ideas pop up, new ways of seeing things, a different angle on a puzzle, and she returns with a sense of perspective. People think she runs to escape her life, she's addicted, crazy the time she spends running when she could invest in relationships, kids, climbing the corporate ladder, saving the world. People can mind their own business.

Willy liked people to mind their own business. After his marriage blew up, he announced he was going to Adelaide.

'What will you do there?' Boring question she realised immediately, like asking a vegetarian where they get their iron from. She liked to say she ordered iron filings in powder form online and washed them down in a smoothie.

'One of me mates, Jase, remember him? He can get me a job at his orchard. Stone fruit, almonds, heaps of citrus, there's loads of work, better pay, weather's good. May as well work on me tan, charm a few snakes.' Willy chucked a tight grin at Rachel. It was higher on one side of his face.

Rachel caught the flatness in his voice, the stiffness in his jaw. He kept his Dirty Dog sunglasses on even though it was dark in the house. His face was a mask where once it was cheeky and open. He'd aged too, or maybe it was the buzz cut. There was a glassiness to him but it was his failure to take the piss out of her for asking the obvious question that broke her heart.

'Willy the snake charmer. I guess that'll liven up your CV.'

'Gotta get away from here for a bit.' He stubbed out his cigarette. 'Cuppa, sis?'

She hesitated. His lack of enthusiasm was a clear signal he was trying to get rid of her. She was already fighting a strong impulse to make her excuses and leave. 'Yeah, tea would be good.'

He glanced around the messy kitchen. 'Tea bags here somewhere.'

Rachel surveyed the forest of cans on the table and in boxes near the bench. There were even a few balanced on top of the fridge. She retrieved a jar of tea bags, helped herself to two. 'Any mugs?'

Willy opened the dishwasher, rescued two mugs, rinsed them at the sink.

'Change will be good.' Rachel wondered as she said this whether she was talking about Willy or her own job. She'd carried her uncertainty like a poorly adjusted backpack for so long she only recognised the ache in her shoulders when she saw it in others. She pushed the thought aside, conscious of the luxury of her position compared with the stark choices her little brother faced. 'When do you leave?'

'Next week. Olds are going ape-shit. You want milk?'

'No milk. Yeah, Mum treated me to a twenty-minute rant, could not get a word in, I'm walking back to my car, she's following me still going on about it. Dad didn't get a look in.'

Willy rolled his eyes. 'Old man is the same. Doesn't play well at the golf club when your youngest has fallen off the rails, messing with the evil smokes and drugs.' Willy tugged at the fridge door and a few cans spilled off the top. He ignored them, pulled out the milk, poured a splash into his tea.

Rachel wrinkled her nose. 'Remember his thing about John Denver?'

He shot her a sideways glance, and for a second the old Willy was back. 'Enlighten me. Don't say he's been playing his old country and western tapes? Sure sign he's off his rocker.'

'No, nothing like that. He was a big Denver fan until he overdosed, then Dad went really dark on him, used to sit on the couch and go on about how he couldn't understand how the guy could sing about nature while all the time he was taking drugs.' Rachel realised she'd picked the wrong anecdote but she was committed now. 'Good old Jim, he took it personally, as if most singers don't take stuff.' She blushed into the silence. 'Will you keep your phone number? I'll call you, see how it's going.'

'Yeah.' Willy was scowling into his tea.

His edginess had Rachel gulping hers down, burning her tongue.

'Serves the old man right. Denver's music, sentimental crap,' Willy said.

Rachel wouldn't mind some sentimental crap, better than the Radio Sport blasting out of Di's car radio. It's the only channel that seems to work. She fiddles the dials with her left hand, trying to find the off button. The front piece comes off in her hand. Silence at last. She stuffs the plastic moulding in the glove box.

It's eerie driving the narrow winding road through the mist but by the time she crests the hill the fog has lifted. A few more minutes and it'll be like it never existed. The ability to move on would be handy. The east coast rises like an invitation. The lines of beach houses don't spoil the promise from this distance.

At the foot of the rise, she passes the street where Willy used to flat. Although he's had a few places, this one was the best. That dwelling's long since been bulldozed to make way for mansions laid out grid-style around neat cul-de-sacs. Each house comes with an opulent boat and trailer, and an electric car but often a big four-wheel drive or ute as well.

The village itself, with its cluster of cafés and shops peddling homewares, Scandinavian furniture, beach clothing and fine art, is deserted. Too early for the bach owners and day-trippers. A few locals in the business of servicing the visitors are setting out fresh baking, lining up produce, catching up on the gossip, practising their marketing lines. All while sipping espressos. Rachel wouldn't mind a coffee herself but she needs a run more. The day is preparing to steam. She can already feel sweat beading her forehead.

She parks at the lagoon and heads straight up past the pōhutukawa standing sentry at the summit. The ridge is a series of rolling curves above a grey water glaze. Other peninsulas extend like fingers pointing eastward. The familiar islands are a hazy blur, curtained by the warming air. There are no cattle today and it's too early for hikers or mountain bikers. The kikuyu is slick with dew and moisture soaks through her trainers, numbing her feet even as her head clears. She drops into the crescent bay before climbing again towards the predator-proof fence. There's a park ranger with a hammer in one hand, a box with wire sticking out of it in the other. He looks a bit like Neil Finn.

'You've got a great office, I'm jealous.'

The ranger smiles, studies Rachel, an inquiring expression on his face. 'Terrible hours but otherwise not bad. I used to run round here, knees aren't so keen on it anymore. Have you been on the trails by the lagoon?'

'The new ones? I'm lucky, my parents live nearby. When I visit I always come here.'

'Ah, I thought you must be a local. You seem to know your way around. I saw a runner above the lagoon, I'm guessing it was you. How long does that circuit take?'

'About an hour, depends if you go out to the point and back.' Rachel's unaccustomed to people taking an interest in her movements. She isn't sure she likes it, though the ranger is only being friendly, probably a fairly solitary job. 'I guess I should leave you to it.'

'What's your surname?'

Rachel hesitates. 'Carlton.'

'Ha, you're Rachel Carlton. I used to play cricket with Jack.' He drops his box and holds out his hand. 'Clive Stringer.'

Rachel can't immediately place this Clive. She doesn't keep in touch with anyone from school.

'You don't remember me, do you?'

'Um, no.'

'My sister Sophey was in your class.'

There's something in his voice when he says Sophey. He's a couple of years younger than her. Not like his sister. Sophey was obsessed with getting good marks, treated it like a sports game. If anyone did better, she wouldn't speak to them. Held on to things. Almost like her grudges were her friends. That didn't work so well when you were both on the school debating team.

Rachel and Carole wanted to meet Sophey to go over their arguments. They were heading down to Auckland for the regionals, a big deal for the school. Sophey had a talent for constructing a good case, an instinct for logical flow that didn't apply to her emotional life. Although neither she nor Carole enjoyed it, their team worked because they overlooked Sophey's compulsive need to patronise. Usually they talked points through and honed them. Not this time. Sophey gave them several pages of notes outlining what she thought they should say. 'What's her problem?' Rachel asked Carole. Carole had rolled her eyes. 'You got a better mark than her in the biology test last week.'

'So you work for the council?'

'Yeah, all around the district, I love it. Hey, you'll get cold, say hello to Jack from me.'

'Okay, seeya Clive.'

Clive watches her run down the hill towards the beach, her cap bobbing up and down. Her single-mindedness reminds him of his sister.

Descending to the beach Rachel is careful to watch her feet, not wanting to roll an ankle on the uneven ground. Tomorrow she plans to circumnavigate the peninsula. She wonders what Sophey is doing. They went to the same law school but hadn't interacted. Rachel had greeted her a few times and Sophey had blanked her which, if she was honest, suited her. Probably in charge of some multinational corporation, Rachel decided.

From the beach she traces the shoreline back to the sheltered bay, a perfect white sand crescent. There are a few surfers, taking advantage of the swell the bored nor'easter dutifully sweeps into uniform sets for shoreward dispatch. Campers are starting to drift down from their tents, joining the first of the day-trippers. Soon the car park will be full, vehicles spilling onto the access road. The beach is a postcard, a selfie, a tourist brochure. Its gentle curves framed by distinguished pōhutukawa and their younger siblings. Slim groves of nīkau and squat clumps of harakeke pay homage, tittering in the breeze. Obese kererū cling to branches that bend under their weight while tūī ravage the flax flowers and each other. To the north, the reef draws up its skirt at low tide to reveal rocky platforms punctuated by pools filled with Neptune's necklace, limpets, periwinkles and sand crabs. At the southern end, beyond the harakeke and raupō, there are sea caves and arches.

At the car Rachel removes her wet shoes. She gazes towards the faint path tickling the lagoon. She needs to check the tides for tomorrow.

Instead of heading straight back to the farm she follows the road further east till she reaches the small coastal village where Kiri and Willy lived when they were married. The village remains low-key. A single café and a fish-and-chip shop with queues out the door. She squeezes into the fish-and-chip place to study the tide chart while she sips her coffee.

Willy liked to tease her about what he referred to as her coffee snobbery.

'You'll be wanting a coffee, sis, probably only had four today so far, am I right? I got in some Nescafé special blend specially.'

'It's not the same as fresh.'

'True story. It's heaps cheaper, less mess and quieter to make. Those machines, like being in the cowshed at peak of milking.'

'Ha ha. Nestlé is an evil company.'

'Whatever, where do you think those cafés get their beans from, not round here, and how much do they pay those barista types to get sore wrists and wrinkles round their mouths from thousand-mile smiles?'

'I don't mind instant actually.'

'Kia ora,' Willy raises his cup and clinks it against Rachel's, gives her a wink. 'I can tell when you're fibbing your pants off, sis.'

Adelaide's horticulture scene hadn't satisfied Willy. The orchards were remote, the heat oppressive, and the labour physically demanding and tedious. The isolation was the worst, it didn't suit his gregarious nature. Within months he was back. Rachel was relieved, had feared he'd get caught up in the drug scene over there. Still, even when he was back, it was difficult to keep track of him. Her job kept her travelling in and out of the country and she could hardly keep track of herself.

The few times they did manage to meet up, she couldn't get much out of him. The snippets of information that did filter through, usually second or third hand, filled her with a mix of helplessness and dread.

'He's running around with that girl from your class, used to pinch everyone's lunches.' That Di hadn't volunteered this information, Rachel had to ask, was in itself disturbing. Usually her mother hoovered up evidence of any little indiscretion, packaged it up with a few of her own judgements and passed it on with relish. Rachel would hang up from phone calls trying not to think about what her mother must be saying to her siblings about her.

'No, he's not with the shady lady anymore,' she said the next time. 'Oops, shouldn't call her that, she got in trouble with the cops for benefit fraud though, so she is shady. Shenanigans didn't stop her holding on to her kids.'

'Who's he with now?' Rachel interrupted.

'The Barclay girl. Remember her? Her kids are teenagers. They're living in the spare house on the Barclay farm.'

'Isn't she married?' Rachel vaguely recalls the girl Di is referring to.

'Oh yes. Husband's in jail for methamphetamine. That how you say it? Cops did him for distribution. Thought you knew about that. You need to stay in the country more.'

'I am over the travelling.' There were days Rachel thought if she saw another airport she'd throw up. She wondered if Willy's relationships with older women meant she was failing him as a sister. She mentioned this to Jack when she called him.

'He's always preferred being bossed around by mature women. Kiri was older,' Jack said. 'The latest chick, she married young too, maybe they have that in common. Look, we could all do more. Having kids takes over your life. I could try getting him into squash. He's hard to talk to, gets all defensive. Can't be eating, real skinny, it's like he hates the lot of us. His Mrs looks anorexic, but wired, like an Energizer bunny, nervous, super friendly. She's just got some puppies, brought them over to show Jim and Di. I was mowing the lawn for them, popped in for a look, they're cute. She can't keep still. She was sitting on the couch and her knees were wobbling. She was loud at school too though.'

'She's probably on meth.'

'Probably.'

The following day, crossing the mouth of the lagoon, the first few kilometres are like stepping into another world. Bush down to the beach, kererū and tūī in the ponga, pūriri and pōhutukawa. Pōhutukawa leaves on the sand, mixing with fragments of shells and driftwood. Craggy rocks glistening in the sun, the muted greens and blues of the sparkling water. In the distance, no more than a murky smudge, another peninsula dotted with houses. Intermittently a small boat appears trailing a milky signature. Shags perch on a cluster of rocks tortured into the shape of a scow. Their washed-out shit streaks the stone like a varnish of tears. Boy, has she missed this.

At primary school, she was part of a small group who spent lunchtimes up on the pōhutukawa-lined bank that separated the classrooms from the main road. They played doctors and nurses, sharing out the roles by unspoken agreement. The leaves were used as medicines. Red leaves had special healing powers if pressed lightly on an injured limb, the more common crunchy brown leaves with dark spots were dispensed for minor aches and pains. For something really serious you had to harvest green leaves off a tree.

The school pōhutukawa were well established, with no low-lying branches. The doctor would remove their sandals and scale the fat lower limbs while the others kept a look-out for teachers. You'd edge carefully higher and higher till you could reach the leaves. Returning with stuffed pockets was more complicated. You were reliant on feel and memory, the brush of your feet against the rough branches, toes searching out little divots to grip hold of, arms hugging the naked trunk. It was the illicit thrill of returning with a haul of green leaves, rather than the welfare of the patient, that made the game so addictive.

Negotiating the sand is sluggish work, like taking a meeting while jetlagged, the slick grains too slack for her trainers to gain traction. Rachel lopes along at the tide line where the waves bully the sand till it's hard and flat. She keeps an eye out for treasures hidden in the smashed shells and broken pieces of seaweed that mark the curl of the tide. She adores the ram's horns, their delicate white spirals remind her of ponga fronds. The way patterns repeat in nature is reassuring until you see them corrupted. The vulnerability of ecosystems. Occasionally she bends to retrieve a piece of plastic, usually fishing debris or a muesli bar wrapper. She stuffs this rubbish in her pack.

Rachel is glad when sand surrenders to rock. Rock travel is slow too, but all sense of time evaporates when she's absorbed in foot placement decisions. Her job used to give her this sensation but lately she struggles to outrun her doubts. For the first scramble she uses hand holds to climb, avoiding the sea with its lining of increasingly large rock pools. The greywacke sandpapers her hands, unless it crumbles and leaves a sticky salt residue on her fingertips. She glimpses fist-sized green and purple crabs signalled by a lightning splash as they flee. Their speed, they must have fast twitch muscles. The brown necklace seaweed sunbathes in shallow pools, but there's less than there used to be, fewer limpets too. The evidence is everywhere if you care to pay attention. Kelp flaps, flops, slaps and swirls, like a car wash. Its rubbery feel underwater gives her the creeps. Such a contrast to the brittle texture of the dark, dehydrated branches abandoned on the shore. In the water, the kelp's frenzied movement, charged up by the currents and tide, make it hard to gauge the depth of the sea, to figure out where the limits are.

They didn't arrest him exactly. Fortunate to live in a small town where Jim and Di were pillars of the community. Out of respect for them, the local cops used their discretion. The deal was Willy had to stay at their house while the police tracked the supplier, the bigger fish. Rachel sat in her hotel room in Bonn trying to imagine her parents. They'd have no idea about meth withdrawal.

Willy was delivered by a cop with nothing but the clothes he was wearing. Initially he slept, would get up in the afternoon and eat whatever was in the fridge. Jack took Willy's car down to his place so Willy couldn't leave.

The Barclay girl came round a few times, though Jim and Di made it clear she wasn't welcome. At first, she brought clothes for Willy but there was concern about what else she might bring. Di swallowed her shame and asked the cops to stop her coming. The police were driving past daily to check Willy was still there, which helped. The supplier was arrested a few weeks later. Willy refused to come to the phone when Rachel rang.

'Are you okay?' she asked Di. 'Sorry to ring at such a weird time. In meetings all your night.'

'I'll put your father on.'

'Dad, are you guys okay?'

'Where are you?'

'I'm still in Germany, I'll be back at the end of the month, when the negotiations are over.'

'Oh. We want him out of here, he's a criminal, hangs out with criminals. That girl keeps coming round, we don't want her round here. He shouts at your mother.'

Rachel wasn't sure what shocked her more, Willy's behaviour or the disgust in her father's voice.

'Here's your mother.'

'He doesn't want to talk about it. We've had it up to our eyeballs.'

Rachel was unclear whether she meant Jim or Willy. Both, she supposed. Di sounded like she was about to cry. 'Can he go somewhere else?' Rachel asked.

'Jack won't have him, doesn't want him near his kids and fair enough. Best to keep him away from that Barclay girl. There isn't anywhere else, only reason he isn't in jail is cos he's here. I'm going to get Tui to come talk to him.'

'Good. That's good Mum.' Rachel was relieved. Tui might be able to get through to Willy. Even if she couldn't, she would help Di and Jim.

Rachel stared at her hotel window. All she could see was the reflection of interior lighting, horribly distorted. Glass that offered no clear sense of what was beyond. Inside, trapped on the other side of the world, she imagined her parents and her brother, swept from their familiar routine into a maelstrom. Like poor swimmers out of their depth, struggling to surface, bewildered and afraid of drowning as waves of shame and grief crashed over them. Unable to get back to shore. And Willy. She pictured him too.

*

There are places where the cliffs drop abruptly to the sea. She can't touch the bottom while hanging on to the rock; her legs kick about in a salty murky void. The currents are strong, causing the water to heave and surge, like a runner on the charge sensing an opportunity to overtake. Rachel concentrates on climbing up and over the rocky bits, focused on the process of figuring out foot and hand holds, getting her weight over the placements. In the back of her mind is the practicality of reversing the moves if she reaches a point where retreat becomes necessary.

She pauses to take a sip from her Camelbak. The onshore breeze steals the sweat from her skin. At least with the heat she doesn't feel hungry. Some of the rock is metamorphic, tiny fossils visible through the dull, sandy soft surface. She can see a sailboat out in the main channel and, high up on the shoreline, occasional markers indicating where a trap has been placed to catch rats or possums. She once tried to follow a trapping line, working her way up a cliff, before realising the devices were laid horizontally. It was a devil of a job to down-climb and she emerged with a fresh collection of gorse scratches which stung when exposed to the salty air and bled more than seemed possible.

It's hard to read the tide. It seemed low when Rachel started, should still be drifting out. She climbs her way around the point, spots the old rope across the miniature sandy inlet below. The sea is inscrutable. There isn't enough space between water and rock to judge the tide's rhythm. At the base of the cliff, she scrambles up without using the rope. Her trainers have excellent grip but if she has to come back, the rope will be helpful. On top she treads carefully along the skinny ridge, inspecting the other side for descent points, checking out the rock fringe for lines she can traverse without resorting to swimming.

She is prepared to swim if necessary although she'd have to keep her phone dry. It's the swell and currents she doesn't much care for. Once in the water it wouldn't be easy to get out. She would need to keep hold of the rock with one hand. There were places around here, thin inlets like tongues in the ocean that run between the rock towers. The ocean surges in and out of these slits with a ferocity that is out of keeping with the friendly scenery. The bursts of energy are particularly strong on an incoming tide. In the narrow passages lurk kelp, crabs and unidentifiable creatures Rachel doesn't want brushing against her bare legs.

At low tide there is a ledge around the edge of the rock towers near the main point. If she can access this and she wins the race against the tide she should be able to traverse all the way around, eventually emerging on the southern end of the crescent bay. She can see the start of the ledge and what looks like a feasible way down to it. The ledge disappears underwater every time the swell moves in, reveals itself again when the water retreats. Her feet and legs drip as she makes her way forward looking for holds, trying to avoid the clutching kelp. A sense of urgency rises up in her body, with the rolling water. A few times she considers her vertical options. There is at least one place where up and over is the better route, but from her low-angled vantage point every rock tower looks similar to the last.

The ledge doesn't seem to extend around the next corner. This must be an up or swim point. Below, the kelp looks menacing. She cautiously dips her right leg into the sea. No indication of the bottom. The swell, stronger now as she approaches the point where the peninsula faces the open sea, has churned up a thick soup. It isn't possible to see further down than a calf's length. She pulls her leg back up, uneasy. So far, the climbing has been good, mostly solid rock, but it would be difficult to back-track.

Earlier, while on the top of the ridge, she'd spotted a couple of blokes fishing several hundred metres further round. They would have arrived by boat. There was a small one anchored further out at sea. She had seen their fishing rods more clearly than the men, as they had their backs to her. Occasionally she catches fragments of speech. If they are aware of her presence, they give no sign. It's comforting there are people nearby, but she knows if she falls and cries out they are unlikely to hear her above the sea, and even if they do, she could easily drown before they come to her assistance. She hasn't told anyone where she's gone, and while Jack will guess, it's a big area to search. The coast wouldn't be the logical place to start as there are no marked trails.

She scans the cliffs above her. There are distinct horizontal lines indicating where the greywacke and fossil-filled rock gives way to crumbly orange clay. Vegetation clings to the land but even from this distance she can see the gorse, harakeke and clumps of grass. Anchorage is tenuous. If she weighted anything, it would come off. Worse, on closer inspection, the lip of the cliff is overhung.

Ascend and risk a fall, or keep going and risk getting smashed against the sharp rocks by the swell, tangled among the kelp and those crabs and whatever else lurks down there, ruined phone, good chance of drinking seawater if she panics. She decides to retreat a bit and climb toward the safety of the grass high above. It will be easier than it looks from here.

She had reached the point in her career where she had to choose. Either base herself in Europe or return here properly. Returning felt like retreating, a short step away from retiring, yet the shuttling between, the hypocrisy of it, shamed her. If she stayed here, there were ties binding her. She was afraid they would slowly choke the life out of her. She would miss the mountains, but the idea that Aotearoa was some kind of nature paradise was, to her, a myth. Plenty of beautiful wild places offshore wherever you chose to look, much of it appreciated far more than here. It sat beside the ugly, yin and yang. Complacency, it's a transmissible disease in her home country. She found this disturbing, even as she knew she was complicit. This collective refusal to join the dots, to think the islands were immune to overcrowding, pollution, warming, habitat destruction, hard to see it ending well.

By the time she returned from Bonn, Willy had left the Carltons. Rachel was baffled when Di told her where he was living. 'Who's Natasha?'

'One of the Smith kids, a few years behind Willy at school, brother in his class, Nathan.'

'What's Natasha like?'

'She's all right, good family. Cops were happy for him to move.'

Rachel considered this. The Barclay family had been decent too. Addiction was an equal-opportunity condition as far as she could see, and she decided to let it go. Her mother didn't need her hope deflated. It wasn't as though Rachel had done anything to help.

She talked to Jack. 'What's going on?'

'Natasha's a lifesaver. Dunno how she found out.'

Rachel had a sudden thought. 'Does she know Tui?'

'Oh yeah, she would know Tui, think they are sorta related. Anyway, Natasha started coming round when the other chick wasn't there, got on okay with Di, incredible tolerance right there. Came up with a plan, squared it with the cops. Next thing she's collected Willy. Seems they like each other, might be a case of star-crossed lovers.'

'Jesus, Jack don't go all Shakespearean on me, that whole star-crossed biz never ends well.'

'The valley edition might, sis. Limited options, you get less choosy. She kicked her husband out a few years back, he was into P, her kids have left home. She's a gem.'

'She sounds too good to be true.'

'Mum and Dad deserve a break.'

It must be close to noon. At the base of the cliff Rachel can feel sunlight blowtorching her exposed neck. She swivels her cap around so the fastening digs into her forehead. She has sunscreen in her pack but its application would only serve as a distraction and lubricated fingers would undermine the friction she needs when her fingers touch the rock. As it is, the temperature, combined with anticipation of the climb, are making her hands slippery. She rubs them on her shorts.

She takes a few deep breaths while she studies the terrain, figuring out a sequence of moves that will direct her towards the least overhung section of cliff top. A final sip of her water, willing herself to stay calm, she climbs in small precise pushes, pulling on pieces of vegetation softly to test them, determined to proceed only when she has two, ideally three, solid holds. Staring at the puzzle in the foreground she suppresses the sneaking thought that going back the way she came would be sensible. She's committed now.

A couple of times she sends showers of soil and loose rock trickling to the sea below. Of the vegetation, the gorse seems most securely attached to the precipice. Her hands are scratched and bleeding. A scoop in the cliff face provides relief. It comprises a series of eroded steps she can wriggle her way up.

The crux comes when she has to exit the steps and haul herself over the lip. There's a fat harakeke bush, but it looks only loosely connected to the precipice, there is little soil in which to anchor its roots. She jerks the closest piece. It shifts but doesn't give way. She inches up beside the clump. To her relief there is some gorse beside it. Looking up, she tries to estimate the distance to the top.

With her left hand she grasps a handful of gorse, with her right she grips the harakeke near its base and hauls, pushing down with her trainers at the same time. As the harakeke bush rips, she grabs the next piece and continues to pull from above and push from below. She manages to get her right hand to the top of the cliff, scrabbles with her feet, wriggles her chest up, and then she is over on her hands and knees, dizzy and shaking. Her arms sting, her legs and torso are covered in clay crumbs, yet she feels clean. She slumps over on her back, drinks some water, her eyes closed. A minute passes, she opens her eyes and sits up, brushes some debris off her hands.

When Rachel stands, the point is visible only ten metres away from her, a few hundred metres above the trickiest part to traverse. She's hungry now and low on water. Her watch is smeared with clay and gorse fragments. Once she rubs the face against her shirt she sees it's past noon already and she's come all of six kilometres. With a final look towards the point, she heads in the direction of the car park.

The sun is behind him, but she knows it's Clive standing beside her car.

'Hello again,' Rachel says.

'You look like you've been in the wars.'

'Yeah, I went around the coast and climbed up.'

'It's a bit dangerous round there.'

Rachel remembers the tone in Clive's voice when he

mentioned Sophey. 'What's Sophey up to these days?'

'You don't know about that?'

'About what?' Rachel has a sinking suspicion she has said the wrong thing. She'd only asked to change the subject, not out of any real interest.

'She was killed in a car crash. Four years and five months ago, drunk driver.'

'I'm sorry Clive. I had no idea.'

Clive keeps looking at her, his face the only cloud in the sky. 'A waste all right. You should be careful climbing those cliffs.'

Rachel glances over her shoulder. The dazzling afternoon light is polishing the bland water in the lagoon, giving its surface the harsh glow that reminds her of fluorescent office light. For a moment she wishes she hadn't left her sunglasses in the car. The water is running away to the sea which surrounds her and Clive on three sides. Lit up, every little horizontal wrinkle is clearly visible, like the ridges on pipi shells. All around her the peninsula is yielding to the sea's rough embrace. Hundreds of years from now, its link with the mainland will erode completely, creating an island.

She turns back, squints at Clive. The sun's fierce heat has plenty more hours to live. The inevitable bruises and muscle soreness, bycatches from her morning, will take a day to show up, but when they do, she knows they'll pass as surely as she knows not every pōhutakawa sapling planted by the lagoon will flourish. She has no answers, only a sense she needs to keep moving, to search beyond the haze.

Trailblazer

Your bedroom is a waiting room. When sunlight heats the bed into a sauna, you kick off your blankets, lie reading and eating ice cream. In the cooler evenings you venture outside. Sunsets bubble up from the dark fields, reminding you of a witches' cauldron. Tangerine flames melt into the yellow of your grandmother's fake daffodils. Blush-pink infusions are stirred by a froth of boiling clouds. Clive and Harriet party, play cricket, tennis, surf and visit friends. Clive starts a band with a couple of his mates. Harriet brings a boyfriend home. Your parents are bemused. Harriet's only fifteen.

Your mother appears at your bedroom doorway. 'Sophey, phone for you.' Her hands are floury, so is her apron, so is the phone.

'Congratulations.'

You recognise the golden syrup voice. Your geography teacher. He's got so many freckles it's hard to tell where his ginger hair ends and his face begins. Everyone calls him Monkeyface.

You know your mother is hovering just out of sight.

'Um, I haven't seen my results. The mail doesn't come till after three.'

'That was one of your teachers?' your mother asks from the doorway.

You wipe the phone on your sheet and give it back to her.

'What did he want?'

'Nothing.'

'What's got into you? He wouldn't ring for nothing.'

'Are you in the middle of baking? He thought we get mail first thing, like in Hereford.'

'Has he not heard of rural delivery? Be lucky to get the *Herald* before your father goes to milk.'

You smile to yourself.

'He knows how you got on?' Your mother glances back towards the kitchen.

'Dunno.'

For a few seconds she stares in your direction. You keep your eyes on the page.

'Kiwi biscuits,' she finally says.

All year your special mission has been to remember everything the teachers say so you can repeat it back to them come exam time. With exams over, it's like somebody snuck into your room and hoovered up your life, or a pet died.

Your town clings to the edge of the highway like a limpet or a weed. You aren't alone in expecting it to collapse, like an old barn emptied of hay bales and left vulnerable to the wind. Hereford's resilience is surprising. Clive jokes that the town has tap roots. Acing the exams is your ticket out. You imagine there are places where you might fit in, you're counting on it. After seventeen years you know what you want to get away from. There is nothing near Hereford except farms and surf breaks.

At the mailbox you feel around inside the folds of newspaper for the envelope.

Your mother makes you ring your teachers. Like suspects with well-rehearsed alibis, they downplay their involvement.

'I didn't do anything, you did it all yourself.'

Winning a scholarship, it's as if it happened to someone else. Polite congratulations scarcely interrupt the test cricket commentary. A neighbour leaves a card, like it's your birthday. Harriet complains that you've eaten all the ice cream.

You help Clive pick peas and shell them for freezing. The two of you pop the smallest, sweetest, juiciest ones into your mouths.

'Looking forward to the big smoke?' Clive asks. 'You can go see bands, go to pubs.'

'I'll be studying, plus I'm underage.'

'You need to suss everything out for when I come next year.' Clive shells with an enthusiasm that outstrips his co-ordination. Some of his peas miss the ice-cream container and roll onto the lino. 'Oops.'

You savour a mouthful of sweet baby peas. No more school.

Clive cracks open another pea pod, flicks the peas into the container, inserts the pod into his mouth over his teeth. When he grins his mouth is green.

'You're the trail blazer, Soph.'

As toddlers you and Clive would search the garden for small things. The snails you placed on the dewy path sat motionless. One night, after your baths, you snuck back outside. Several of the snails had emerged from their shells. Tiny tentacles quivered like silver pins caught in the pale light of the moon. As you watched, one glided forward leaving a faint fringe of slime in its wake.

In four weeks you leave for Auckland. You wouldn't mind if Clive tagged along.

*

You remember it all beginning, winter school holidays at your grandmother's. You were fourth form, Clive third form. Rain-filled days, a long muddy skid of boredom. Smearing the greasy condensation on the window to clear a porthole, hoping the rain had lost interest. Sick with cabin fever. Your frustration swelled. For two straight weeks it rained, a few pauses when the sun tried to sidestep the clouds. Nobody told the rain about the holidays.

'We should play pool Soph,' Clive said.

'How?'

'You've watched Pot Black. Deploy long skinny stick so as to shunt brightly coloured ball into little pockets.'

The table had experience. It was there in the faded green felt and the square of blue chalk you rubbed the tips of your cues with.

You watched for gaps in the rain and snatched a few glorious hours running around the waterlogged paddocks. Gumboots slipping on the slick grass. Fuelled by the soft kiss of the tepid easterly and constant moisture, the grass blades grew thick and lush as a monster's eyelashes. Returning to the house you'd peel off your muddy clothes and deposit them in the wash house for your grandmother to deal with. Mostly you played pool, read textbooks and made notes.

Lip aside, the pool table made a reasonable study. Unlike your house, small, cluttered and full of Harriet, your grandmother's house was spacious and quiet. You could run and get out of breath before you got to the end of her hallway, if you were allowed to run inside her house which you weren't. There were three bedrooms off the corridor, each with sets of single beds covered by matching pastel-shaded candlewick bedspreads. Grandma's intricate hand-crocheted doilies dozed

151

on the dressing tables beneath vases filled with hideous artificial flowers.

You didn't get why Grandma spent hours meticulously crafting fake blooms out of coloured plastic, wire and dull green florist ribbon. She had a big garden, heaving with fragrant daphnes, delphiniums, daisies, irises, pansies, gladioli, marigolds, dahlias and camellias. In spring, bluebells, freesias, snowdrops and daffodils cut swaths through her orchard, surviving long after the citrus succumbed to root rot.

There were more bedrooms up the front. Children slept in those rooms once. The pool table was an early move in a gradual repurposing of Grandma's house. It began with careful consultation and her eventual consent, accelerated in her later years, culminated in her unceremonious removal, first to live with her eldest and later in a hospice.

The rain gave up when school resumed. By then you'd caught the study habit, it grew like winter grass into the bloodstream of the part of you that said and did, and for reasons as mysterious as your grandmother's fascination with fake flowers, it never abated.

An agriculture service town, that's what Monkeyface called Hereford. He had a way of telling stories that stuck. Students took turns asking him questions just to keep him talking. Monkeyface tolerated the game, actually seemed to enjoy it. He had an expansive take on his allocated subject, could loop his way back regardless of how tangential an inquiry seemed. Everyone loved him for it.

'Your school chums, they'll scatter to the four winds, but the friends you make at university will be your mates for life.'

You didn't have any school friends. The closest university

was in Auckland. Geography lessons had left you more familiar with the agricultural systems and weather patterns of Africa, Asia and Europe. Your parents considered Auckland a foreign country. Biannual excursions were undertaken to the North Shore to purchase lace-ups from Hannahs. Someone drafted in for the afternoon milking. Pocket money allocated for spending on inexpensive items normally forbidden. Store-bought ham sandwiches for lunch. Your mother complained, rightly, they weren't as good as hers. Those day trips were the closest your father got to a holiday. He drove, so he called the shots.

Sometimes he drove you over the harbour bridge to Eden Park. You hated those expeditions. Squashed in the back seat suffering arguments about the route, traffic and parking. The long walk to the stadium. Waiting for something to happen before the game started, and during – you could scarcely tell the difference. The crowd heckling as you stood up, assuming the premature departure indicated a lack of faith in the Black Caps. You wanted to explain, all it was, your father wanting to beat the traffic. The car radio blurting the result.

You needed to figure out where to go by end of term. Your parents left school at the first opportunity, didn't go far. The map was the territory for everyone you knew. You didn't think consulting your penpals in Germany and America would help.

Monkeyface suggested law. You were doubtful, read *Twelve Angry Men* for English, didn't know any lawyers.

Nicole whose dad had disappeared to Australia said, 'You need to learn heaps of cases and rules off by heart, then argue all day.'

The class laughed. You wished you could do equations in your head like her. Nicole was like a Teflon-coated butterfly, cushioned from conflict by cheerleaders. She shook her long glossy strands of chocolate chip hair so it rippled. You couldn't see her as a lawyer.

Back in primary school, the two of you were punted up a class halfway through term. Some discussion must have taken place, parents informed.

'You girls are special. We want you to be challenged.' The principal didn't look at you, gestured to follow him down the corridor. There's a humming feeling in your stomach, like flies caught in a web. You wanted to ask, what challenge?

One moment you were surrounded by familiar kids and routines, the next, a bunch of strangers. Reading a pecking order was different to reading a book. Nicole's assigned table was a refuge for the quiet and the docile, her assimilation was seamless. Your desk was down the back – the Rottweiler pack howling with laughter and trying to stab each other with compasses. You looked around checking for the exit, all the while telling yourself you're not a baby, you won't cry.

Later, Clive tried to cheer you up by singing 'I Got You' by Split Enz. 'Hate it when you sulk Soph. What if you sang them a song?'

'They're horrible wild animals and stupid.'

Clive switched to 'I Hope I Never'. When he got to the chorus you joined in, couldn't help yourself. Clive and Nicole surfed sets of tunes to a better mood. You saw the wave too late, got dragged to the bottom, emerged gasping, still clutching your grievances, even as you took a breath.

'You're good at debating, Sophey,' Monkeyface said kindly. He glanced towards the back of the classroom. 'Rachel's going to study law.'

You stiffened at mention of Rachel, forced yourself to turn and look over your shoulder. Rachel hunched lower in her chair, avoiding your gaze. You stared through her to the wall then faced the front again, a mix of satisfaction and shame. That biology quiz aside, you got better marks. Your planning self wondered if people who did bad things could still be lawyers.

You practised being a lawyer as you executed your homework at a miniature desk your father made before he got good at woodwork. First you wedged your desk between bed and wall so your bed hugged the line drawn on the floor. Every time an item of clothing or a book of your sister's crossed the line, you tossed it back, consistent with your zero-tolerance policy. Harriet tried erasing the boundary. You redrew it.

'Mum, Sophey's moved her bed into the middle.'

When you heard your mother in the wash house removing her gumboots, you had your evidence ready.

'Mum!' Harriet said.

'Are the spuds on?' Your mother sounded tired.

'Yes,' you called from your desk.

'What about the chooks?'

'All fed.'

'Mum,' Harriet whined.

'What's all this.' Your mother appeared in the doorway, still in her shed overalls. She smelled of wet calf and sour milk.

You looked up from your wobbly desk. 'Harriet wouldn't leave me alone. I need space and quiet to study for School C.'

Mum looked around, your neatly made bed, Harriet's pigsty.

'Harriet hasn't set the table for tea.'

'Sophey ate all the toasties.'

'You two stop fighting. When we're at the shed you're to behave. Do your chores and schoolwork. Not shriek like banshees. Harriet, set the table.'

'I was just about to.' Harriet glared at you. 'Dad,' she called.

You heard your father emerge from the bathroom, where he would've been washing cow shit off his hands. 'You heard your mother, set the table.' He poked his head around the door, surveyed the bedroom, caught your eye, offered a disapproving look then headed for the lounge.

Even Harriet knew not to push it before Dad had his tea. A few weeks earlier you'd all been watching *Country Calendar*.

'Be quiet Harriet. I want to hear the programme.'

'Docking is an animal welfare issue,' Harriet said. 'There are other ways to guard against leptospirosis or fly strike.'

Your father grabbed one of your mother's books and threw it. For a moment you wondered if you'd imagined it, but the book was splayed on the carpet beside Harriet's chair where it landed, its spine an exclamation mark.

For a few stretched-out seconds, the room was on mute.

'That was pretty childish Dad. We should be able to discuss things. There is more than one point of view.' Harriet's voice sounded shriller than usual, the way it got when she was upset.

'Tea's ready I reckon.' Clive glanced towards the kitchen, got up and poked his head into the dining room. 'Yeah, it's ready.' He retrieved the hardback and returned it close to its original spot, just out of your father's reach.

'Thanks Clive,' Harriet said.

'Not much of a throw on ya, Dad.' Clive gave your father a shaky smile.

Your father looked sheepish. 'People should shut up when they're told to.'

You, the planning part, wondered if Harriet was too young

to know, or had forgotten, the weeks your father was off work with lepto.

The space wars petered out when summer breezed in, its humid breath announcing the end of the school year. The days swelled and arced, each building off the back of the last, yawning at the deep blue sky, a rolling maul of spritzed heat. You melted like a tub of hokey pokey left on the bench. Everyone took to the water, emerging only for bouts of cricket, haymaking and strawberry hunting. In the interlude between School C and University Entrance, the need for schoolwork and lawyer practice evaporated.

With the hay out of the way, your father's builder mates finally finished fitting out the inside of the Skyline garage. Like waiting for new books, you and Clive could hardly contain your impatience. The garage sat off the veranda, separate from the house. You shared it with your mother's sewing stuff, your grandfather's old piano, the freezer and a table tennis table. The building was supposed to be a rumpus room. You didn't mind. About to turn sixteen, fifteen in Clive's case, you had your own rooms. Harriet too. Clive's old bedroom immediately filled with *Dairy Exporter* magazines, spring bulbs, hockey sticks, ice-cream containers and old clothes.

'Grandma might need Clive's room one day,' your mother said as she stashed cake tins under the bed.

The new bedrooms were intended to fit like matchboxes, but the cheap materials weren't suited to Northland's humid climate. The louvre windows warped against the plasterboard. Their best design feature, not widely promoted by the manufacturer, was the efficient collection of spider webs and mould. There was no gap for a desk. You and Clive set yourselves up at either end of the table tennis table. Clive drew the short straw. His bedroom was closest to the sliding door through which people entered. You claimed the back bedroom by the rear exit door, which wasn't properly hung and therefore barely opened.

Every few days you pulled on gumboots to walk down the road to visit your grandmother. Your jobs were to pick grapefruit and squeeze the juice for her so she could freeze it. She couldn't squeeze them herself on account of the arthritis in her wrists.

'Could do with a bit of rain. The garden's getting dry. What do you think of these ones?'

Your grandmother was working on artificial daffodils now. The yellow matched the grapefruits, so you nodded.

'How long does it take?' You were curious despite yourself. Could see she took the job seriously, found it satisfying. Maybe it was because she couldn't squeeze grapefruit anymore.

'Few days. Sometimes they aren't quite right, I have to remove the fabric from the wires and start again. These ones are for Harriet's birthday next month.'

You tried not to think about the old fake flowers, the ones that she had made with acrylic paint. The ones someone poked holes in. You liked the soothing sound of her voice, the way she didn't let swollen wrists stop her doing stuff, even if it was weird stuff. You sat with her in the sunroom, ate ginger biscuits and drank grapefruit juice. The juice was as sour as the baking was sweet. You were not required to say anything. You thought about asking your grandmother what people did for jobs beyond Hereford but watching her busy herself all around her house and garden, the words wouldn't form.

'Well, I'd better head home Grandma, it's nearly time for tea.'

Your grandmother always followed you down her path.

She pointed out the latest flowers in bloom and the places in her garden where slugs or caterpillars had tried to invade. Although she stopped at her gate you could feel her watching. Halfway down the drive you turned and waved. She waved back. Wandering beside the road, you looked for blackberries among the wildflowers. Your feet slipped around in your gumboots. By the time you got home, your feet were covered in slimy toe jam.

You imagined your grandmother standing at her gate, her floral dress, her pink apron so faded it was nearly white. Her hair reminded you of dandelion seed heads, luminous and light. There was a trick, you blew on a dandelion head, the number of attempts it took to demolish the head was supposed to tell you the time. People said you had the same eyes, blue as gravel. Her industry, you were unsure if it kept her free or fenced in. You wondered too if she knew who'd ruined the flowers.

She was right about needing rain. The crescendo of cicada chants, and emergence of black crickets like miniature trolls from the cracks in the parched grass, signalled the end of the holidays. There was talk of drought. Your study habit resumed.

All the studying paid off. You regularly scored top marks. Your parents were surprised, and slightly bewildered. Said you didn't get it from them. The way they said 'it', they weren't sure what 'it' was, or whether 'it' was a good thing. Your mother was assiduous about going to parent–teacher sessions. Your teachers must have sung your praise, because she returned satisfied.

'You know they call you brain box,' Clive said. He was sitting at the other end of the table tennis table doing some sketches for his technical drawing class.

'I don't care.' This was a lie. You enjoyed the attention,

considered brain box an advance on string bean.

'It's not much fun for me and Harriet.'

'Why?'

'Teachers expect us to get good marks. They're always saying to Harriet, "You're Sophey's sister." Kids think we must be swots too. Worst is Mum going on about it.'

'Do you guys get teased?' It hadn't occurred to you that high marks reflected on anyone but you. You'd overheard your mother on the phone telling her friends your scores and cringed. It was like she was talking about someone else.

'It's worse for Harriet.' Clive glanced up from his drawing. 'I know it's not your fault.'

You made more of an effort to keep your head down. School, the rules were crystal. Do whatever you like under the radar. You avoided telling your parents your marks.

'I'm going to take debating. Will you do singing?' you asked Clive.

'Choir sounds lame. Bet they do Neil Diamond songs. I wouldn't mind being in a band. Do you think I look like Neil Finn? I should be in the First XI this year. Going to be so good, Jack's a mint captain!'

'Jack?'

'Jack Carlton ya gumboot, he's in your class, he's captain.'

You weren't sure whether Clive meant cricket or hockey. Clive did look a little bit like Neil Finn but you weren't about to say so.

'Soph, wanna come and play hockey with us?' Harriet asked. When you said no, she got Clive to ask. You considered wasting most of Saturday excessive. Harriet was tall, coordinated and confident. She played centre forward, scored the most goals. Jim Carlton, your coach, also trained Clive's team and provided lifts to games.

'Sophey, you play fullback first half and left half second,' Jim Carlton said. 'Swap with Rachel. You don't have Harriet's vision and aggression, but I like the way you never give up. Eldest kids make the best defenders.'

Playing hockey with your little sister, you understood how she felt when exam results came out and people compared the two of you. On the hockey field you were Harriet's sister.

'You'd be pretty good if you practised, big sis. You stopped a few goals today,' Harriet said.

'I've got better things to do than chase a ball round with a stick.'

'Don't let Dad hear you say that.'

'I'm being responsible,' you snapped.

'How so? Clive and I do our homework as well. Practice makes perfect.'

'Really? Could have sworn it made you obnoxious.'

You wanted to tell Harriet she was like a mosquito buzzing and biting. Bugger off and do your own thing. But you thought about your mission and the A you got for your history essay instead.

Your constant mulling on university was interrupted when Grandma fell down her front steps. The kerfuffle that followed was punctuated by a week of tense phone conversations. Your parents would vanish into town, return hours later to growl at you because you hadn't got the tea on. Clive made toasted sandwiches.

'Sophey, I want you to visit your grandmother on the weekend.' Your mother had been in a bad mood all week.

'I can't Mum, I have study to do.'

'It's not optional. You'll get your backside down the road on

Saturday. The rest of us have sport. You don't have to stay there all day, just check on her.'

Your grandmother was set up in the sunroom. The walking frame beside her chair made her look small. You had to squeeze past it.

'Hello dear, I wasn't expecting anyone. I thought you'd be studying.'

You didn't know what to say, what your role was. It was a familiar feeling, although you didn't usually experience it with your grandmother.

'Shall I make you a cuppa?'

'I don't need any tea thank you. '

She looked like a worn-out dishcloth. You wanted to go home.

'Shall I get your magazines?'

'They're right here, child. There's biscuits in the tins, help yourself.'

In the kitchen you were surprised to see a few unwashed dishes. You rummaged around in the tins. Selected a couple of your favourite gingernuts, put them on a plate. Then, thinking maybe your grandmother wanted some as well, added a few more.

'Bicky?'

'Thank you.'

Your grandmother rested a gingernut on the arm of her chair. Gave you a faint smile. Her arm was bandaged.

'They were your grandfather's favourite too. Used to dunk them in his tea.'

'Ha, yeah I remember.' And you do remember the elaborate afternoon teas, plates of biscuits and cakes all over the table.

Salty crackers with lumps of rock-hard Tasty cheese chiselled from a kilogram block bought from the dairy factory. Tea that tasted like soapy water, sculled when it was cold to wash away the lumps of sugary paste that clung to your teeth. Your parents only let you have one biscuit for afternoon tea. Your grandmother let you have as many as you wanted. There was always a telling off to be had when you got home and had no room for dinner.

When you'd eaten the gingernuts, you thought about escaping. You should have brought your books down. You could have studied here, kept an eye on her, except your grandmother didn't seem to want company.

'Will you be okay if I head home Grandma, do you want me to get you anything?'

'I'm fine. Maybe those pills on the kitchen table, and a glass of milk.'

You found the medicine, Meloxicam, read the back of the pack. It was for osteoarthritis.

'Here you go.'

'Thanks, dear. You better head home. Get on with your studies. Your mother said you're going to university next year, clever girl. Got your whole life ahead of you.'

You blushed and stood, unsure how to exit.

'Off you go. I might just stay here. The walker's a bit hard to get up and down the steps. Your father's going to make me a ramp.'

You dawdled down the garden path. Everywhere weeds taunted the flowering plants, spoiling for a fight. They didn't have the numbers yet, but unless someone intervened it was only a matter of time. You wanted to stop and grab handfuls of them, imagined wrenching them out and hurling them over the fence while yelling 'Get in behind' like your father did with his dogs.

You fiddled with the gate, wondering if your fingers would go numb. When you turned around to pull it shut you searched for your grandmother and waved. She was watching of course. She didn't wave exactly, more a slow lift of the hand that wasn't bandaged, halfway up, and a surrender. You turned and trudged home, glad nobody was there to see you, because if they asked you why you were crying you wouldn't have been able to say.

How could you forget? Debating, weekend hockey, learner's licence test, your planning self dropped the ball. Anxiety prickled your arms, leaving a pink rash. You sat beside Carole, who tried to talk about the upcoming debate. You flicked through the textbook, hoping Larson the new biology teacher would skip his weekly quiz. You weren't the only one.

'Mr Larson, I forgot. Could we, like possibly, do it next week instead?' Nobody had to look to know that Vanessa, who had a reputation based on her pashing rather than her marks, was batting her eyelashes and deploying her most devastating smile.

A glimmer of amusement ruffled Larson's face. He was young, tanned the colour of kelp, rumoured to have taken the job because he was into surfing. His head shook.

'Actions have consequences, Vanessa. Everyone else is prepared and anxious to take the quiz.'

Breaths were sucked in. A low-level murmur spread around the classroom. You thought about the driving test. You and Clive had driven quads and tractors for years, but you needed car practice. Having a licence would mean you could drive to exams.

'Wouldn't be cool to skip it.' Larson smiled like a bloody shark. 'It is a weekly quiz.'

You considered feigning sunstroke. Didn't think you'd be able to pull it off. Carole was good at biology. You glanced sideways. Some kids liked to shield their papers with their arms to protect against wandering eyes, but you never bothered and nor did Carole. Larsen, who usually stayed at his desk, decided to cruise the classroom. His gaze dusted the rows. Vanessa made eyes at him. You kept glancing sideways, checking answers matched. The rest of the class kept scribbling letters. At the conclusion of the quiz, as was customary, you swapped papers for marking.

'Anyone hang a ten?' The class laughed.

Half the front row glanced over their shoulders in your direction. You studied the stainless steel of the lab bench, the way the light hit the cold, slick surface, bulletproof.

'Nine?'

'Um yep.' Rachel Carlton half raised two fingers in a crooked peace sign for a moment, before her hand dropped to her lap.

'Groovy Rachel. Bring your paper up.'

'Eight?'

You and Carole raised your hands.

'Coolio. Sophey, bring your paper up.' Carole half rose. 'No worries, Carole, two checks are plenty.'

You walked up the front, wondering if Larson was going to comment on you only getting an eight. He gave your sheet a cursory glance, you an appraising stare.

'Can see your buddy's sheet if you care to look.' Larson spoke quietly so only you could hear.

Panic blew through you. It felt like white petals, gusts of them, shaken off a camellia bush in the wind. The petals turned brown almost right away when they hit the ground. It was strange the way they did that.

'Something to be aware of, yes?'

You blinked, nodded.

'Back you go.'

You were late for an exam, driving across flooded roads and detouring around broken bridges. Always, at the point when brown camellia petals started falling like bruised snowflakes, you'd wake up, sweating and hyper alert. You used the opportunity to get in an hour or two of study before breakfast. The more you studied, the more you realised you didn't know. More needed to be done to create the creamy feeling in your stomach when all the petals stayed on the blooms. After school, you studied until bedtime. At the weekends, if you had to go with everyone else to a sports event, you'd sit in the car, read and highlight key passages. Frequently you were given permission to stay home. Your parents preferred not to explain to their friends why their daughter wouldn't leave the car.

'What do you do all day Soph?'

Clive was a clown with his zinc-lined lips, a sunburned face streaked with pale tide marks where sweat had dried. His cricket whites had grass stains at the knees. The side of his right thigh was red where he'd rubbed the ball before bowling an over. He smelt of stale perspiration and leather.

'Study till I'm tired. Walk the paddocks repeating stuff in my head so I remember.'

'There's nobody to talk to. Don't you get lonely?'

'No. There would be nobody to talk to if I came to cricket.' You didn't say you would rather learn history than watch other people race around in the heat. It was what you admired about your grandmother, she wasn't a spectator, did lots of her own things by herself.

'There's heaps of people. The tennis girls come to the

clubrooms after their games.'

'And chat about tennis and eyeliner. Hold me back!'

Clive wiggled his hips and flung his arms about while he sang a few lines of 'The Brain That Wouldn't Die' by the Tall Dwarfs.

You scowled at him. 'I'm not a zombie. Thought you wanted to be Neil Finn. What's wrong with using your brain anyway? I make instant, put hokey pokey ice cream in it. The coffee softens the toffee. I read.'

'If you came to cricket you'd get money for ice creams from Mum. I do want to be Neil Finn, he's cool.'

'If I came to cricket I'd have to study in the car, it's hot.' Even though you craved routine, you longed for release. Which one was really you?

'We go to the beach ya gumboot! Swim in the lagoon. Water's warm and deep, no rips. Remember? You used to swim with us.'

For a moment you can see yourself in the lagoon, floating on your back, arms and legs spread out like a starfish, face turned to the clouds, mellow and weightless. 'Go take a shower. You stink like a polecat.'

Clive's smile faded.

'Sorry, but you do. Worse than cow shit.'

Partway through the final term a new kid arrived. Like Larson he was into surfing, fluent in a kind of laid-back charm that you didn't get. Girls captivated by his smile. When he asked about scholarship exams, he surprised everyone. Hereford boys channelled all their energy into sport. You wanted to sit the tests too. Teachers shrugged, whatever.

'Ya kidding me sis, three more exams?' Clive said.

'I like exams.'

167

'What about those wicked migraines you get?'

Your headaches started a few months ago, around the time your grandmother had her fall, Saturday mornings like clockwork. Numb fingers, every sound magnified, then blurry vision. Not being able to see properly, lines of text wiggling in and out of focus, frightened you. The fear was worse than the head pain and nightmares.

'Panadol makes them go away.' You took Panadol whenever you lost feeling in your fingers. The packets went everywhere with you just in case.

The weeks of study break, the lead-up to the end of high school, were a series of melting moments, a textbook blur. The humidity clung to you like a quieter version of Harriet. You sweated, studied, walked the farm memorising key points, drunk ice-cream coffees. It was too hot to sleep. Sometimes you thought about swimming in cool water but there'd be plenty of time for that after exams. Clive studied for university entrance at the other end of the table.

'Surfing,' Clive said. 'It's the cool thing to do this year. Stay over for parties at the Surf Club.'

You gave him a death stare. 'Studying hard at practical biology and chemistry?'

He laughed and started singing 'Counting the Beat' by the Swingers. 'I wouldn't mind a party, can't wait till the exams are over.'

Doing well in the exams was your getaway plan.

What happened after the exams was an unlined notebook. More visits with Grandma perhaps, if she was still there.

It was the last day of the school holidays, back when you loathed primary school. Thoughts of Rottweilers and taunts of 'string bean' swirled in your head like clouds of dust kicked up by a rotary hoe. You and your cousins were at your grandmother's. Everyone was outside playing Go Home Stay Home in the sunshine. You'd come in to use the toilet. You knew you wouldn't be found, since inside was out of bounds. You wandered into the lounge, which was cool, shadowy and silent, like the vat room after the hubbub of milking.

You remembered your arrival in the new classroom, how it was greeted with resentment, curiosity, contempt.

'Hey string bean!' The boy's compass was bloody.

'Me?' you asked, heart in ankle.

'Yeah, string bean, borrow ya pen?'

The boy helped himself, giving one of your pigtails a hard pull so your eyes watered. The teacher, trying to get the class to do a writing exercise, didn't notice. A girl on your other side snatched your exercise book and passed it round the table.

'Can I have my pen back, and my book?'

The teacher looked over. 'No talking.'

'Finder's keepers.'

'Give it back.'

'Gonna make me? I've lost it.'

'I'll tell on you.'

'Telltale tit.'

'Give it back.'

'String bean's a telltale tit.'

The only way you could see to get your pen back was to put your hand up. The pen returned only after the teacher asked you what you wanted, leaving you scarlet, tongue-tied, fighting back tears.

*

The wire stalks covered in green florist ribbon looked grey in the half light. They reminded you of the bloody compass. You must have looked away for a moment. A few of the flowers had holes in their petals. What had you done? You had a pencil. Wanted to see how much pressure they could withstand. Not much, all it took was a prod. The jagged gaps in the pink brought on an instant hit of creaminess. Working the pencil, making little pricks, a few more petals a little less perfect.

Back in the garden, once your eyes adjusted to the harsh light you studied the fleshy white camellias with their lemon pollen icing and realised there were no holes. Slugs, snails and the skinny green caterpillars preferred the new growth, the buds and leaves. Your tongue tasted like grapefruit.

The damage did not go unnoticed for long. Plastic coating doesn't rip itself.

'I don't know,' you muttered. You were just the one watching.

'It wasn't me!' Harriet insisted. 'I was outside with Clive.'

'Wasn't the bloody tooth fairy,' your father said. 'Someone's lying. Your grandmother put a lot of work into those flowers, now she'll have to redo them.'

'Could've been your nieces,' your mother pointed out. You could see she wanted to believe it. They both did. 'I would hope you three know to respect other people's property,' she said. 'If it was one of you, the right thing to do is to own up and apologise. Think about it carefully.'

You glanced at Clive. He was looking at Harriet, who was shaking her head. You looked at Harriet as well.

'It wasn't me,' Harriet insisted.

'We didn't raise you to be liars,' your father said.

You realised you should be ashamed but it was dark in your grandmother's house where the flowers were kept on top of the big china cabinet, among the family photos and silver sports cups. It was hard to see anything. Maybe you weren't even there. Maybe it was a dream.

After the exams, your mother ejects you from your bedroom and sends you down to visit your grandmother, and you find her sitting in her sunroom surrounded by fur pelts.

'What are you making?'

'Not sure yet dear. I think I might stitch these together to make toy bears.'

You study the pelts; they look too small for possums.

'What skins are they?'

'Some stoats were coming round the hen house stealing the eggs.'

'Oh.'

'If I make bears, I couldn't give them to grandchildren, the pelts are a bit smelly. I'm experimenting to see how flexible they are. Might just stitch them together for floor coverings. Look at my legs!'

Your grandmother's legs are covered with faint scratch marks.

'Cat does it, to get attention.'

She doesn't have a cat. You wonder whether your grandmother is losing her marbles.

'Your father found it in one of the barns, brought it down. It isn't tame. It's a ginger. Like those biscuits you're so fond of. Drinks milk, comes and goes as it pleases.' She notices your confusion. 'Your father didn't tell you about the cat, I'm guessing. Heard you passed your exams and you're off soon?'

'Yeah.' You watch her working with the pelts. After a few minutes she looks up again.

'I can only do this for short stints then I have to rest my

arms, they get achy. Can't do the garden anymore.'

The arthritis medicine in the pill container must work. You think about your migraines, which vanished when the exams were over.

'You aren't making flowers anymore?'

'It was time for a change. After my fall I couldn't do much of anything. Now, with the cat, it won't let me muck around with paint. I tried, he chased the ribbon, put a paw through a bloom I had drying, ruined it. Didn't do it on purpose, not his fault, he's curious. He's scared of these pelts. Must be the smell, lets me get on with it.'

You can feel her gravel eyes on you.

'For someone off to university you don't look excited.'

You pull a face. 'It'll be a big change.' What you are heading towards remains stubbornly out of focus. You understand your life won't be the same.

'I don't know anything about university. I imagine there'll be smart people like you with the same interests. New pastures. You'll be back to visit too.'

'Where is the cat?'

She gestures towards the side of the house. 'Probably round the back. He's still getting used to being here, might not even stay. He likes milk.' She points to the empty saucer by the door.

When it's time for you to leave, she leads the way down her footpath. The garden feels diminished. A carpet of ground covers designed to suffocate any weeds. Squads of herbs of the most robust, utilitarian varieties – parsley, mint and thyme – guard the northern corner near the gate. Geraniums sit impounded in terracotta pots, belligerent sentinels. Their lurid red and pink blooms dare anyone to question their legitimacy.

You can't see any monarchs, or the fluffy bumblebees that used to amble around like drunks smooching every second flower, or even any snails.

'I don't know if I want to be a lawyer.'

Your grandmother stops and points her walking stick at splotches of vivid pink. A shaft of sunlight is forcing its way between two of the pots, illuminating a thicket of ice plants. Their spiky petals are folded out like deck chairs to reveal luminous yellow hearts. There's a simple genius in the way they open and shut with the sun.

'Nobody does till they give it a try, dear.'

When you turn and wave goodbye, your grandmother waves back. You want to think you catch a glimpse of a ginger cat. It could have been something else.

Tramp

'Jack it's incredible, verging on sublime!'

Kyle has this idea to show me a certain hut on a hill up north. We figure to stay overnight. I'm intrigued, didn't think there were many places to tramp up there. A little nervous because, well, Kyle. Greg agrees to come, three seals the deal. Safety in numbers.

I'm hunting for my cap. I hate it when things aren't where you left them. My cap is where I should've looked for it first, the tray of the ute, by the pig bucket, under a stack of clothing that only sees intermittent use. It isn't in great shape my hat, certainly not clean, but I'm not in great shape for a tramp either, though I'm at least freshly laundered. Sniffing the cap, it smells like pig tucker, rotting food scraps basically.

The kids spot Kyle and Greg first.

'Your friends are here, Dad,' Ellen calls from the kitchen.

'It's a white mini. Way to go Dad!' Jed says.

'Seeya later.'

Kyle is a couple of hours later into the afternoon than promised. Greg will want to get the show on the road.

The passenger door opens. Sounds like it could do with

a drink of CRC. A leg that wouldn't look out of place on a wētā reveals itself, followed by a second. Greg. He looks at my Macpac, a sturdy roomy beast. Overkill for an overnighter, but it's what I have. A reminder of my younger days, when I got out more. The driver door opens. Kyle. The pair of them extracting themselves from Mozart is like opening stiff blades on a Swiss army knife. Fully extended, both are close to six foot.

'We could take the ute maybe?'

Greg has a bungee cord in his hand. He hesitates, glances at Kyle.

'Oh, Mozart'll be fine. He's a trooper.'

Mozart's backside is held shut with an ingenious bungee arrangement. A disembowelled pack is wedged between black vinyl seats, its contents nearby. No attempt made to put it all back together. Would be like trying to return toothpaste to the tube. We wrestle my beast onto Mozart's head. Greg fixes the bungee to the roof rack, binds it hostage style. We stand back to study our efforts and wipe away perspiration.

'Humid for winter.' Greg rubs his hands on the sides of his narrow legs.

The first time I met Greg, I couldn't take my eyes off his legs. Two cables of muscle with squash-ball-sized calves.

'I didn't think you'd get up a sweat, with all your cycling?' For every hour in the office, Greg probably cycles three or four. Like my twin sister Rachel, except with her it's running.

'Don't get out as much as I used to with the kids and work. Commutes and big weekend stuff only. Always seems warmer up here.'

'It's about to rain. You guys want a drink before we go?' Kyle looks like he might.

'No. We need to get going.' Greg glances at Kyle. 'You okay to keep driving?'

Kyle nods with his teeth. They're whiter than his face, a real optimistic shine to them. He waves to the kids who are bug-eyed at the kitchen window. I give them a bugger off wave. I know they're laughing at Mozart, and Greg's legs. They wave back, drop their hands to their mouths to hide their giggling. I squeeze in beside the leaky pack. Kyle turns Mozart with a degree of effort commensurate with handling an overloaded vehicle in an unfamiliar space.

I have a feeling my knees are sticking into Kyle's back. 'You okay Kyle, got enough room?'

'Golly yes, tonnes of space thanks.'

Kyle pretty much always says the opposite of what he means so I wriggle around to relieve the pressure on his back. If I move my legs sideways rather than straight, I achieve it. The result is a pain in my hip.

Kyle is in good spirits. Greg seems slightly on edge, like he's recently been in good spirits, can still remember what it's like, typical Greg. He turns his head to look at me. You could slice bread with his cheekbones, if you had a need.

'How's Gemma?'

'In Auckland with her mates for the Blues game. We're leaving the kids home alone.' I don't mention my wife needs a break as much as me. She's my worry doll and vice versa. You might have seen them, little bags with tiny dolls inside, tell one a worry, put it under your pillow et cetera. Gemma listens to me venting about Jim's antics, sweating the weather. I get to hear the crazy committee goings on she's caught up in. Nets of intricacies pertaining to feuds and fiefdoms born of ego, boredom and everyone knowing each other's business. People eh, some doozies lurking round Hereford way. Us too I suppose.

'It's great once they're old enough to be left to their own devices,' Greg says.

'Funny you should mention devices, Jed's addicted. He was falling asleep during the day. Gemma thought he might be low on iron, or glandular fever, one of those chronic fatigue things. We took him to the doctor. Gemma's sister figured it out when she stayed. He was spending half the night on his laptop playing games. We have a box for devices now. Stash them in there at bedtime.'

Greg doesn't care. 'This bush we're heading to Kyle, I didn't know it existed?'

'Oh boy. I had no idea either till we visited for a territorial training exercise. To be honest I thought Northland was mostly beaches and gravel roads. Beautiful white sandy beaches. I didn't know about the forest.'

There is a certain extravagance to Kyle's gestures. Greg ducks his gesticulating hand in the interest of keeping both eyes.

'It's pristine bush. I mean really unspoilt. You should see it. Fantastic, thick forest down to the water's edge with a couple of streams full of the clearest, coldest water you've ever tasted. It's like the streams are fed by a glacier or something. Amazing birdlife, could be in an aviary. The dawn chorus, fantastic, honestly the sounds our natives make, it puts classical music to shame, the pure notes and the way the rest of the birds join in with the first soloists. And the symphony just builds. You really could be in a concert hall listening to a grand orchestra.'

'There are tracks right?' Greg has pulled a map up on BackCountry Navigator. It's too small to see properly. He squints like a swimwear model looking into the noon sun.

'Oops.' Kyle swerves to avoid a sheep in the middle of the road. 'Yeah, a few tracks. I believe DOC is going to open some terrific new ones. It's paradise. You guys will love this spot. Not many people know about it. You have to get permission from the forestry company to access the roads.'

'Yeah, I hadn't heard of it.' Greg points out another sheep. 'You got the okay, eh?'

Mozart comes much closer to colliding with the second sheep. It freezes, bolts at the eleventh hour. Weird when road sheep play chicken.

'Absolutely, I phoned the forestry people last week. Explained I was Army. The lovely lady confirmed the gate access code. Assured me it would be fine and dandy.'

I'm not feeling fine and dandy in the back seat. I wriggle to relieve my hip pain. A tightness seeps down my iliotibial band, but I'm used to feeling cramped. Farming with the old man is like that.

I told Jim to relax, I would only be away for two days. He gets stressed if he doesn't know what's going on. Sometimes forgets, or remembers a different version, one that appeals to him more. I take comfort in knowing he'll be limited in his ability to go off script, what with his wrist, and his Mule out of action. His wrist is munted since his attempt to lift a dead cow. Poor bugger, Jim, the cow too of course, but nothing could be done about the cow. Wrist was painful, more than he usually endures with his arthritis. Sufficient for him to make a doctor's appointment though he had to wait a fortnight. She'll be right. Medical receptionist likely didn't ask about the pain, and Jim wouldn't have volunteered the information.

The frontline medics hardly last a season. Difficult role trying to keep the herd from bolting through the gate. Infants and children with ailments they lack the words to describe, and stoic elderly patients. Some of them, like Jim, are a bit deaf. It's tricky discerning whose needs are urgent versus merely routine, genuine versus fabricated. Mostly patients volunteer only the vaguest descriptions. Some, like the seasonal vegetable and fruit pickers from the islands, are shy or struggle with English.

Others have specific needs, not strictly legal. Painkillers. I listen to the docs talking shop down the squash club. Seems to me, the primary ailment, which you can't get a script for, is loneliness.

The wrist thing hasn't kept Jim off the farm. He's devised a nifty habit of approaching gates sideways and nudging them open with his Mule. I guess he figures his Mule is a side-by-side vehicle, so why not? Because the brake lever is situated on the outside at floor level is why. This morning, before I left for the tramp, Jim snagged the lever in a gate and it snapped off. Mechanical types are easier to source than medics in our valley. We towed the Mule to the neighbour with the yard full of broken vehicles and empty beer bottles. Looked to have a few regrets the neighbour, waking up being one of them. Eyed the Mule from the vantage point of his front veranda for a couple of minutes. Either he has exceptional long-range vision or the model was as familiar to him as an old girlfriend. Reckoned leave it with him. He had a reasonable show of putting the lever back where it belonged.

As we drive north I'm feeling good having exchanged the confines of the farm for the temporary cramp of Mozart. Late autumn is easiest. Pre-calving lull is for fencing. I'm sure fencing will be the death of me, turns my stomach just thinking about it, but it has to be done. Maintenance, weed control and riparian planting too. Less urgent, easier-to-put-off tasks.

I like to take a break if an opportunity presents itself. See my mates infrequently at best. Threat of rain for this trip, runs to its own schedule the weather. Likes to keep forecasters guessing. Whatever. Tramping is like a fence post. Doesn't really need good weather.

'Need gumboots!' Greg stalks the kitchen window at the backpackers, stops to rub a blurry patch in the condensation with the sleeve of his raincoat. The sticky grey looks back at him, like a visitor who fails to realise they've outstayed their welcome.

I check the forecast on my phone. Changeable, with scattered showers clearing Monday, light nor'west breeze turning southerly. I hope the rain will ease for the sake of the cows. I have them up near the airstrip eating the high grass before I move them closer to the shed, in preparation for calving. It's the best way to conserve grass. So far, autumn has been mild and grass growth no problem, but as it gets colder, the kikuyu will chuck it in, doesn't like frosts. Usually I check the forecast as soon as I get up. I check each time I return to the house. There is a Norwegian site that's really good. I keep a whole suite of different weather sites constantly updating. As Gemma is fond of pointing out, I can hardly blame Jed for his device addiction.

We hadn't planned to sleep in but we must have been tired after work, then the drive, and the beer and hot chips. The pub kitchen was closed by the time we got there. No worries. Kyle reckons it's only a few hours' tramp up the hill to the hut.

Nobody but Kyle is permitted to drive Mozart so once we cram everything back in, Greg fires up Google Maps to navigate. Ten minutes, we've driven out of coverage.

'Gosh the region is crying out for infrastructure. Would be tricky if you didn't know your way,' Kyle says.

Greg's lifted a pile of paper towels from the backpackers and he uses them to wipe the condensation off Mozart's windshield. We have the windows down. After a few detours we arrive at what seems like the correct road. Kyle gets out and punches in the access code. Mozart doesn't fancy the coarse metal so we crawl the first kilometre at walking pace then figure to leg it.

'It'll add a tiny bit to the tramp,' Kyle says.

'How much do you reckon?' I'm wondering about my fitness. Squash fit doesn't translate to tramping. On the other hand, I reckon I'm probably more up for it than Kyle. He works stupid hours in the lab. If things are going well, he sleeps there.

'Just a tad. We had four-wheel drives when we came, so I'm not totally sure, a few kilometres?' Kyle blinks the rain out of his eyes.

Greg has already extracted and shouldered his pack. He waits on the roadside for Kyle and me to get organised. Kyle needs to put on his tramping boots. I fish out my old cap, it'll be sweet for keeping the rain off.

Drops of water plop in puddles and tickle the back of our necks. Tall pines are on parade either side of us behind the fences, which I suppose we should have expected. The fences mean business. Good nick, expensive fit-out, complete with electrics, impenetrable, flasher than mine. Forestry company isn't short of cash. Greg's old trainers are soaked.

'We'll be in bush in a minute,' Kyle reckons.

'Seems dark.' Greg squints at the concrete sky.

'Botheration.' Kyle stops. I nearly walk into him. 'Think I might've left the headlights on.'

Greg ditches his pack and holds out his hand for the keys. 'I'll go.'

Kyle looks like he wants to object, but he sheds his pack and pulls out his keys. We watch Greg jog away on his pin legs. The squelch of his sneakers drowns out the rain and Kyle's chagrin for a couple of seconds.

'Better to be sure. We don't want to come out to a flat battery eh.'

We swat mosquitoes. I spot a circle of red toadstools tricked out with white flecks. Light smacks their rain-glazed tops, flickering like little screens.

'Fairy ring.'

Kyle turns for a look.

'We had a good crop on the farm this year. Think it was the dry start to autumn, then we had a few solid dollops of rain.' I can recall what the weather was for any given week. I keep a diary. Early March was the most stressful, the district on the verge of drought even with irrigation. Thanks to my bore, Jim's bore, we were okay. Old man had the foresight to put it in twenty years ago, before droughts were more frequent. Mid-March there was rain, again a week later. The water was a godsend, especially for the neighbouring farms that lack irrigation. Brought out the mosquitoes, and when it stopped raining the sandflies.

'I love mushrooms,' Kyle says.

'Not magic ones I hope.' Greg has freckles of mud on his legs. The car headlights were off. Kyle tells us about the time he helped out in A&E and they had to pump the stomachs of some kids who'd eaten too many shrooms.

'What about meth?' I want to know. 'See much of that?'

'Evil stuff. I'd rather treat alcohol or cannabis related conditions any day. It used to be just alcohol we dealt with, mostly, especially on weekends. You did see some meth. You could score it by buying diet pills at the chemist and grinding them up, till they stopped that in the 70s. But it's chronic now.' Kyle shudders. 'Turns people into devious maniacs.'

'Yeah.'

Kyle and Greg don't know about my little brother Willy. Willy's good company if you don't mind having the piss taken out of you. Sharp wit and cutting insights, but underneath the bravado there's something darker and more brittle. And Rachel, unwilling to commit to a place, job, relationship, all the conventional trappings, well, traps, in her opinion. I try to understand and get on with them both, but you have to be realistic, take the good with the bad, like the weather.

It's like the rain can suss my mood. Backs off, replaced by a cloying mist drifting between the trees. As Kyle promised, where the road peters out and the track kicks in, the plantation forest vanishes. Initially signs replace pines. I didn't expect the first one starring a rubbish bag with a line through it. The other is a skull-and-crossbones one, warning of 1080 drops.

The first sign is a waste of time. A potpourri of rubbish and weeds fringe the track, same as too many roadsides. Plastic bottles and soiled plastic bags, the little snap locks and the bigger supermarket ones, a few cans, takeaway coffee cups, tissues and toilet paper lie amongst the flat green docks, prickly bearded scotch thistles, yellow flowers of the gorse, broom, ragwort, dandelions and buttercups, crumpled blackberry bushes, clumps of twitch grass, sticky paspalum and biddy-bids.

Biddy-bids, so practical and enterprising the way they hitch a ride on our socks. Like Jim and Di. I get the farm but they come with it, part pragmatic, part sticky little balls of need. Fair, they raised me after all, but a kind of torture. We pass nightshades with their gothic berries glistening as if they've just stepped out of the shower. Fine-stemmed rushes wrestle bracken and toetoe. Toetoe bows to mānuka and hebe bushes with their friendly pale pink blooms. I like how both flower in winter. Their way of adapting to the pressures and struggles, how plants get along, make space for themselves, a kind of sibling rivalry.

The track winds on, climbing gradually. The rain hasn't really left, merely changed into something more comfortable. If it was a party you'd recognise various guests, Mr Humidity Hangover and Ms Pregnant Cloud. Mrs Mist Accompaniment,

183

she's the one that drifts like a sulk halfway towards the treeline.

The mānuka and kānuka zone with its stores of dirty brown and fluro orange fungi sit next to scraggly groves of nīkau. I reach up to see if I can touch a green bulb. Northland nīkau always look wasted to me. Strung-out, shabby and stunted. It wasn't till I walked the Heaphy and clocked the platoons of southern nīkau that I realised the difference. Down south the palms line the banks of the river, where the tea water gains girth and volume in its final run to join the feral Tasman Sea. It's quite a sight, the refined Heaphy pouring into the Tasman. The sea smashes the sand, punting salt spray into the spiralling mist. Clinging on for dear life with their shallow roots, those nīkau take a right pummelling, but they lean into the power of the collective. By sticking together no single tree is easily dislodged. Sandflies do it too, clouds of the voracious little buggers, eat you alive given a chance. Funny what you notice and what you won't look at. Up here, easy to confuse the benign climate and the green veneer of cultivation with a taming of the land. As if fences equate with civilisation, as if litterers obey signs. As if checking the forecast all the time will stop global warming.

As kids we used to sneak over to the remnant bush in the gully, gather up the dead nīkau bulbs, use them to hoon downhill. Things change, we grow up in different ways. When you have a family of your own, your first one fades. What kind of future will Ellen and Jed have?

I'm like a cow chewing its cud on the walk up that hill. A few of the nīkau have bright orange and crimson berries on them still. Like someone's strung up a few bunches of Smarties for us to pluck and eat.

'I missed the bush when we were in London.' Kyle sees me tag the nīkau bulb.

184

'Yeah,' Greg says. 'Loads of interesting stuff but nothing like this. In England I missed our beaches and peaks, in Dubai, I used to dream of rain.'

'When I went overseas, have to say, the bush was all right. And I met a few German tourists who came to stay and help out on the farm for a bit so, you know, it was win-win.'

'Ha ha. Yeah, the South Island bush is amazing with those mountain views.' Greg sounds wistful. 'When the kids are older I'm going back down there to do more tramping.'

'I don't get time.' Kyle runs his hand along the silver underside of a ponga. 'I get really into some good project then I don't want to stop until we've got somewhere. There are always more avenues.'

'That's true,' Greg says. 'Cancer research is bloody important mate. Speaking of important, shall we stop for lunch?' He points to a log off to the left.

'Golly, wish I had more time to spend with my kids and Justine,' Kyle says.

I wondered. At university Kyle was a workaholic, often pulling all-nighters to cram for his exams and staying on after his hospital shifts. Justine holds the fort now when Kyle disappears to conferences and research trips. That's one of the good things about farming. My work is home. When the kids were little, I was around, had the flexibility to go to school stuff and sports. Jim was around too, but strict and blunt. He had good intentions but the criticism – like water on rock it wears you down, pushes people away, they hide stuff. Not my style. I want Ellen and Jed to be free to pursue their interests.

All afternoon we plod uphill. Happen by stocky, prickly tōtara, pūriri, their branches all twisted and spewing pink flowers

185

onto the track. Furry baby rimu, no kahikatea or kauri though, unsurprisingly. The bush will have been logged, the kauri gum dug up and sold. No rātā either, possibly still too many possums sampling their old favourite. The rain stages a comeback. Once you're wet, it makes little difference, you stop noticing. It's the failing light that switches me from past to present. We stop to grab our head torches.

'I thought we'd be there by now,' Kyle admits.

'Probably just a bit further than you remember,' I say.

Greg offers round his barley sugars. 'Seen that set of footprints?' He shines his torch on some welts in the mud. 'Reckon there'll be anyone at the hut?'

'No. Maybe they're old prints. Not many people know about the place,' Kyle says.

We're sucking on the orange sweets when we spot the green hut, right where the track seems to peter out.

A four-bunker furnished with a small table, a couple of rickety benches, pot belly stove and some dry wood.

'Sweet!' Greg's well pleased. 'We should see if there's more wood.'

There is a shed round the back that contains dry wood and a couple of axes. We haul wood inside. Greg gets the stove going and sets his soaked trainers beside it. As our numb fingers permit, we drag off our wet gear, exchanging it for dry. Our breath escapes our noses and lips, steaming up the cold air. Dragon's breath. It's when I'm wrestling my sleeping bag onto one of the top bunks that I notice the other bunk.

'Hey, there's stuff here already!' An old synthetic sleeping bag slouches like a hibernating bear. It smells of smoke and mould. It might have been abandoned, the way trampers leave fuel canisters and empty wine bottles behind, except there's a leather sheath, the type that normally contains a knife. Still has the price sticker. A couple of hunting magazines, several empty Lion Red cans and some yellow packets of instant beef-flavoured noodles round out the stash.

'Hunter?' Greg has a look as well.

The discovery dampens our mood slightly. I can't put my finger on why exactly. Maybe the empty sheath. It gets me wondering if there's someone wandering around outside with a knife. Greg makes a brew and sets water on for the rice. Kyle has some tins of tuna. We are hungry enough to eat the wood. The hut even has a couple of candles, which we light. After tuna and rice, a hot Milo goes down a treat. Everything thaws out. A pleasant ache settles into our middle-aged muscles. Kyle complains about his wet hair. Greg and I laugh, two beanie-wearing baldies. Greg points out we haven't heard many birds. Wet has sent them packing we reckon. Pit time. You can imagine the scene, after a long day in the rain, three mates snuggled on our bunks, dry for the first time. Warm and listening to the rain whacking the corrugated iron roof. The guttering leaking less than the same at my house. Cosy. Bring on the snoring and the possums.

I've been awake for a while, debating how much longer I can put off leaving my warm pit versus venturing outside for a cold but necessary pee. I've made it to the ground soundlessly, thanks to years of experience protecting the family from my early starts. I put my head torch on and then I'm seriously tempted to sneak outside in my bare feet and piss off the balcony, but for some reason, maybe because it's been a long time since my last overnighter, I decide to be a masochist. I get the worst part over. Force my toasty feet into yesterday's sodden socks without cursing aloud. It's a truly horrible feeling putting on cold saturated socks. I'm doing a half-arsed lace of my still wet boots, enough so I won't trip, but not the full nine yards, when I hear a scrabbling sound and light flicks at the window and the hut door flings open. A big chap stamps in. He's carrying a rifle and a bad attitude. His scowl half fills the hut. The gun goes on the table. He shines his head torch into my eyes and beyond. I hear the others stirring.

'Who youse?'

He stands still for a moment, dripping water into a puddle, then turns and slams the door shut. The hut shakes. I have a feeling my legs might be shaking a little bit.

'We're trampers,' Greg calls from his bunk, somewhat unnecessarily.

'Pardon us. We're heading back down tomorrow, um, golly, I mean today,' Kyle says.

His eyes narrow. 'Youse been into my stuff?' He strides over to the spare bunk, lifts the mattress and feels underneath. Whatever he's stored under there must have remained untouched. He seems to relax slightly and turns back to the middle of the room.

I set about lighting the stove.

'Um, good idea. It is chilly in here,' Kyle says.

I can't see Kyle but I can tell from his tone he's offering his best smile.

'We have tea bags if you'd like some, um, tea.'

'Tea?' The bloke spits the word out like he is telling us to fuck off.

He gives me a long smouldering look. His eyes remind me of embers, the ones you poke and underneath they are red. Good for toasting marshmallows. I turn and focus on the stove. It takes a bit for the kindling to catch. Greg is better at lighting it than me.

'You guys want breakfast?' I ask.

Ember Eyes yanks open the door and pulls a slimy pack inside. It's one of those old external frame jobbies. It must have been uncomfortable, and at some stage it must have been green. Now it's grey and even though it's wet there are dark stains. Blood stains? Mud probably. I look at my watch, 4:30am, no wonder I'm awake, milking time.

'It's about breakfast time?'

'Yeah.' Greg is getting out of his sleeping bag slowly. I want him to hurry up, I'm not doing a flash job with the stove.

I can see now Ember Eyes is wearing a green swannie, the same shade as his beanie, City Mission or Army Surplus store fit-out. Canterbury Rugby shorts, cheap gumboots. I feel a little bit sorry for him, those gummies are useless, no drainage or ankle support, bugger all traction, no wonder his legs and bum are muddy. He watches as Greg and Kyle get up. I stuff my sleeping bag into my pack with the rest of my damp gear.

'I'll do it.' Greg takes over the stove project.

I give a half-hearted nod as if this was my plan all along, which in fact it was. I want Ember Eyes to see it was my plan. He is watching me.

He points. 'You. Youse were up when I come in eh.'

I nod.

'We should have a cuppa. Are you sure you don't fancy one?' Kyle's voice is squeaky.

Ember Eyes has seated himself on the stool nearest the door. He reaches into the pocket of his swannie and extracts a butcher's knife. It's the knife that belongs in the sheath on the bunk. And there are times in its history, I feel sure, when it has been cleaner.

'Do you want your sheath?' I realise instantly it isn't a very smart thing to say.

He half rises. 'Youse been going through my stuff!'

'Um, nah mate, just happened to see the sheath when I climbed up there to get in the bunk. My bunk, not your bunk. Good-looking sheath that.'

Greg says, 'Hot drink mate? Will warm you up.'

The billy of water is beginning to steam already. Greg sits beside me on the bench by the bunks.

Ember Eyes glares at the billy. For a moment I think he's going to pick it up and throw it outside. He glances up at his bunk again, then back at the billy. The pupils in his eyes are so big. That's what is making his eyes look black like embers, but also like possum eyes, a cornered possum. I would have preferred a cornered cow, or a small child, as I have some experience with those. I very much hope none of us say the wrong thing, even as I realise we have no idea what the wrong thing might be. The best course of action is probably to say as little as possible. I turn so he can't see my face, but the others can, and press my index finger against my lips. Trouble is, Greg and Kyle can't take their eyes off Ember Eyes.

Ember Eyes sits back down.

'Just going out to water a tree,' Kyle says.

Ember Eyes sticks a hand out towards the door.

'Youse aren't going nowhere.'

Kyle sits down on the edge of his bunk. I turn and do my finger over lip thing again. Kyle widens his eyes in response. I look at Greg. He nods without looking. We wait for the billy to boil and for Greg and Kyle to finish packing.

Ember Eyes picks up his gun off the table and sets it down against the door. He keeps his knife in his right hand. Right-handed.

'You guys got your cups ready?' Greg sounds matter-of-fact.

Greg has his cup. Somehow, he's found the teabags. Kyle

190

and I have packed our cups. We don't want tea. Kyle and I open our packs to find our cups.

'Want a barley sugar?' Greg asks Ember Eyes.

'Eh?'

Greg sets the soggy packet on the table where the gun used to be. Ember Eyes puts down his knife to pick the packet up. His hand shakes as he tips it upside down. Barley sugars rain onto the table. He swishes them about with his finger. His finger is stained. It's blood on his finger, I'm sure.

He looks up at Greg. 'Lollies?' His tone is one of disbelief. 'What youse playing at?'

'Tramping,' Kyle squeaks. 'We're expected back in a few hours.'

Ember Eyes ignores Kyle. The billy boils. Greg pours the water into our cups, watched over by Ember Eyes. There is confusion in his face. He doesn't know what to do about us I suppose. I'm impressed Greg pours the water without any spillage. I really have to concentrate on keeping a steady hand as I offer my cup to Ember Eyes. He takes it and sets it down.

Then he points at my hand.

'Where's your finger?'

I look at my finger. I lost the tip years ago, another inch or so and I'd have lost a hand. The nail has grown back. Not many people notice, I hardly notice myself these days, though it was excruciatingly painful at the time. I blacked out. Weary of post rammers ever since.

'Lost it in a fencing accident.'

A conspiratorial look of recognition passes over Ember Eyes.

'Knew it. Think I seen youse before.' He points his knife at me. 'Who youse fencing for? Not the Mongrels.'

'You know I can't tell you,' I improvise, ignoring Kyle's gasp.

Ember Eyes keeps staring. I give him a gentle stare in return.

Ember Eyes lays his left hand flat on the table. His pinkie finger is missing. Kyle's gasp is a bit louder this time. We're not paying Kyle any attention.

'Same thing happen to you?' I ask. I can feel Greg stiffen beside me. I risk a quick look in Kyle's direction. His lips move but no sound comes out. Later he will tell us he was praying.

'What happens if ya don't look after ya stuff.'

Ember Eyes glances again up to his bunk. Steam is rising off his swannie even as it rises off the hot drinks.

I gesture to the cup. 'Made that tea especially for you.' I turn to the other two.

'Do we have biscuits? I have some muesli bars. Want some breakfast? It's about that time. You can keep an eye on your stuff while having a feed and a drink.'

I slowly open the zip at the top of my pack and extract a snap lock containing muesli bars and dried apricots. I unlock the bag and lay it on the table between us.

'Chocolate?'

Greg has dug into his pack too. He breaks up a few pieces, puts one piece in his mouth. I reach across and help myself, it looks better than dried apricots. I offer a piece to Ember Eyes. He still has those eyes locked on me but he wavers, flicks a glance at the chocolate. Takes the piece. He stares across at Greg while he finishes eating his square. I pop my bit in my mouth which is so dry I have difficulty getting the chocolate down.

Only when Greg and I have both chewed and swallowed our pieces does Ember Eyes move his square. He doesn't put it into his mouth, he drops it into the mug of tea.

'Want some more? You making hot chocolate?' I ask.

Our eyes lock as he reaches across and breaks off a big chunk of chocolate and wedges it into the cup. He drops eye contact, looking around for something to stir the chocolate with. He picks up his knife. It won't fit into the cup. Displaced liquid sloshes onto the table.

'No worries, the chocolate will melt in no time,' I say. At that moment I almost wish I had a cup of tea. As if he can read my mind, Kyle pushes his untouched mug past Greg towards me. I lift it up and take a sip. It's an average cuppa, only lukewarm.

'Good tea.' I nod to Greg graciously, like I'm the Queen or something.

'You going to try it?' I ask Ember Eyes.

His eyes narrow again but he seems more at ease. We both drink from our cups. I think about the Heaphy River, tannin-stained, how the colour gets diluted when it reaches the Tasman.

Ember Eyes bites at his lump of chocolate where it hasn't melted. He gets chocolate on his nose, and his lip.

'What did you shoot?' I have an idea, hope the others will catch on.

'Goat.'

'You sure? Need good skills to nab a goat round here.'

He studies me, takes another slug from the mug.

Without saying anything he rises, moves the gun and opens the door. I follow. I still have my torch on my head, as does he. We stand just outside the door adjusting our eyes to the darkness and the rain. We walk over to the edge of the bush where a small goat, not much bigger than a possum, lies on the ground. I bend down and shine my light on it. It's dark brown, the colour of a beef animal. It doesn't have much head left. The gun Ember Eyes is running around in the bush shooting things with is too powerful for the job.

'Choice bro.' I sound like Willy when I say that.

Behind me I can hear Greg and Kyle trying to quietly exit the hut. I hope they've had the nous to grab my pack. Ember Eyes doesn't seem to notice. He bends down and touches the goat

193

briefly. After he straightens up, he stares off into the bush. He might be reliving his killing spree, or perhaps he's just lost focus.

'Gotta piss.' He moves off a little bit.

I turn and sprint down the track. I have never run so fast for my life.

When I catch up to the other two, I gasp, 'We need to get off the track.' As we keep jogging down the hill we scan the forest for entry points.

'Animal track?' I say.

We shine our torches into the bush. 'Let's go in here, hide for a bit and see if he comes.'

We plunge into the wet undergrowth for a few metres, then stop, kill our lights, and listen. We're all shaking. All we can hear is our panting and the beating of our hearts. All we can see is little puffs of mist, our own breath. Puffballs of aliveness. After a few excruciating minutes Greg turns his head torch back on, directing the beam at the undergrowth. A lone korimako issues its pure call, and another answers, and another. I recognise tūī and the lilting call of a riroriro.

'Can you remember Kyle if there are trapping lines or anything?' Greg whispers.

Kyle looks like a ghost. 'Yes, somewhere. Parallel to the track I think.'

'I'll scout, you guys stay here and keep quiet.' Greg vanishes into the rain.

Kyle is still shaking. I reach out and set my old cap on his wet head.

'Smells a bit but keeps the water off. We'll be okay Kyle, dawn chorus,' I whisper.

'Pissed myself,' Kyle whispers.

*

194

Greg must have been away only a few minutes but it feels like longer. Kyle and I are shivering and swaying like a pair of drunks.

'I found some pink tape. Going to be tough to follow, the bush is thick.'

'Did you move his gun?'

'No, we took your pack and bolted.'

I nod. 'Good plan. I don't think he'd shoot us.'

'He shot a goat!' Kyle says.

'You don't go to prison for shooting a goat, Kyle.'

'He's under the influence of illicit substances,' Kyle says.

'Off his face,' Greg agrees.

'Possibly. He went for a slash. He might forget about us,' I say.

'Um, we left our cups and your Snaplock on the table,' Greg says.

'You did good. I reckon he'll stay with his stuff. We should follow the tape for a bit,' I say. 'Kyle?'

'Yes please.'

Greg leads the way. The dark has faded to a matte grey, enough so we don't need our head torches, but gloomy. The bush acts like a shower nozzle controlling the rain pressure. Lucky for us the trapping line merges with the more established animal trails. Our four-legged explorers, having both a lower centre of gravity and free of the need to lug packs, tend to opt for direct downhill passage. We cling to branches for purchase, lest momentum take our feet out from under us. A couple of times I land on my bum. Start, slide, stop. We go for a few metres then strike an obstacle like treefall, bush lawyer or a pile of vines. The vines are fit for their purpose of catching everything and the lawyer takes its cuts where it can. Nature is a fine architect. At the back, my job becomes liberating Kyle from vines and prickles while ensuring I evade their overtures. Greg seems better at avoiding them. If he does tangle, Kyle is there to free him.

Elastic hula hoops, serrated edges, ties that bounce, wobble, rip and bind. There we are wrestling our way through the bush. Possibly we are saving each other's lives. How dangerous Ember Eyes is, we can't know.

I think about the farm, how it's taken more than a fingertip. I doubt I'll walk away. Leave it, leave them, not yet anyway. A bind, but an anchor too, a home base for family in need of attachment. Kyle and Greg have their research and their families. Even Ember Eyes seems bound to his stuff, whatever it is.

The trail we are following is very steep. The magnitude of which reveals itself when Greg drops off a cliff. We hear his yelp.

'Sup?'

'Nothing. Bit of a drop-off eh.'

Kyle and I lower our packs to Greg then slide down ourselves. All three of us covered in mud, like elephants.

'Onwards?' Greg asks.

'May as well.' There is no obvious way to remove the mud.

A few minutes later the bush thins. We stumble into a sizeable clearing. A new carpark with fresh green and yellow branded signs announces a reserve. Fifty metres away, on the other side of the gravel, a cluster of black and green umbrellas stand all quiet and serious like a grove of pongas. Under the umbrellas are officials, most decked out in tidy suits and leather shoes. They look like local dignitaries, iwi representatives, volunteer types, landowners perhaps.

Heads turn in our direction briefly then back to the speaker. The minister, I recognise her from television, is wrapping things up. Light applause follows. Kyle joins in. The spectators split into small groups. Heads turn our way again. We're all out of hiding places, though we could have ventured towards the new toilet block if we'd seen it sooner. A middle-aged lady in a pink dress makes her way towards us and offers her umbrella.

'Um, you probably need it more than us,' Greg says.

'Pardon us for intruding on your, um, opening?' Kyle is blushing. He looks slightly better with a bit of colour on him.

'Good to see the reserve getting used,' she beams.

A man in Department of Conservation uniform comes up. He has a handful of track brochures. He offers them round. Greg accepts one on behalf of the three of us.

'Oh look.' The pink lady points east. A section of sky has let out a breath the colour of Kyle's face, an offering of dusky roses fringed with grey. As we watch, the colour expands, pushing in front of the grey clouds, the way rainbows sometimes do, especially in winter. Pretty soon we'll have to figure out a few things. Where Mozart is in relation to us springs to mind. But in this moment, standing filthy in the flash carpark, we settle for pushing our embarrassment to one side to gaze in silence at random beauty beyond our control.

Road

The silver handle squeaks as it turns but the door won't open. It takes Rachel a moment to realise it's locked. She tries again to make sure. It is not yet 7am. She was woken up first by Jack heading out to milk, then again by the chorus of cicadas. The cicadas were promptly drowned out by the rumble of quarry trucks. She figured she may as well walk down to her parents' place. The trucks when fully laden are enormous, indestructible, like tanks. Yellow and green branded beasts, with long, swinging trailers and wheels the size of tractors. Rachel has felt their giants' breath as they thunder past inches away. People who go on about earthquakes have no idea.

Jim will be watching TV in the lounge. She should go around and tap on the back door. And she would have if she hadn't caught a glimpse of the dusty, cobweb-infested top windows of the wash house. She retraces her steps along the concrete path, back past the garage to the rear of the house. Below her old bedroom, an identical set of windows are limp and unlatched. Scanning the surroundings, she selects a wooden apple box, an heirloom from Di's father's apple orchard. Emptied of its cargo of old plant pots, and placed on the concrete under the sill, it makes a rudimentary ladder.

She climbs onto it, weight over her feet. The window yields to her push, revealing a promising gap. One leg twists through the slit onto the inside sill. She scrunches her trunk and head up close and levers herself through the slot, leaning as far forward as she can without toppling to the floor. Last comes her other leg. Safely on the ground, she rights herself, brushes at a few cobwebs and quietly returns the window to its original position.

Emerging into the hallway she can hardly hear the TV above the snoring coming from the master bedroom. As a child, she'd perch on the edge of the bed in that room to watch her mother apply her make-up before going into town. Now the room has an abandoned doll's house feel, though her parents probably spend more time here than ever before. Di's head is resting on a light blue pillow. Rachel studies her mother's pale face, wondering if she is feigning sleep, but the snoring is so loud. Jim's snoring has got worse too. Once, it was a mild irritation, like a persistent cough, something to make wry jokes about after a night trying to block out the noise. Di's snoring is an indication she's breathing.

Rachel continues to the end of the hallway, opens the kitchen door. Three steps through the dining room. Two large cellophane-wrapped cakes and two boxes of medications fill the table. The packet of needles sitting on a stack of mail are new. She pokes her head around the doorway separating the dining room from the lounge.

Jim lies on the chocolate couch. His silver hair needs cutting, there are big bags under his eyes. His face is red with a white undercoat showing through. He's in his good trousers and jumper, cleanish socks by the looks of it, no pieces of hay falling off them at least. The remnants of his breakfast cling to the coffee table, one of Jack's old woodwork projects. The breakfast tray is competing for space with stacks of newspapers, bags of cashews and jellybeans, and plastic water bottles. A golf tournament is on TV.

'Still alive?'

Jim starts. He looks in her direction and his eyes widen. He makes an effort to sit up. 'How did you get in?'

'The window. I knocked but you didn't hear.' This isn't true. She hadn't wished to wake Di, wanted to catch Jim alone before he disappeared to the clubrooms.

'What window?' Jim uses his remote to turn the sound down.

'Bedroom.' It's childish, but she's chuffed she climbed in. She sits down in Di's clapped-out La-Z-Boy, careful not to disturb the piles of brightly coloured wool and half-finished toys either side.

'You climbed in. When did you get up?' Jim asks.

'Jack picked me up last night. How's Mum?'

Jim pulls a face. 'Still alive.'

As a child she'd hated being ill. The way time slowed down, her world reduced to the scratch of the old towel Di folded over her duvet, the faded yellow plastic basin beside the bed in case she needed to throw up. The glass of flat lemonade on the bedside table. Nothing to do except try to sleep or count stains and cobwebs on the ceiling, wondering if daylight would penetrate the curtains before she needed to go for a pee. Listening for the throb of the motorbike engine signalling Jim's return from the cowshed. She would hear the front door squeak, the thump of his steps down the hallway. A pause followed by the sound of running water in the bathroom as he washed up. More thumps and silence. She wouldn't be able to resist opening her eyes. He'd be standing in the doorway. 'Is the patient still alive?' She would squirm beneath her sheets before replying. Even though she knew he said the same thing to Jack and Willy when they were sick, it felt for a wonderful moment like she was his only child.

'Golf?'

Jim looks at the clock on the wall. 'Soon.'

When Rachel, Jack and Willy were little, winter Saturday golf was Jim's time off the farm and their time with their mother. They would help her make special lunches. Pancakes, bacon and egg pie, fried scones, or their favourite, potato bird's nest. Years later, Rachel encountered the grown-up version in a restaurant. She eyed the limp, overpriced fritter oozing yellow fat like dishwashing liquid, and thought warmly of Di.

A quarry truck rumbles past, shaking the room, making conversation impossible for a moment. She wonders about the locked door. Have her parents reached the stage where they feel they need to lock the world out and view it through the TV, or are they worried about intruders?

'I'll get Mum.' Jim raises his voice: 'You're wanted!' Then, more quietly, 'She's usually up before now, watches the six o'clock news.' He inches himself upright, preparing to swing his long legs to the floor so he can start the process of levering himself up from the depths of the couch.

Rachel pretends not to notice.

'Don't worry. I'll be back later. I'm off for a run, just checking in first.'

'I didn't know you were coming.'

Jim has a way of repeating himself. Rachel always took it for granted, found it comforting, until her mother started doing it. It was then she realised it's a habit associated with forgetfulness, with aging. Maybe other people found it odd when Jim did it as a young man. Visiting her parents intermittently has sharpened her ability to notice little changes, like the spots of mould on the bathroom ceiling.

'You're wanted!'

Jim is sat on the edge of the couch now. He waves the remote and starts to explain what is wrong with a particular golfer's technique when Di appears in the doorway. She looks like her favourite blue heron. Her blue towelling dressing gown has lost most of its fluff and fails to hide her stick legs. Around her slender face rest tight silver curls that remind Rachel of the little metallic balls that used to be popular on iced Christmas cakes. A good way to break a tooth, biting one of those. Di shuffles the two steps to her newish La-Z-Boy, in between the old one Rachel has claimed and Jim's couch.

Di attempts to set her glass of water on the box of wool beside her chair. Her hand is trembling, so even with the glass only half full there is some doubt as to whether she'll land it without spillage. Rachel half rises to assist but thinks better of it. Mission accomplished. Di clasps her hands together in her lap.

Rachel is trying to work out whether her mother's tremor is worse than the last time she saw her. Jim's eyes dart in her direction then away.

'I caught a burglar,' he says.

There is a pause as Di appears to gather her thoughts. She turns to Rachel as if she is a visitor. 'When did you get up?'

'Last night. Thought I'd surprise you. Go back to bed Mum. I'm going for a run.'

Di points at Jim.

'He hasn't been drinking enough water. I put a bottle beside him but he doesn't drink. Perhaps he'll listen to his daughter. '

'She doesn't eat anything!' Jim says.

'Quarry trucks woke me up,' Rachel says. 'Have they started working longer hours?'

'5am, six days a week,' Di replies.

'Are there more companies? I remember the green and yellow trucks but not the red ones.'

'Three trucking outfits, two routes, truck every few minutes.'

Trucks were the reason Rachel and Jack were useless at cycling. Her parents banned bicycles, fearing if the kids ventured onto the road they'd be flattened. When they were growing up the road was gravel, its maintenance a low priority. Winter floods regularly stripped the gravel surface, mixed stone fragments with dust, and deposited the resulting metallic sludge in adjacent paddocks, where it found its way into the creek. The trucks wove unsteadily between potholes as they transported their cargo. Spotting a kid on a bike amid the dust clouds would've been difficult.

'At least there isn't the dust, with the road sealed,' Rachel says.

When her parents built their house, they chose a site close to the road rather than opting for a long driveway as was common in the valley. By the time the sealing eventuated, she had long departed the district. In those intervening dust-filled decades they'd countered civic indifference with do-it-yourself solutions. Jim planted clumps of fast-growing bamboo to ward off the grime, other hedges too, though Rachel remembers the bamboo most, partly because remnants remain. The bamboo spread like an enthusiastic protest march, shedding crisp brown leaves that crackled underfoot like empty chip bags and stuck to everything, particularly the dirt. As with any battle, there was collateral damage. Dead leaves clogged the guttering, creating fountains when it rained. No one in the family suffered from asthma, but anyone who did knew not to visit.

One summer holiday Rachel returned to find the road sealed. 'Finally found enough councillors who live on the other side of the gravel to get something done,' was Di's assessment. Willy organised a mock opening ceremony. Jim's mother was coaxed down the driveway to her mailbox to cut the ribbon they'd strung across the road.

'You supported the resource consent for the new quarry?' Rachel asks Di now, without looking at her.

'Sara rang and asked us to.'

'Oh Mum, really?'

'Hippies in the village were kicking up a fuss, even though it's them that need the metal for their roads and houses. They've turned into Nimbys. Hate quarries, and they hate farmers as well, except for pretend organic egg-farming like what's going on behind the airstrip. Our hens are more organic.'

Rachel turns to Jim. 'She didn't ask you?'

'Your father doesn't answer the phone as you're well aware, but he doesn't have any objection, do you?' Di looks at Jim.

Jim shrugs. 'Sara's land. Long as I don't have to listen to her. Talks your ear off. Had a nosey at the quarry last week. Lots of new machinery, big operation, mountains of metal, computers like you use, it's changed.'

'It's like mining. It is mining. Mining greywacke.'

'Quarries give people jobs. Not everyone's good at studying. Better they have something to do around here than unemployed and taking drugs.' Jim has gotten himself into a standing position. 'Gotta go to golf.'

At the doorway he turns. 'Old quarry, they wanted to lease some of the acres they sold me over by where those campervans are parked by the creek. Told 'em needed it for pasture.'

Rachel doesn't say anything. She rises and gathers up her running pack as Jim goes out.

'What are you having for breakfast?' she asks Di.

'I have an Up and Go. I'll get it.' Di stands. 'Afterwards I'll go on my walk. What did you have for breakfast?'

Rachel is glad she resisted the impulse to tell her mother Up and Gos are not a healthy choice. 'I'll have breakfast later.'

Di stands at the front door, watching as Rachel pulls on her running pack.

'Which way are you going?'

'Towards the beach, away from the trucks.'

'You don't have to live here like we do,' Di says. 'Have a nice run.'

Rachel prefers to run off-road, but asphalt is better than risking a sprained ankle on the lumpy paddocks. Back only a few hours and she's fallen into her old pattern. It's a convenient way to assess the lay of the land. Now everything is sealed, an effort has been made to ensure floodwater drains off the surface. A ditch separates road from fenced fields. It traps the occasional vehicle travelling too fast and also acts as a collection site for rubbish. The sheer volume of bottles, cans and disposable cups surprises her.

City folk, or people from Hereford? The local beach isn't a popular tourist destination. Apart from the old campground, most of the ocean front is Māori land with restricted access. One of the few places resisting development. The beach is guarded by fierce rips, and thanks to its exposure to the prevailing nor'easter, monster swells. A place possessed of a feral energy and unadorned beauty that frustrates those seeking regular features and placid water for swimming, fishing and picnics. Not Insta-friendly. As if to underline the point there are homemade signs: No Dogs, No Guns, No Trespassing. Rusted machinery skulks among corrugated-iron shacks and decaying fences. Patches of singed grass and oil stains share real estate with crumpled cans and plastic bags fumed by salt spray and the stench of urine.

On her last visit Rachel noticed recent dune plantings. Probably linked to the walking trail that passes nearby. All the unmodified bush and the best views are locked up behind tall gates guarding mansions and helicopter pads. If walkers realised before setting off that they'd be toiling on a muddy rutted trail through distinctly mediocre corridors of bush, their only reward a few glimpses of the coast through the kānuka and clag, they surely wouldn't bother.

There's a feeling that the buildings on the roadside have had the life sucked out of them and deposited in the more glamorous estuary and surf village to the north and the millionaires' playground to the south. She recalls reading cases at law school challenging the practice of dredging sand from the foreshore to install on Auckland's eastern bays. Relocation of sand from some remote site to a more convenient spot for people to have barbecues. The thought causes her to increase her pace till her sunscreen melts down her forehead and she has to slow to wipe her eyes with the sleeve of her shirt. Monetising sand under the guise of mitigating coastal erosion is nothing new, but when it's your childhood beach it stings.

From the top of the hill she has a clear view to the beach, though she won't run as far as the shoreline today. Cantering down the hill generates the same joyful feeling of climbing through her old bedroom window. A kind of awe at what her body can do. She thinks about her parents, how they are anchored to the farm. Her work is in her head. It goes where she does, as variable and intangible as a spring breeze whose presence is felt in rippling flags of toetoe or a pool of pink petals at the base of a plum tree. A portable existence. Di is right, she doesn't have to live here.

From the bottom it's a long, undulating slog to the tiny township where she and Jack nearly went to school.

It was raining the morning the Education Department lady turned up, otherwise her mother would have sent her and Jack outside. Di made the woman a cup of tea and set her down at the dining room table. Rachel and Jack were in the lounge, listening while pretending to play with their toy farm. The beachside school needed its roll bolstered in order to remain open. Benefits included less travel time, lots of individual attention for better learning outcomes, socialisation across a range of ages.

'My daughter is shy,' Di said. 'Took long enough to settle her into Hereford Primary. I would prefer not to change her again.'

'Your two seem cute as buttons. You've done a fine job considering your isolation. She seems outgoing and well-adjusted to me.'

They could hear the condescension in her voice, as sour as marmalade.

Di spoke in the slicing tone she normally reserved for when someone dared to venture inside with their muddy gumboots on. 'She's at home with her twin brother, I would hope so. And how does the teacher ensure they learn when there are pupils from five years old to twelve in the same class?'

They didn't have to go to the small school. The lady must have found some more pliable families in other valleys. Rachel and Jack continued to make the half-hour bus trip to Hereford. It wasn't that Rachel wouldn't have adjusted to a small school, but it would have made returning to Hereford for high school harder. She had seen it when kids arrived from the remote schools. They were picked on, bullied, forced to battle for acceptance. Di had protected her then, as she'd done countless times throughout her childhood. Rachel wishes she could protect Di now, Jim too.

She's nearly at the school. A woman in a bright red headscarf waves from the side road opposite. Tui. Rachel hesitates but there is nowhere to hide. She jogs towards her.

'Rachel! I'd recognise those legs anywhere, same as your mother's. You must be ready for a rest if you've run over that hill. Come in for a coffee.'

Rachel searches for a graceful way to refuse.

'Don't worry if you need to be back, I can always give you a lift. Defeats the whole exercise purpose I know, but you're as skinny as a scratch match, won't do you any harm.'

Rachel smiles to cover her awkwardness and follows Tui into her house. She hadn't realised Tui lived next to the school.

'Sit down there my dear. Jug will boil in a sec. Peaceful at the moment, Hori's up the coast fishing. How are your mum and dad, pleased to see you I bet?'

'I hadn't seen them for a bit, they've aged I guess.'

'Oh, they're getting old all right, but they're keeping active, your dad with his golf and tinkering around on the farm, your mother walking all around the place and helping me with baking and sewing for the hospice.'

'Do people buy the dolls?'

Tui winks. 'Oh, they do. We donated some to Starship, Gemma's niece works there. They were short of soft toys. Anything homemade. Di makes real quirky ones, lime-green hair with gold flecks, some with gold earrings, all blinged up. She's mostly doing woolly hats and scarves at the moment, good for winter.'

'She walks along the road.'

'Yeah, I heard. My grandson works at the quarries. He's told her it's not the best place to exercise. Here you are running along them, setting your mother a fine example. You Carltons always on the go.'

Rachel blushes and shivers at the same time. She reaches into her pack for her jacket.

'Ever think of moving back?'

She pulls her jacket over her head. The nylon feels clammy against her arms. She wishes she'd driven to the peninsula to run. 'It's all right for a visit, I mean the coast is beautiful. But it's changed. Too many people, tourists, and all the Aucklanders who've moved up too. It would be okay if you didn't know what it used to be like. Some things are better I guess.' Rachel pauses. Nothing 'better' springs to mind, but she wants to say the right words so as not to appear negative or, worse, pretentious. 'There aren't any jobs I could do.' She doesn't add, although it hovers in the air between them, that she'd prefer to keep her distance from her parents.

Tui nods. 'I thought when my Denise came back from Aussie, nearly twenty years ago now, she'd struggle to find a job, but she's done all right. Oscar too. Course you're a professor type.'

'You mean no practical skills or business experience.' Rachel isn't sure who Denise and Oscar are. Tui must see her confusion.

'Oscar's Denise's boy. His outfit, they got contracts for nine quarries. Busy as bees with bums full of honey digging out metal. They grade it like apples or something, send it off for roads, houses and concrete-making, all over the show, like NZ Post. Well, like the post used to be.'

Rachel imagines people in red-and-white uniforms driving

up and down the country roads leaving small deposits of blue-grey metal in mailboxes like dog shit. She almost spits her mouthful of coffee back into her cup. She's still coughing when Tui points to a picture she's brought up on her tablet. Rachel studies it. Denise is a younger version of Tui, same oval face, dark hair, tortoiseshell eyes. Oscar is all open rolling curves, from his moon-face to the arch of his eyebrows guarding thick eyelashes and brown eyes. Glowstick smile.

'What qualifications do you need for quarry work?'

'On the job training, online training. In his blood. His dad worked in the mines in Aussie. He's got a knack with people, works his socks off. Nearly finished his quarry management thing. He'll probably head off down the island or across the ditch. Enjoying having him around while we can. Always good having whānau close.'

'Does he live with you?'

'Cripes, no room here!' Tui extends her arms in either direction and her fingernails nearly touch the faded floral wallpaper. 'He's camping out with Denise, down at the beach.'

'The settlement looked a bit rundown last time I was there.'

'Yeah, bit of argy-bargy going on over whether to subdivide but most of them don't want it thank goodness. Enough people round here wearing cashflow cards like sunglasses.'

Rachel nods. Jack has mentioned the helicopters flying overhead on their way up the coast. She's remembering now, something her parents told her about Tui and Lotto. 'Well, I guess I should get going before my legs seize up.'

'Us mothers, we miss our kids when they aren't around. Your mum, few like her locally. Poor old Eileen down the other end of the valley, and Sara by the quarry, kids in the city or overseas, husbands gone. Roosting in their houses, not really into those modern community activities like yoga, going to cafés and what have you, bit too fragile for sports. Di doesn't like golf?'

'She hates it. Dad wouldn't want her near the golf club, would cramp his style.'

Tui rises and collects up their mugs.

Rachel imagines her parents know everyone in the district, have known them all their lives. 'Funerals, Tui. Di and Jim attend funerals.'

'Ha ha. Too right.'

'And there's the grandkids,' Rachel says. Di relays whatever her grandchildren have been up to when she rings.

'Oh yeah, they're lucky on that front. Can't wait for Oscar to give me some mokopuna. Well, say howdy to Di and Jim from me, tell them I'll stop by, probably be over in a few days. How long are you up for?'

'Just the weekend.'

'Eh, not long. I guess you have to work.'

Yeah right. Rachel winces. Work, running, the distance. Any number of justifications for doing exactly as she likes. Would it really cost her much to come up more often, considering the pleasure it would give her parents?

'Seeya Tui, thanks for the coffee.' She wants to say thanks for looking out for Di, but she feels it would offend Tui. She is the type who looks out for people.

Retracing her steps up the hill the only sound is the buzz of cicadas and soft pad of her trainers hitting the asphalt. Near the summit a couple of desultory ponga squat among the paspalum, the only hint the hillside was once covered in bush. Paspalum oozes sticky brown sap that sticks to her legs, a Sellotape feel, hard to rub off, even with water. At least Tui hadn't asked her about kids. She imagines herself as Tui must see her, as a daughter. It's not a role she considers often. Her friends talk about their work and their hobbies more than their parents. Most shuttle back and forth between cities and countries, family scattered all over the world. Like her they're more comfortable with legal puzzles, things that they believe, with enough practice and attention, they can solve.

As she enters her parents' kitchen again there is a hiss of air brakes releasing. One of the trucks is slowing.

'That'll be Oscar.'

Her mother is suddenly beside her.

'Oscar?'

'Come for the cakes. He's going to take them to town for me.'

Rachel retraces her steps to the driveway. A guy with a round face wearing Dirty Dog sunglasses and steel-capped work boots climbs down from the cab. He shoots her a smile.

The door to the house opens and Di appears.

'He's here for the cakes.'

If the driver wonders who she is he gives no hint of it. He heads towards the house, Rachel following. He pauses at the front door as if to remove his boots.

'Don't worry about those Oscar, how are you doing, want some water?'

Rachel watches, astonished, as the driver accepts the glass Di offers him. She looks into the lounge where Jim has hauled himself upright on the couch. She edges past Di and Oscar to join him.

'Banana cakes?' Rachel asks.

'One's for St John's, one's for the police.' Jim nods as if confirming to himself he has this right. Over the noise of the TV Rachel can hear Di telling Oscar how she hides any baking from Jim because of his diabetes. 'He doesn't drink enough water.' Jim pulls a face, sits back and resumes watching TV. He's changed out of his good clothes into his threadbare fleece pants and holey green jumper. She can smell his thick woollen socks from the doorway, cow shit mixed with stale hay. Rachel points to the water bottles on the coffee table, catches Jim's eye. He shakes his head.

She studies Oscar's shorts and singlet, his large brown arms. He's pushed his sunglasses back onto his bald head, revealing soft brown eyes. He is younger than she'd first thought, early twenties maybe. There is something about him, Rachel can't put her finger on it. He has an aura of calmness, open-mindedness, perhaps it's humility. Whatever it is, he seems to be a confidant to her mother. After several minutes he begins to signal his exit, explaining he can't leave the truck parked on the roadside for long.

'Boss installed GPS in all the cabs so we won't sneak off to the pub, eh.'

'There aren't any pubs round here!'

Oscar inches towards the front door. Rachel picks up one of the cakes. It's unexpectedly heavy. He follows with the remaining cake, Di bringing up the rear with a plastic container full of biscuits. They pause at the side of the road. Oscar balances his cake on top of the mailbox and tells Di he'll go and make room. He crosses the road, opens his cab, hauls himself up, starts shifting papers. Rachel follows him across with her cake.

'It's good of you to do this, thank you.'

'Do anything for Di, she's a good sort eh.' There's a pause as Oscar looks across to where Di is stooped by the mailbox. He pulls his sunglasses down. 'She probably shouldn't walk up and down the road eh, lotta trucks, not much space.'

Rachel crosses the road again to collect the other cake as Di watches. Back at the truck Rachel hands up the second cake.

'Sorry they're heavy.'

'No worries.'

She turns to find Di standing beside her, the container of biscuits in both hands.

'Mum, you should not be on the road.'

Di looks up into the cab. 'These are for you Oscar. Few Anzacs. Say hi to Denise.'

Rachel reaches for the container and passes it up.

'Oh, wow, thanks Mrs C. Well, I guess I should get going.'

As the cab door shuts Di calls out, 'Thanks.'

'Thank you,' Rachel repeats. She should be carting these cakes into town herself, not some driver on the clock.

Safely back across the road, they wave through the whistle of the air brake. It feels like a long time before the big machine eases back onto the road.

'What was that about?'

'Nothing. Ambulance has taken me down to hospital often enough and you know how the police helped with the Willy business.'

'Mum, it's their jobs!'

Di ignores her. Rachel follows her back inside. Now Oscar has left, Jim finds his tongue.

'You're back! Where have you been?'

'The run took a bit longer than I expected.'

'You've got goosebumps!'

'It was a bit colder than I expected too. I saw Tui. How was golf?'

'Tui. You went all the way to the school?'

'Does Oscar stop by often?'

'That's Denise's boy. Tui's grandson. Works at the quarry as a driver, used to play cricket, not much chop. Jack is teaching him squash. Good guy like Des, helluva good guy, should put him in charge.' Jim settles back down. 'Bob Charles can rest easy. Didn't play my best golf.'

'Do you know this Oscar person?' Rachel is irritated. She isn't sure why, maybe she needs to eat something.

'Works at the quarries, his mother fills in at the supermarket sometimes. Mum always spends ages in there yarning to her if she's on,' Jack says.

'He plays squash?'

Jack gives her a sideways look, then grins. 'About as well as you do. Want to play him? I'm supposed to be giving him a game tonight. Reckon he's trying squash to meet more people his age. May as well tag along, won't be out there long.'

They're sitting on his veranda, Jack with a cold beer, Rachel enjoying the play of the dusty evening light on the green fields. She picks a cicada skeleton off the deck. The buzz of the insects is synonymous with summer sliding into autumn. Back in primary school she thought the sound mournful, associates it still with the end of the holidays. She shows the skeleton to Jack.

'You used to collect these, kept them in a shoebox.'

Without his family Jack seems smaller, like a dried-out puddle. She brushes aside the thought she's a poor substitute for Gemma and the kids. They're away visiting Gemma's sister.

'You used to try and catch ladybirds,' Jack says.

Rachel doesn't remember, though she recalls them both chasing monarchs. She remembers her dislike of the tiny aphids the ladybirds cleaned off Di's rosebuds.

'You know broadband is taking as long as the tarseal did. I

have to upgrade our measurement of the milk temperature in the vat. Dairy inspector wants greater precision to be certain the milk is safe. The latest company-supplied devices work off cellular tech.'

Rachel rolls her eyes as she knows she's meant to. The lack of cellular coverage this far down the valley is a long-held grievance. Jack seldom has an audience upon which to vent his frustrations.

'I had a bloke call in last week. He wanted to know if the cows in the paddock beside the house were mine.'

'Like you'd sit here and let someone else's cows graze your grass?'

'Well, people do, the chap over the road does, but my point, he told me he was from the transport agency and they're introducing regulation so I'd have to pay for any stock damage to the road surface.'

Although they share a chuckle, Rachel can see that for Jack the joke is wearing thin.

'How's the planting going?

'Two steps forward, one step back. Every time there's a flood we lose about a third, fences too if it's a bad one. Aphids don't get a look-in, it's possums and birds feasting on the fruit trees.'

'Bugger. Floods used to mean a day off school. Remember Dad's favourite dog?'

'Rover?'

It's these moments when Rachel misses her brother the most. The comfort of having someone who knows what you are talking about when you mention a name, an incident from decades ago. Rover used to sleep in the potholes, safest part of the road as vehicles swerved to avoid them. Holes deep enough a truck could run over Rover's nest and he'd emerge unscathed.

'Hard case eh.'

'Seen the harriers?'

'I've seen falcons down south, beautiful but territorial, like to peck you on the head, worse than magpies. Where? Not on the road?'

'They're fearless, come down to feed on the possum and rabbit corpses, sometimes they get hit by cars. It's not like they understand the danger.'

'Crikey.' They sit in silence, imagining a harrier being smashed by a car. Rachel wonders if the harriers are resorting to roadkill because of a lack of other options, or whether they are simply unable to resist the convenience of fast food.

'Be good if you could talk to Mum about her morning walks. She needs to go on the farm races rather than playing Russian roulette with the trucks.'

On the drive out to squash Rachel tells Jack about the banana cakes.

'Since she got Oscar's email, she gets him to do things for her. She knows most of the truck drivers from walking on the road, they wave and toot and stuff.'

She stares out the car window. Every time she visits there are more houses, artificial ponds, campervans, fences. Jack drives slowly, usually Gemma does the driving. She should have offered to drive. 'I guess the walking on the road in her fluoro vest, and the baking for people, it's about being seen. Tui reckons she's lonely stuck at home by herself.'

'Probably. She's been home by herself for years though, well, not alone really, Jim's there. And she's always given away baking. She gives it to us, Gemma gets a bit fed up, reckons Di thinks she can't bake.'

Rachel considers this. 'It's a competitive thing. Mum is the best baker. She is good at it.'

'Yeah, nah. It's more how she shows she cares. Trouble is she doesn't know when to stop.'

Rachel pictures her kitchen cupboard overflowing with plastic containers that once housed Di's baking. The time she moved apartments, Jim drove down with his trailer bringing Anzacs and an old clothes dryer she'd told him she didn't want. It took up half the lounge.

'Addicted to baking!'

'Worse things to be addicted to.'

She tells Jack about all the rubbish she saw on the side of the road.

'When did it start getting like that? It's disgusting.'

'All the takeaway coffee cups and Pump bottles?'

'I have a KeepCup and my reusable running bottles now.'

They're silent for a few minutes, then Jack sighs.

'Lot more traffic now the roads are better. There are clean-ups. Gemma organised a couple. It's worse closer to Hereford. Di sometimes takes a bag out with her when she goes on her walks, though she has trouble bending down.'

It's close to twilight when they arrive at the golf clubhouse that also houses Hereford's squash courts.

'Not so lively in the evenings.' Jack switches on the lights on the ground floor, illuminating the basement where the two court entrance doors sit off the corridor. A couple of members have arrived already. Jack goes over to chat with them and see if they need an umpire.

Rachel's been here enough times to recall the layout. The changing rooms are on ground floor. Up a narrow set of stairs is a small kitchenette and seating with views down onto the courts. The windows by the kitchen sink look out on the final few holes on the golf course. The clubrooms smell of musty, stale sweat and old rubber. She opens a couple of windows.

The main building is the golfers' domain. A large open-plan space filled with Formica tables and wooden chairs. The seats are uncomfortable but light enough to shift to the sides of the room and resilient enough for stacking. Honour boards line the wood-stained walls above trophy cabinets filled with silver cups in need of a polish and black-and-white photos of champions. The small servery and bar are near the entrance. Rachel sometimes sat in here with Jim after his round. Jim's companions always shook her hand and said, 'Oh you're Jim's daughter, the one who lives down south, you run marathons,' or something similar. Apparently, Jim liked showing off his seldom-seen daughter. Some of the golfers had known her when she was little but none recognised the adult version, nor she them. The names were sometimes familiar, but the only way to place them was a shared memory. If one mentioned a particular cricket game, calf club or fishing event, she might be able to place him and his family, but otherwise they all looked the same. Rundown, but not unhappy. Enjoying each other's company along with their sandwiches and pints. It was Rachel who didn't fit. In her presence conversation tended to vanish down the plug hole. If Jack accompanied her, everyone had more to say. They knew Jack. He was no golfer but he had a good nose for everyone's business, a fluency in Hereford-speak Rachel hadn't learned as a young girl and never would now. Jack had an ear out on permanent loan and a knack for shelving pints.

Tonight, the small group sitting drinking are younger than Jim's vets. She figures they've been at their table for most of the day. One of them is the bartender. Their table is littered with glasses and plates and there's a familiar sour smell of spilt beer. Out the window she can see a solitary bloke practising his driving on the fairway nearest the clubhouse. He finishes his hitting and power-walks up the green to collect each of his balls. He paces out the distance from the green to his closest attempt. She vaguely recalls some rule that you aren't allowed to practise putting on the greens outside of games. Golf has as many protocols as law or accounting. Probably a good idea to stick to the rules, given the infamous five who are busy drowning their sorrows have a view onto the fairway. Not that the audience is well behaved. The bartender is known to resent the fact that the squash club shares the premises. Jack has told her he sometimes turns the lights off on squash players while they're getting changed.

The way things are – small-town foibles, petty irritants, stuff to take in your stride. All of this is familiar to Rachel, if not the nuances. Jack is well practised at deploying a bit of tolerance and a lot of conflict avoidance to secure an easier, less stressful life. No point taking stuff personally, no matter how personally it's intended. How it is. Rachel wanders off to find Jack.

He's talking to Oscar.

'Do you play squash?' Oscar asks her.

'Just thought I'd tag along.' Rachel supposes she looks as restless as she feels.

Jack digs around in the club locker for a racquet and a new ball. Rachel watches the game from above. The grey smears on the sides of the court where balls have crashed into concrete remind Rachel of insect splatter on her car windshield. It's particularly bad at night, the impact pulverising their small bodies. Squash seems equally violent. She shuts her eyes for a moment. The muffled thud of ball on concrete, the high-pitched squeak of trainers scuffing the tired red service line. The players' grunts as they engage in their jerky dance. Courtside, her brother owns the cramped space, patrolling it with the understated athleticism he's had since childhood, hitting the ball with delicate precision and control. Oscar flounders round the court as if his trainers are the wrong size, using his racquet like a fly swat, connecting with the ball only intermittently. After another game they make themselves cups of tea.

'How's quarry life?' Jack asks.

'I'm on the morning shift.'

'Ha, so we're both getting up at the crack of dawn. I'll remember that when you start beating me. Won't be able to say Oscar gets more sleep.'

'Don't think I'll ever be up to your standard, Jack. It's good to get out and meet some people though, hard to do when you're on nights.'

'How's Denise?'

'Mum's primo. Reckon she could cut back her hours but she likes looking after the new trainees straight out of school, and talking to people like Di, eh.'

Rachel imagines Di doing the rounds of the supermarket aisles. It would be an abbreviated version of her visits to the Hereford shops when Rachel was young. Dropping into the fabric shop, the butcher's for luncheon sausage, gossiping with acquaintances in the Post Office queue. 'It'll only take a minute,' she'd tell Rachel, who would accompany her. There was the popping into the chemist, the one Di approved of, not the one beside the fruit shop. And frequent stops on the street. The itinerary seemed to flow and expand like a king tide. Di knew everyone. For Rachel the anticipation and excitement of a trip off the farm ebbed away as she stood there awkwardly, gazing into space or pretending to study her shoes as she waited for Di to finish her updates and enquiries. The worst part, what really had her grinding her teeth, was when Di's friends remarked on how much she resembled her mother. It was the comparison that killed her interest in the trips. She must have been about ten, and liked to think of herself as different.

'Kind of like a little community over there,' Jack says. 'I heard Denise found Di some bags of split peas out the back they've stopped stocking out front. She uses them in her vege soup.'

'Yeah, she told me. Mum doesn't like kids quitting school for the supermarket. Reckons it's a lure of easy money, what she calls the bright lights blinding them so they don't think long term. They'll get bored stacking shelves, better off sticking with school.'

'Maybe the kids want to decide for themselves when to move on,' Rachel says.

'Yeah, good point,' Oscar says.

Jack beckons some squash people over so he can introduce them to Oscar. Rachel can't shake the image of insects hitting a windscreen. She lets the banter drift over her. The pattern is similar to how things go with her running mates. Hardly anyone talks about squash apart from a perfunctory opening line about a game. Sports administrators around the region must fulfil the role that vicars used to fill back in the day, Rachel thinks, when people were more inclined to go to church. There may not have ever been such a time, of course. There certainly weren't many functioning churches in the district, most had been converted into housing. For as long as she can remember, the locals have worshipped at the clubrooms and sports fields.

'Do you reckon you'll stay once you've finished your training?' she asks Oscar.

'Probably not, the quarries round here have managers, plus I want to have a family, stop working shifts, settle in somewhere, save for a house. I mean, it's comfy here but I need some fresh challenges. What about you, would you come back up here to live?'

'No. I like it where I am.' She thinks about the electric bus service some entrepreneurial types have started for commuters. She's tried it, can see its possibilities, reducing road congestion and carbon emissions. She considers Jim and Di, how they're set to stay. Most of their peers have sold up and shifted to small, low-maintenance lives or assisted living places outside the district. 'Hope you don't mind me asking, where's your father?'

'Stroke when I was seven. Don't really remember him, though after what happened to Des . . .' Oscar sets down his cup of tea. 'But you know, Dad worked in the mines, so I'm sort of following in his footsteps.'

The overhead light pools around his shaven head like a halo. It occurs to Rachel that as it gets dark mosquitoes and cicadas will come in through the open windows. She thinks about Jack carrying on the farm. 'We need more people like you Oscar. I feel like a middle-aged grump when I'm up here. Too busy holding on to the past, resenting every little change. Your generation might get some things done.'

'What do you mean?'

'Figure out some better ways of doing stuff.'

Oscar squints at her. She wonders if he still doesn't understand what she's trying to say. 'You know the worst day at my job?'

Jack, who wandered off earlier, returns to stand beside Oscar. He has his squash bag over his shoulder, car key in his hand.

'Worst day?'

Oscar and Jack exchange a look. Jack says, 'Des? Bad day that.'

'What?' Rachel wants to go and shut the windows.

'You know how when it's real early before sunrise and the valley is full of fog?'

Rachel has driven at dawn. Sometimes you can't see anything but the roads are empty. She enjoys how fog hangs low, waiting for the moment the sun crests the ridgeline. That moment when its heat evaporates the water vapour, rendering it translucent, then transparent.

'Yeah, hard to see, even with headlights.'

'One of my mates, mentor really, Des Richmond, do you know the Richmonds?'

The name is familiar. She looks at Jack. 'Was his wife a Sunday school teacher? From the other end of the valley?'

'Bingo. Des was Eileen's husband,' Jack says.

Oscar continues. 'Des was taking the first load of metal for the day over the hill. On the flat near the new quarry, he would have been going real slow cos of the fog.'

She looks from Oscar to Jack.

'Des hit a beef animal,' Oscar says.

Jack says, 'Poor old Des.'

'Yeah. Had a heart attack in the cab.' Oscar is staring at his cup.

'Oscar was first on the scene, eh Oscar, in the next truck,' Jack says.

'Yeah. The animal was dead and nothing I could do for Des either. He was only sixty-seven. Still on the job part-time, company had asked him to mentor the management trainees. He agreed cos he lives locally and you know, he loved the metal. Worked it for thirty-three years, started when he was twenty-three. Wasn't so keen on the driving anymore, hardly ever drove. That morning he was filling in for one of the young guys who didn't show up for work. Thing is, I offered to take the first run. It should've been me on the road not seeing the animal, or maybe I would've seen it. Des's eyesight probably not the best in poor light.'

'Horrible.' Rachel understands now why he doesn't want Di walking on the road.

'It's been eighteen months. I still look in on Eileen. Des was my work dad.'

All Rachel can recall about Eileen is ginger hair and the owlish way she looked down her glasses when someone failed to remember their Bible reading. She has no recollection of Des.

'Never know when something random could happen,' Jack says. 'Pillar of the community old Des, huge funeral, loads of speeches from the big wigs, citation from the New Zealand Institute of Quarrying.'

'Yeah, he had a good send-off. Gotta look out for each other, eh.'

Rachel drives them home. The route they bussed twice a day for school and have driven thousands of times since. There's more safety infrastructure these days, cats' eyes that glow in the dark, lines indicating where corners are coming up, warning signs the colour of ladybirds. She passes the tightest bend where Willy's mate went over and drowned in the creek. The long undulating straight where everyone used to speed now has a 30-kilometre limit on account of the undulations obscuring oncoming vehicles. Past the panel beater's place with its dead vehicles like a herd of metallic cows. As she crosses the junction that leads to the quarry where Des would have hit a beef animal her hands tighten on the wheel. A few minutes later, almost at Jack's turn-off, they pass their grandparents' old mailbox where they'd celebrated the arrival of the tarseal. At Jack's driveway, they cross the little bridge by his fruit trees, possum traps below, quarter orange moon above.

Rachel parks outside Jack's garage and opens the car door. Without the car engine the warm air is thick with the high-pitched buzz of cicadas. Although she can't see them she knows they haven't got long to live. Tui is right, her parents are doing okay in the valley. She doesn't think she'll be telling Di to stay off the road, not yet. Tomorrow she'll head south, a strand in a web of connections that spin out from this place.

Survivor

Flash of blue and orange. Glimpse of a dagger beak. The way it perches on a fencepost, like the one that visits our garden. Heaps of times I've made sketches. None do it justice. Sweet colour combinations. Somehow the turquoise on the wings melts into azure, teal and a Cheezle-coloured underside. When it flies, the kōtare is a comet hurtling sky to sunset.

Here, listening to the soft plop of rain on nylon, our tent and our spirits are sagging. Water puddles all the wrinkly bits where we haven't pulled the nylon tight. Poles are sick of standing to attention.

We're thinking it's okay to sleep on the back lawn when it's dry. Soft grass, toilet and shower close by. Camp has one lousy toilet block, the only shower the rain currently rinsing the tent. There is a swampy smell, the tent probably leaks.

Yesterday when Mum and Dad were doing that thing, talking about me but not to me, Dad said the forecast was rubbish and I'd better take his raincoat. Mum went on about how weird the weather was, tropical cyclone one minute, drought the next. I wanted to say duh, its global warming. For them to get it, to realise it's not something you just read online.

What do I know? I can't even pitch a tent.

'Year 10 camp. Living the dream!' Amy wriggles in her sleeping bag. The tent wriggles back.

More pork, more pork.

'Ruru eh?' Trish sounds scared.

'Just a ruru.' The word 'morepork' reminds me of the sausages we had for tea. Better than the ready-made coleslaw sliding out of its bag like scraps from the pig bucket. Scraps soaked in PVA. I wouldn't mind a bit of pork, the greasy chewy crackling.

'Saves us making up ghost stories,' Amy says.

I open my eyes. Amy slept in her sunglasses. I fish around for mine. The ones with yellow lenses. It isn't properly light yet. What the fuck, nobody born this century thinks sunglasses are about glare protection. The rain has packed it in so we hit the beach to see if there's a sunrise. Sky's grey as a school uniform. Should send Mum a picture.

'What are those?' Amy points to the black and white birds with bright orange beaks and long legs strutting the sand runway.

'Oystercatchers.' Their swagger reminds me of her.

'You know your birds, Ellen.'

I'm surprised I know. I guess you absorb stuff without noticing. Like without looking we know there are two teachers behind us sitting on a piece of driftwood having a quiet vape.

Trish asks them if they can help us with our tent.

The teachers follow us. Our tent could pass for a half-set lime jelly. For a few minutes we watch them wrestling with it.

'Our tent doesn't wanna be tamed,' Amy says.

We decide to get breakfast. As she eats her toast Amy

228

touches her hair. 'Oh my god!' She inclines her head in my direction and I put down my peanut butter toast to touch her hair. It looks okay, but she's right, it feels like bailing twine. I touch my own hair. Same coarse texture. Horrible, like my fingernails I can't stop biting.

'Not much we can do. Doubt I could get my brush through mine.' Did I even bring a brush? Probably, heaps of damp gear going mouldy in the tent. I return to my toast. 'Have you tried peanut butter and Marmite? Could be yummy.'

'I'm gonna find my brush.' Amy looks at the peanut butter. 'Would not normally touch that disgusting stuff, it looks like, you know . . . but I'm starving. We're tramping today aren't we?'

I'm hungry too. 'I'll get us some Milo.'

'Put heaps of teaspoons in.'

'On it.' I make two cups of brown paste. It smells amazing. We spoon it into our mouths. I chew my longest nail, the one I've been saving, and daydream about the world of difference colour-wise between peanut butter and Milo. I don't want to think about my hair, how it might rain again, or the tramp.

'Ellen, this is genius. Oh my god, this is like *Survivor*!' We laugh. In daylight and without the rain, we're both thinking this whole camping thing is so bad, it's good.

I offer Trish a teaspoonful of the Milo paste. She manages to get some before the teachers notice the rate at which it's disappearing, seal the lid and hide it under the table.

Dad said the camp was an opportunity. He's always going on about embracing the natural world. When I think about the kōtare I feel better. It will either have insects for breakfast or pop down to the beach for baby crabs. Up front the Magpie pecks away as if we're five-year-olds. My sunglasses make everything darker when it's overcast so all I can see is black hair, raisin eyes, sandy face.

The Magpie's a prefect. She's only two years older than us but if school was a forest ecosystem she'd be canopy, us saplings. Hopefully I'd be a rātā sapling since they last for like eight hundred years. Sometimes I like imagining people's futures, and what they'll turn out like. I wonder what will happen to the Magpie. Next year she's leaving to do teacher training, probably make deputy principal at one of those big schools up Bay of Islands way. I reckon her heart isn't in it though. She lasts a year, then chucks it in to organise community solar and tidal energy schemes. I can see her encouraging people to save electricity too by putting in energy-efficient lights and insulation in their houses, schools, and squash clubrooms.

Meanwhile, the Magpie practises bossing us. Each tent must pair with another tent. After my Milo hack, and with us rocking our sunglasses, our tent is sought after. We have a whispered conference. I know we'll be pairing with Dion's tent because Amy fancies Dion. He does have a well-pitched tent. I'm kind of hoping Dion and freckly Tim are better at tramping than they are at squash. The other guy, Mark, turned up from South Africa last term. Arriving late is his thing. He appears from the direction of the carpark just as the Magpie shuts her beak.

We have to make our lunches. After a day of camp, we've got this. I queue for fruit, Amy does sandwiches, Trish fills our water bottles and writes us on the whiteboard. Trish shows us the bottles, they're traffic cone orange. The same shade as her T-shirt, which hangs loose like it's outgrown her.

'What the fuck?' Amy says.

'Some kind of cordial. You know, like *Survivor*. Sugar will keep us going.'

Teachers remind prefects to check daypacks.

'My aunt gave me a first-aid kit, reckon bring it?' I ask Amy.

'Has your aunt like, ever needed it on a tramp?'

'She takes it on runs.' I imagine Aunty Rachel with her red daypack. Inside it there's a baby running pack, also red. When she and Dad were watching me pack they definitely said stuff about first aid. 'She does heaps of tramping, carries a bigger one for that.'

'Fit in your bag?' Amy looks at it again. 'Hey, I have an idea!'

When our group assembles for checking, Amy offers the kit to Dion. 'Can you put this in your pack? It's important.'

Dion hesitates.

'If you want to tramp with us, we need this kit. Drugs and stuff.'

Dion shrugs, stuffs it into his pack.

The Magpie takes a quick look in our daypacks. When she sees my raincoat she yells at everyone else, 'If you've got a raincoat put it in your bag just in case.'

Amy does one of her eye rolls. 'Do you guys have coats? Look at the sky, probably going to rain.'

Tim raises his eyebrows and his freckles move too. 'Why are you two wearing sunglasses then?' We ignore him. Trish doesn't have a coat. She looks like she might cry.

Dion leads his mates back to their tent. They all have coats. Detouring past the lunch-making area he returns with a couple of large plastic bags. 'If it rains these can be ponchos.'

Amy looks at the plastic then at me. I nod. There is way too much plastic in the world but we might need it. Amy treats Dion to one of her best smiles.

'Good thinking Dion. You guys carry them,' she says.

I nudge Amy. Dion's got his sunglasses on.

That's how we end up a group of six. Amy, Dion and me,

half blind in our sunglasses, Trish in her emergency T-shirt. Freckly Tim, and the late dude, Mark. We think we know where we're headed, we're following an obvious trail after all.

Trish hands the map to Tim.

'Do you think he knows what he's doing?' I ask Amy quietly. 'Do you want it?'

I don't. One thing I noticed on our family walks, the map was more of a complaint licence than a path-finding tool. Everyone not in possession of it got to direct all their grievances at the map-carrier. 'Nah,' I say to Amy. 'Who cares?' I don't know why I say this. I do care, I just don't want the responsibility wearing away at me like sand when it gets in your socks.

On one side of the camp is the estuary, with its unruly flock of burly mangroves, and on the other is a herd of flash baches. Mum said this might be the last time the school comes here because the landowner has sold to developers. Sandspit is out of bounds so no chance of spotting any tara iti. I really hope they don't get kicked out and sent to Hauturu where I'll have no chance of seeing them. Bush near the camp is mostly a network of trails through toe toe, harakeke and mānuka, with a few ponga and other scrubby things, but further in I recognise rimu, pūriri and horopito with its red leaves.

Amy takes a few pictures on her phone. She's the only one of us brazen enough to ignore the phone ban. We share a fist bump then pose for a group selfie by a big tree with lots of little plants growing on it.

'Epiphytes.' Trish surprises us. 'Nature's social climbers.'

Before I can ask her more, freckly Tim interrupts. 'I like your T-shirt.'

Trish blushes. What is this, the Bachelorette New Zealand?

I'm thinking about how there are three guys and three girls as we pass yet another intersection where we could take any number of tracks. We're following Tim. As far as I can tell we're selecting trails at random. I don't see Tim consulting the map but I assume he does. We're supposed to find spots and record clues. Every group has been sent in a different direction, which kind of sucks. We won't be able to compare answers. Trish and I stop to wait for Amy while she waters a tree. The guys carry on.

'How's it going?' I ask Trish.

She looks pensive. 'Do you think Tim's recording the clues?'

I shrug. Tim is kind of easygoing. At squash he doesn't call a block to get a point replayed if you obstruct him, he waits for the ref. I like that about him. I just want to enjoy the bush and I want Trish to relax. Actually I want to get the tramp over and done with. Trish reminds me of Pipi wanting to go outside then tapping on the door to be let back in. I get distracted watching out for her and burn my toast. I'm working on a design for a cat door, in the shape of a cat. I'm not sure what colour it should be, something between the shade of horopito leaves and the colour of Trish's face when she blushes, cerise maybe.

Trish is looking at the long skinny trunk and finger-shaped leaves of horoeka.

'Dad reckons they look like something out of Dr Seuss,' I say.

'These ones are juveniles. Adult ones have short fat leaves and round crowns.'

'Wowser. Reckon you'll keep doing botany?'

'I think so. You know – ' She fiddles with the hem of her T-shirt.

'Know what?'

'Sometimes I can't stop thinking. About how the planet is

warming up, the waterways getting dirtier, birds like the tara iti. And you know all the plastic, like those sheets Dion got, it doesn't break down.'

I nod. I think about the David Attenborough doco all the time too, when I'm not thinking about the plastic ocean one. We watched the David Attenborough one in science.

'I stopped eating meat. Mum doesn't want me to be vegan. That coleslaw last night made me feel sick,' she says.

'Oh my god. It was disgusting, that coleslaw!' Amy's back. She strokes the leaves of the horoeka with her perfect nails. 'Doubt anyone ate it. Bet the prefects ditched it. These trees look dead!'

The leaves feel smooth but the edges are knotty. They point earthwards rather than skywards, like they've given up on the sun. 'You're right Trish, it's hard to know what to do, and we're running out of time.'

'Oh my god, Ellen.' Amy is pointing at my chewed-down nails. 'Gross!' Then she says to Trish, 'I'm only kidding. Her hands are gross though.'

I want to mention her bailing twine hair. 'What about climate change, Amy?'

She wrinkles her nose. 'I dunno.'

'Not eating meat is a thing, I guess. I like meat but cows are bad, methane eh, pollute the water if you don't fence. Dad fences and plants trees. Pipi catches birds sometimes, sparrows.' I can see from the look on Trish's face that I'm not making sense.

Amy says, 'It's us burning fossil fuels, not the cows and cats Ellen. That doco was like, work together to fix up your mess peeps, and by the way, there are too many of you fuckers. All right for Attenborough though, he's ancient, won't be around.'

'Yeah, but like, over his, our grandparents' lifetime, all the changes, it's real gradual but past a certain point it's going to speed up, then we might not be able to back-pedal, that's the scary bit eh Trish?' But I'm thinking Amy is onto something too. Easy to see the signs, to tell people what to do, harder to get them to do it. Like us with the tent, now this rogaine. We gave Tim the map.

'You have to break it down to get your head around it,' Trish says.

I shut my eyes for a moment and think up Trish's future. I can see her being awarded a science scholarship and using it to research horoeka. She's good at fieldwork, she loves it and gets invited all round the world to do it. Like a female version of Attenborough, except she doesn't make docos, she's hands on, might give some talks in schools and stuff, yes that would be cool. She'll come home to see her parents when they're getting older and work at a conservation park near Kerikeri. Plenty of rich dudes up there to fund it, and people like Dad and Aunty Rachel will pay subscriptions like they do for Netflix and Neon. By then, the replanting of natives and getting rid of weeds and pests will be happening everywhere. I reckon she teams up with local greenie Clive Stringer and eventually replaces him as CEO. Not sure what the park will be called, Te Tai Tokerau maybe. I wonder if she'll ever think about our Year 10 camp then.

'Chocolate?' I pull off my pack and retrieve my bag of mini-Snickers. I'm tempted to tell Trish the story I just made up about her but I can't rip open the bag with my nails. I'm about to use my teeth when Amy snatches it off me and tears it open. She helps herself and offers it to Trish.

'Comfort food. Sugar and fat, bloody good,' Amy says with

her mouth full. 'Vegan probably Trish, maybe a bit of gelatine, but no worries. You collecting the wrappers, Ellen? Better not leave rubbish.'

I look at Trish as I help myself. 'Reckon Amy's even carrying anything in that pack of hers?'

Trish smiles as I hold out my hand for her wrapper. 'Nail polish?'

Amy laughs. 'True!' She slides her pack off her shoulder and pretends to look inside. 'Yeah nah. But like, seriously Ellen, you gotta try that stuff that tastes disgusting you can paint on your nails. Take it as a first step towards sorting out the planet eh.'

We nearly walk right past the guys but they yell out to us. Tim is in the bush taking a leak and happens to spot Trish's orange top. We push our way through the trees and vines for ages, aiming for his voice.

Dad always goes on about, when you're tramping in groups, you need to stick together. It seems a bit late to mention the sticking together thing. Dad had asked Mum a thousand questions about the camp. Would the prefects know what they were doing? Who would keep an eye on them? Where was it exactly? Dad is usually so chill. Mum had to tell him to pull his head in.

Eventually we emerge on the shoreline. Mint spot. The guys are reclining on the sand beside a big log. A curved sandy beach piled high with driftwood and shells, nīkau with their tattooed trunks and vermilion berry necklaces woven together in loops. Behind them are clumps of harakeke, hebe bushes and dusty piles of crunchy nīkau fronds.

'Anyone seen anything interesting?' Dion has his mouth full of sandwich. Mark is onto his orange. I like the pūriri flowers but don't want to say so. We marvel at the quantity of driftwood. The guys have started collecting it into piles. Amy and I pull out our lunch. Trish says she'll eat hers later.

'Why not eat it now?' Mark says.

'Not hungry. Do you want it?'

'I could eat it for sure, but it's yours, you hold on to it.' He turns to the rest of us. 'Is all the coast and forest round here like this?'

'Duh, yeah,' Amy says. 'Have you not been in the bush?'

'Not here. You're lucky having the beach so close. Back home we hardly ever went, big trip, too crowded.'

'We were talking about that,' Trish says. 'How we take it for granted.'

'Meaning?'

'We aren't doing anything to reduce our carbon emissions. Sea level will rise from the warming. This beach will go underwater, the bush too. Plants and animals will die.'

Mark considers this. 'Everyone drives everywhere, I've noticed that. Less emissions here than in Cape Town, doesn't seem polluted.'

'The emissions warm the atmosphere everywhere, it's a joined-up thing. Everyone, everywhere needs to do their bit.' I look at Trish as I say this. I want to know if I'm making sense this time.

Mark says, 'People should work together more, we're supposed to be tribal.'

I hope he didn't see how saggy our tent was before we got the teachers to fix it.

'Teams man, like with sports.' Tim shoots Trish a look so hopeful I have to chew my thumb. Above us diluted sunlight pours through a plate-sized gap in the cloud. I'm not sure if it's a reward or a warning. Tim's freckles are like glitter where the light catches them. Trish reaches into her bag, pulls out her sunscreen and offers it to him.

It's Mark who suggests we make a tepee. 'Back home we used to build them and sleep in them.'

Amy is busy applying sunscreen to her tanned arms. 'I didn't know South Africa was a third-world country.'

Mark misses the joke, gives her a hard look. 'We live in houses.'

Trish takes the sunscreen tube back. 'We're supposedly first-world, but we don't have enough houses. People live in cars, garages, under bridges and stuff.'

'Those baches at the camp are empty most of the time,' Tim says.

'Ghost houses.' Amy looks at me. She wants me to remember the ruru from last night, but it's the kōtare that's haunting me. It means something, but exactly what is just out of my reach.

We leave Mark and Dion assembling the tepee and continue gathering wood. Mark knows what he's doing. Lines up the dead branches so they're flush, manages to work the alignment so the structure's stable, breaks some sticks to fit. He uses his pocket knife to hack through dead flax leaves then weaves them between key pieces.

'How did you learn to make these?' He really does seem to know what he's doing.

He doesn't look up. 'My dad's an engineer, always building stuff from natural materials.'

I decide I like his accent. 'Are you going to be an engineer?'

He glances at me then. 'Probably. What about you?'

The gentle drop-shot he plays when I'd been expecting a backhand smash. 'Dunno.' It's the best I can come up with.

'You must have some idea?'

I take my finger out of my mouth. 'I like drawing and design but no, I haven't thought that far ahead.' There is no way I'm sharing my dream with anyone yet. I don't want to be laughed at. It's still blurry and it kind of changes all the time and I haven't worked out how I'll do it but I hope to design eco-friendly houses. My idea is they'll change colour depending on the light like the sky does. And they'll be small because we don't need big ones, in the future we won't be buying lots of stuff. Also, they'll be cheap and easy to build so everyone can have one and be able to put them up themselves if they want to, like a tent. Maybe a tent is a bad example. I'm going to call my thing Kōtare Designs, or Halcyon. That's the part I'm most sure about. Kōtare are so quick, colourful and magical.

'Let's put some shells around it so it looks better,' Amy says. There's a pause before she adds, 'So it looks even better than it already looks.' She has a handful of white shells. She and Trish start arranging them around the base, while I pretend to look for periwinkles. Dion comes back with seaweed.

Amy wrinkles her nose. 'It stinks!'

'It'll look good up the top, like dreadlocks.' He arranges a pile of dark seaweed up the top. It does look cool.

Mark says, 'We used to burn seaweed.'

'Really? I thought people eat it.' I sort of want to keep him talking.

'Seaweed? I'm just about hungry enough to, but nuts and berries would be better.'

'Scroggin.'

His eyebrows shoot up.

'That's what we call it,' I say.

'Good black-and-white pattern.' He nods at the shells then looks at me. 'Not a bad example of a joined-up thing. But if we want to do any more construction we'll need to stand on them, then we'll ruin the effect.'

'I'm thinking about interior design.'

He squints. The cloud gap has closed on the sun but its shine persists.

'What about architecture?'

I can feel heat in my face but nobody seems to notice. Amy decides it's time to take a photo. We crowd around while she works out the angles. The guys have to crouch, especially Mark who is the tallest. Eventually Amy surrenders the phone to him on account of his reach. 'I'm a selfie stick,' he says and sort of smiles. It's his way of saying he forgives Amy.

He does a great job on the composition, even manages some black-and-white ones of us all grinning like Jacinda, the tepee an arty blur behind.

'Should we go back?' Trish asks.

Amy checks her phone. 'It's nearly two. Maybe we should.'

'We could walk the beach?' Tim says. We're packing up, but he's checking his shorts pockets and now he looks like he's unpacking.

'Do you think we can get all the way back to camp that way?' I like the thought of walking on the sand rather than crashing through the prickly forest. But I don't know the area, none of us do.

'Aren't we supposed to be doing a loop?' Amy says.

'Clues. We're supposed to use the map to find the clues.' Trish is watching Tim unpack.

'What are you talking about?' Mark says.

'When you were up at the car park you missed the briefing thing,' Dion says. 'We're supposed to be doing a rogaine.'

'Rogaine?'

'Don't you know orienteering? Same thing, you look for points on the map.'

'I thought we were doing a hike.' Mark runs a hand through his hair.

'Where's the map?' Trish asks.

Everyone looks at Tim. He's still searching his bag. 'Yeah, about the map, I think I dropped it before lunch.'

'Jesus, Tim!' Amy says.

'Bugger,' Dion says. Then he shrugs. 'We've come this far without it.'

'We should retrace our steps,' Trish says.

Retrace our steps. Yeah right. We didn't see much the first-time round on account of our stupid sunglasses. If I could retrace my steps, I'd be back at the camp paying attention to the Magpie. I'd have the map out. I'd be studying it and working out a route. We would not be anywhere near the beach. If ever you want a lesson in the difference between theory and practice, just wander round in the bush for half an hour blindfolded. Take the blindfold off and see how you go finding your way back. That's what we're trying to do. Amy, Dion and me at any rate.

With six of us it should be easier, but really we have no idea and nobody wants to admit it.

'We could look for the broken branches,' Dion suggests.

'Oh, you mean those sticks that kept poking me in the eye?' Amy has taken her sunglasses off and put on sarcasm. I want to tell her this is a poor strategy but I have trouble of my own – I've accidentally grabbed hold of a bush that stings. I let out a yelp. 'Something bit me!'

I stop and inspect my hand. There's a line of white welts like giant pin pricks. The pain feels like a wasp sting.

Trish looks at my hand. 'What was it?'

'That bush.' I point to the offending pale green shrub with prickly leaves.

'Ongaonga, type of stinging nettle,' she says.

Mark says, 'Let's go back to the beach.'

We've been bashing around in a circle. The shoreline's nearby, although before we make it Amy gets tangled in a vine and has to be rescued by Dion. Following Mark, I find if I stay close there are less sticks. My hand throbs. I dip it in the water to cool it down.

'Now what?' Amy is brushing leaves out of her hair.

Tim and Dion wear expressions like when I beat them at squash. Kind of sheepish, kind of staunch. I turn to Mark and am disappointed when he shrugs.

It's Trish who takes charge. 'Let's follow the beach back to camp before they send a search party.'

Amy looks like she's about to say something grumpy but I shake my head at her.

'Do you have coverage?' Mark asks her.

She stares at him blankly for a moment then drops her pack to retrieve her phone. 'No.' She does have her bottle full of cordial. Trish and I get ours out too and share them around. Raro has never tasted so good. I think about my bag of mini-Snickers but don't mention it. Something Dad said about always keeping some food for emergencies keeps me quiet, even as my stomach growls and my hand aches.

'Let's stick together eh.'

We walk down the shoreline. There's no way to avoid wet feet. The salt stings our scratches. The shells that were glittering promises an hour ago have lost their lustre, we barely register them. Amy shows me a broken fingernail, then another one. Tim's T-shirt is ripped at the side where he's caught a branch and kept going. We're hungry and generally over it. Resigned to a bit of a hike and having to explain to the teachers why we're so late. A good pecking from the Magpie to look forward to. Tim probably thinks we'll throw him under the bus, what with losing the map and the stupid bush bash. He's likely right, although Trish will stick up for him.

'Just like *Survivor*,' I say to nobody in particular. I mean it as a joke, but it's one of those jokes that's too close to the truth to raise a laugh. I'm feeling mortified till Mark asks if I've seen the South African one. We all scramble to decide which series is best as we walk. I'm not the only one addicted to the All-Stars series, so I end up achieving the distraction I was trying for.

Anyone who's walked a beach knows there are spots where the bush and sea scrum together, forcing a stocktake of sideways options. Sea or sticks. Wade or flail. Sink or swim. Dion offers to try the bush. We sit down to wait. Mark wanders off. Watering a tree, we think. We monitor Dion's progress by the cracking branches, rustling leaves, occasional yelps and curses.

I sit on my hands. I'm angry with myself for not looking at the map, for leaving it to Tim. Last week at squash coaching, the trainer said that when things start going wrong you need to stay in the moment. Focus on the next point, then the next. Don't think about the big picture, especially don't imagine you're going to lose the match, or you will. She had a name for the thing you were supposed to avoid – catastrophising. Are we focusing on each step on the way back to the camp? I think we are. The time we've spent building the tepee bonded us enough so we won't splinter. Of course, if we stayed on the track like we were supposed to it wouldn't be an issue. Finding our way back is one of those situations where I'm realising we're not playing a game.

*

'We're stuck.'

'We'll be fine,' I say, because I want it to be true. 'We'll figure it out, Trish.'

'We haven't got the map!' She's blinking back tears and pulling at her T-shirt.

'Old news, Trish,' Amy says.

'How's it going, Dion?' Tim calls unnecessarily.

There's a pause in the crashing. 'Think we need to try the water.'

Tim walks out to the shoreline and wades in, shading his eyes with one hand. Water rises to his waist. There seems to be a bit of a channel. I'm thinking he'll turn round but he must be keen to atone for the map thing because he carries on.

'Can you see around to the sand?' Amy asks.

'Come back before you drown!' Trish shouts.

Amy glances at her. 'Calm down mate.'

'Come back, Tim!' she shouts.

I pat her arm. 'It's okay.'

Trish gives me a look that stings more than the nettle did. 'It isn't okay Ellen!' She lets out a shrill sound and her shoulders swoop up and down like a seagull. I realise she's crying.

'Trish!' Amy doesn't know what to say so she tackles her with a hug.

Tim squints towards us. A slimy mist has drifted in. It sets about thickening like gravy. Trish must have seen the fog before we did. 'Come back!' I yell.

Tim wades ashore. Water runs from his shorts, leaving dark splotches on the sand. His legs glisten like freshly caught snapper. 'Trish, it's all right if we link up. It's hard to see, but even if we have to, like, swim, there are trees to hold on to.'

Trish goes to put on her jersey.

244

'I wouldn't bother if we're going to get wet.' Amy sounds subdued.

The bush is silent. There aren't even seagulls. After what seems like a long time, but is probably less than a minute, we look at each other. 'Dion!' Tim calls.

'Where's Mark?' I ask.

'Mark!' Amy yells. 'For fuck's sake!'

Trish is starting to lose it a little bit. She sits down, hugs her knees and starts rocking. Amy drops down and strokes her hair. All I have to contribute is a sore hand.

I feel like I need to find Mark. I consider leaving my pack, but Dad and years of squash have schooled me to never leave your bag behind in case you can't find it again. 'Wait here. I won't go out of shouting distance. Keep yelling for Dion.'

Mark is a few hundred metres back along the beach, hunched by some miniature flax.

'Sup? Mark?'

He opens his eyes, gestures to the plants. Watery sunlight tickles the edges of their cylindrical leaves, catching on luminous dots the most intense shade of purple I've ever seen. Smouldering blackcurrants on a diet. My mind feels sluggish. The sugar high from the Raro is long gone, or the berries have hypnotised me so I'm thinking Mark is pointing them out because he knows I like unusual colours and he's too brave to bother me with the news that he's sprained his ankle or been stung by something.

'Are you hurt?'

'Thought they were blueberries.'

My wish-fulfilment fantasy dissolves like sugar in water. I glare at the berries.

'You touched one?'

He nods, his eyes shut.

It's the colour. The way the dots glow, like inkweed, though that isn't what they are. Berries are too small, the leaves the wrong shape and shade of green. I've been brought up not to touch berries unless I can identify them. It's up there with not talking to strangers and mostly wearing black. I try to remember what we learned from first aid. If he'd been unconscious I would have done CPR. I have breathing into those rubbery dolls all dialled in. But by the time we got around to learning about poisoning, my attention had wandered towards stuff like, when's afternoon tea. I have an idea vomiting is good. I regret all the *Survivor* talk, the mention of scroggin, the keeping quiet about my chocolate. Mark probably only touched the berries because he was hungry. Then it hits me. A wave of panic, the weight of a quarry truck. He hasn't just picked one, he's eaten one.

'How many?' I want him to say none. To shake his head, give me the thumbs up and let me off the hook. 'Mark, how many berries did you have?'

He waves his hand.

Does that mean a handful? I have no idea. He's going to die. I yell to the others to come.

'I think he needs to spew to empty his stomach.' I'm furiously wishing I was somewhere else, but I need to keep thinking about what to do right here. The effort is making me dizzy. Amy and I look at Trish. We don't want to upset her even more, but we're not keen on Mark dying just because he's eaten a few poisonous berries and doesn't know how to throw up. You put your fingers down your throat, but I've never tried. I really hate vomiting.

'Maybe if he runs around so he feels sick,' Tim says. 'You know like if you play squash too soon after eating a Big Mac.'

'Jesus Tim,' Amy says.

I expect Trish to start crying again but she gets down on her hands and knees beside Mark, has him roll over onto all-fours. She demonstrates, and he vomits a bit. Lilac sick, or mauve maybe. Surely he only ate a couple of berries. I wipe away tears. Tim passes his water bottle to Mark, who is shuddering.

'Good, Mark. Keep at it,' Amy says. 'Imagine you've eaten a shitload of that disgusting coleslaw we had last night!'

'Whaddya mean, coleslaw was all right,' Tim says. 'Better out than in.' He stands over the berry bushes. 'What are they?'

Nobody is listening to Tim.

'We could go back to the tepee?' he says.

'Shut up, Tim,' Amy says, 'You did great, Trish. Probably saved Mark's life!'

Trish starts crying again.

Tim moves in beside her, places an arm awkwardly around her, trying not to get her wet. 'Put on a jersey eh?' He gets it out of her bag.

I let out my breath and slump to the ground so I can put my arm around Mark. I realise I'm shaking as much as he is. 'All right?' I wonder if we've gained a good story to retell for the rest of our lives, or a nightmare situation where we're about to witness death first-hand.

Mark isn't interested in the death scenario. 'Those berries aren't as bad as a snake.'

'Hey!' Dion appears behind us like glass shattering, and Amy lets out a little shriek. He's out of breath and has fresh scratches on his face. 'Thought you'd left me.' He pauses. 'What's wrong with him?'

We explain to Dion about the berries.

'We thought you'd got lost,' Tim says.

'Jesus, Tim. How could he get any more lost than we already are!' Amy says.

Mark looks up from his vomit. 'We know where we are.'

'We're lost!'

'Only thing we've lost is the map.'

Dion says, 'Found a trail but I don't think it goes anywhere, trapping line maybe.'

'What took you so long?' Amy has her hands on her hips, like she's cooked a roast and it's gotten cold because she's been waiting for Dion. Amy hates waiting. She hates persisting with anything that isn't working. When I imagine her in the future she's trying out different jobs like's she's going through a wardrobe full of clothes, abandoning them item by item till she finds the one that fits. She wants to be an actress for a bit, then a model, then she wants to go to Spain to teach English because she thinks Spaniards look gorgeous. She ends up marrying a Spanish guy and managing his eco resorts business. Once Amy commits she's really focused, so she'll make improvements to ensure a low-carbon footprint. Zero waste, all food grown on the property, definitely water conservation, I don't think Spain has as much water as we do. Transport will be those electric golf cart things like Grandpa Carlton's got. I bet she paints them a decent colour like tangerine or trapping tape pink.

'Was there pink tape?' I ask Dion.

'Didn't see any. I thought maybe the trail went to one of those flash baches, so I followed it for a bit then I shouted. You guys didn't reply so I came back.'

'Right thing to come back,' Mark says. He drinks more of Tim's water then offers it back. All the while, he's keeping hold of my arm. Somehow the weight and warmth of it counters my impulse to flee.

Amy is giving me a knowing look, but for once she remains silent.

We try to remember how far we've come. Even without the mist it's starting to get dark.

'Let's sit a moment and work it through.' I don't know why I'm in charge now. I'm not used to being in charge. I'm thinking poisoning causes people to hallucinate. Magic mushrooms. Where do I get this stuff from? The information. Of all the things that would be useful, hallucinogens are probably not in the top five. I try to grab my thoughts but they're swarming like sandflies, impossible to capture them all. 'What are our options?'

'Stay put till morning, maybe shelter in the bush. It'd be warmer. Or we try wading round the point back to camp.' Dion rattles them off like he's swotted for a test. It occurs to me we should have given him the map rather than Tim, but regrets, like catastrophising and hallucinogens, are outside the top five. When we leave school in three years I reckon Dion and Tim will head to Lincoln, where they'll study horticulture and soil science before convincing their parents to convert from dairy to market gardening. Dion'll cross-breed for resilient traits and will eventually produce a new strain of micro-green that will be sought after locally. Tim'll grow it on his farm too. Dion and Tim make a good team. Dion's inventive, but Tim's easy-going and kind so he'll be good at handling the people side of things. The two of them will go on to revolutionise the micro-greens business in other countries.

'Someone could wade round and get the teachers?' Trish says.

We look at Tim, who says, 'I think we could get around. But like I said, might have to swim.'

I don't want to split up the group.

'Won't the teachers come looking for us anyway?' Trish says.

'What about the trail Dion found? What if it goes to a bach? We could take the trail and break in,' Amy says.

'We can't break into a house.' Mark sounds shocked. 'The owner will shoot us.'

'I'm not sure the trail goes anywhere,' Dion says, his eyes glued to Amy.

No option seems ideal. Other groups might take a vote. 'Stay put?' I'm not sure whether I'm opting for the path of least resistance or making the best choice.

'Yes,' Mark says, as if I'm making perfect sense. I want to hug him.

Trish, Amy and Dion agree.

Tim says, 'Sorry.'

We put on all our clothes and pool our food. My chocolate and two muesli bars. Trish remembers her sandwiches. The raincoats seem the most useful items till Dion inspects my aunty's first-aid kit and finds a square thing that looks like tinfoil. He unwraps it – an emergency survival blanket.

We do some high-fiving then. 'Body heat will keep us warm,' I say.

'Anyone got something to light a fire?' Tim asks.

We don't. None of us are smokers. I'm going to stash this anecdote and pull it out next time someone bangs on about smoking being a health hazard. Hello, being a smoker could actually save your life if you are benighted in the bush. The only person I know who smokes is Uncle Willy. Instead of saying any of this I say, 'I think you can make sparks with a knife rubbing against a branch.'

'Or by rubbing two sticks together,' Amy says.

'Isn't that like, a myth?' Dion says.

'They do it on *Survivor* all the time, but they're in it for prize money, it's like a job, so they practise.'

'I'm going to try.' Tim is wet and therefore the coldest. He rummages in Mark's bag for his pocket knife, then finds a branch.

'Let's set up a camp first,' Dion says.

Mark seems to have stopped spewing, and I ask if he can get up. He grabs hold of me for balance. Dion offers him a piece of driftwood as a crutch.

'Hey Trish,' I say. 'See those plants, do you know what they are?'

Without sunlight the berries are a dull shade of eggplant. Trish plucks one, sniffs it.

'Jesus Trish, don't you try eating them as well,' Amy says.

'Not flax. Turutu, I think. Native blueberry.'

'Poisonous?'

Amy says, 'Mark's been vomiting them up, Ellen. They aren't health food!'

'Um, I don't think they are too bad, in small quantities, but yeah, not health food.'

'Sorry.' Amy tips her gaze in my direction.

'No worries.' Small quantities. I let myself picture it, a future where we still have bush and beaches and it isn't too hot to be outside. I feel a calmness, like my blood has settled and my thoughts are resting on the ground like fallen leaves. Maybe I'm a ninja or something. Not invincible, but capable of breaking things down.

There is a small clearing a few metres into the bush, away from the cold sand. We spread leaves for a mattress and overlay them with the plastic bags Dion rescued, then we huddle on top. We cover ourselves with our raincoats and the survival blanket, and use our packs as pillows. We eat our food. Dion offers round the Panadol from the first-aid kit but nobody's that desperate yet.

Over our breathing we can hear the light plop of the water tapping the beach. It's the same sound as last night's rain on the tent. That was a thousand years ago. I can feel leaves under me. They rustle every time someone moves. Little sticks prod my back through the plastic. Beyond our camp the bush murmurs and groans.

The welts on my hand tingle and I lick them to cool them down. I can smell my sweat mixed with salt crusts in the creases of my eyelids. Tim has his arm around Trish, who is gripping my good hand really hard. Amy is cuddled up with Dion. Someone is shaking, maybe all of us. The raincoat and the emergency blanket tremble.

More pork, more pork.

Beside me, Mark flinches. Amy tells him not to worry. 'We heard one last night. It's a good omen.'

Someone is shining a head torch in my face and telling me to get up. Cobalt blue overalls. It can only be Dad. He says we have to check the possum traps. I tell him it's dark. He replies he's been up since 3am watching the Black Caps play England and we may as well check the traps and plant some more trees before he goes to get the cows. It's the only free time he's got today and otherwise we won't make our daily tally. 'It was your idea, Ellen. It's your future at stake here. You don't want to blow it by sleeping in.' I wake up and realise the light is the moon shining an emergency pathway on the water. The mist has lifted. I need to pee. I wriggle out from under Dad's coat and walk to the shore. It's so quiet I can hear the soft pants of effort coming from the bedraggled waves as their small tongues lick the sand. Moonlight catches on the flotsam and jetsam, where broken necklaces of seaweed form a tidal frill. Further out, a bluey green sheen floats on the water like a shimmery dye.

'Luminescence.' A whisper from behind. Trish, with Amy. The guys, even Mark, are stirring, and soon they're walking towards us.

'Like nail polish,' Amy breathes.

'Low tide?' Dion points down the beach. In the distance we can make out the spot where earlier Tim waded up to his waist in water and Dion went into the bush. There is plenty of space between the sand and the bush now.

I reach out and ruffle the water with my sore hand. It's like stirring glowing jewels or silvery tadpoles maybe. The coolness gives me a little charge of energy. The others reach out their hands too.

The luminescence feels like an invitation mixed with a challenge, or a dare. The colour reminds me of the kōtare perched on the fence at the camp.

'We should head back. We can walk along the beach now.' I look at the others, their moonlit faces. They know it too. We've come this far, no need to wait to be rescued, we can make our own way.

Acknowledgements

Thank you to all the people who helped me write this, my first book, and encouraged me every step of the way.

When I happened by the International Institute of Modern Letters I wasn't expecting an ecstasy of screaming tūī outside the workshop room or a leap of leopards inside it. Thanks to the leopards – Kate Duignan, Phoebe Wright, Clara van Wel, Joey Parker, Janet Holst, Gerard O'Brien, Jayne Costelloe, Anita Nalder, Brendon White and Michaela Tempany for your camaraderie, generosity and insight. The thought of your books being published makes me salivate. They'll be so juicy and delicious I'll want to pounce and dispatch them with a bite on the neck. Thanks to the tūī for your indifference to the happenings on the other side of the glass.

Thanks to Damien Wilkins for your astute guidance and unwavering belief in my potential. Without your mastery of the art of teaching, there would be no book.

Thanks to Katie Hardwick-Smith for the unassuming way you get stuff done. Thanks to everyone who provided helpful feedback on my manuscript including, but not limited to, the leopards, Damien, Kate, Ashleigh Young and Chloe Lane.

Thanks to my other creative writing teachers over the years: Pip Adam at the IILM and Rebecca Styles at the Wellington High School Community Education Centre. Also, Paul Hersey for that non-fiction outdoor adventure writing course. You know, the one at Aoraki NP where we had mint weather and you suggested I try using some dialogue in my stories and you were okay with us spending lots of time outside. Thanks Laurence Fearnley for your appreciation of my writing.

Thanks to the Adam Foundation and Verna Adam for your interest in my work, your kind words and for tolerating a bit of swearing and a lot of speech-making.

It's a privilege to be associated with the team at Te Herenga Waka University Press. Thanks especially Fergus Barrowman and Ashleigh for looking out for me. To be a beneficiary of Ashleigh's perceptive editing and the generous and gracious manner she goes about it is a dream come true.

Thanks to the intrepid Ebony Lamb for scaling a crumbly clay cliff while clutching your most valuable possession, an enormous camera. Your author pictures are as stunning as your commitment to your craft is inspiring.

Sonja Drake allowed us to use the digital image of her lovely watercolour 'Winter Walking with Charlie' for the book cover.

To my friends in the Sustainability Team at Mercury Energy thanks for your ongoing trust, support, good humour and flexibility, especially during the MA year.

Thank you to my close friends and family especially Pat, Mick, John, Heather, PC, Marie Henderson, Robert Kirkby, David Jewell and Kathy Perreau.

The story 'Peninsula' was partly inspired by a Seamus Heaney poem with the same name.